RAVE REVIEWS FOR CATHLEEN CLARE'S REGENCY ROMANCES

MISTRESS OF MISHAP

"A DELICIOUS ROMP"
Romantic Times

FELICIA

"CAPTURES THE FLAVOR OF THE ERA SPLENDIDLY"
Rendezvous

CLARISSA

"DELIGHTFUL . . . A BOOK WITHOUT A SINGLE FALSE NOTE"
Rendezvous

TOURNAMENT OF HEARTS

"AN ABSOLUTE DELIGHT"
Affaire de Coeur

Other Avon Regency Romances by
Cathleen Clare

CLARISSA
FELICIA
LETITIA
TOURNAMENT OF HEARTS

Other **Regency Romances**
from Avon Books

A PROPER TAMING *by Joan Overfield*
THE DANGEROUS MARQUIS *by Barbara Reeves*
AN UNUSUAL INHERITANCE *by Rebecca Robbins*
A MISBEGOTTEN MATCH *by Rita Boucher*
THE IMPOSTOR *by June Drummond*

Coming Soon

AN IMPROPER WIDOW *by Kate Moore*

Midwinter's Bliss

CATHLEEN CLARE

AVON BOOKS NEW YORK

MIDWINTER'S BLISS is an original publication of Avon Books. This work has never before appeared in book form. This work is a novel. Any similarity to actual persons or events is purely coincidental.

AVON BOOKS
A division of
The Hearst Corporation
1350 Avenue of the Americas
New York, New York 10019

Published by arrangement with the author
Library of Congress Catalog Card Number: 94-94478
ISBN: 0-380-77668-5

First Avon Books Printing: January 1995

Printed in the U.S.A.

RA 10 9 8 7 6 5 4 3 2 1

For Mary

1

Teeth chattering, the diminutive ladies' maid turned frightened brown eyes toward her employer. "Oh, my lady, 'tis getting terrible bad out there!"

Staring out the window of the coach, Lady Hope Blissfield nodded anxiously.

The snow had started to fall during their last stop. When Hope, her abigail, Martha, and her companion, Agatha Sommers, had left the warm inn, big fluffy white flakes were fluttering down and lightly dusting the ground. As they continued their journey, a wind had arisen and the precipitation had grown heavier. Now they were in the midst of a full-scale blizzard. The driving snow whipped against the vehicle and swept across the road to form wildly graceful drifts. Lady Hope could scarcely see more than a few feet in any direction.

"What are we going to do?" the maid whined.

"I'm certain that everything will be all right, Martha." She studiously kept her voice calm, for there would be no gain in adding her own distress to that of the excitable girl. "We cannot be too terribly far from Shadyside Park. Though the snow has slowed us somewhat, we shall probably be home in time for supper."

Martha leaned forward, trembling. Quickly peeping out, she drew back against the squabs and pulled the carriage robe even more tightly around her body, so that only her small, heart-shaped face was visible.

"How can John see where he's going?" she wailed. "We'll never get home! We'll have an accident!"

"Now, now," Hope soothed, "we must trust John Coachman. I'll hazard a guess that he is the very best driver in Northumberland!"

"That don't matter, my lady, if he can't see his hand in front of his face. He'll land us in a drift!"

"Perhaps since he is seated high on the box, he can see the road better than we can." For Martha's sake, she tried to speak calmly and confidently, but she doubted her own conjecture. How could John's sight be superior to theirs with the torrents of snow blowing in his face and stinging his eyes?

The maid apparently doubted it too. Shivering, she regarded her mistress with disbelief. She chewed her lip fretfully.

"Are you cold, Martha? Take my robe too." In her fur-lined, woolen cape, Hope was warm enough. She removed the heavy blanket from her lap and laid it across her servant's quivering knees.

"Oh, no, my lady, I couldn't!"

"Of course you can! Now that will be enough of that. Why don't you lie down and close your eyes? It's been a very long day." If the girl couldn't see the storm, Hope reasoned, perhaps she wouldn't be so frightened. Martha's nervousness was beginning to adversely affect her own state of mind as well.

She almost wished that they had never left Blissfield Manor where she had spent the Yuletide season with her brother, the earl, and his growing family. She'd had an enjoyable visit, and she loved playing with her little niece and nephew, but when the excitement of Christmas had waned, Hope soon longed for the solitude of her own home. How could she have known that they would end up in the worst storm she had ever seen?

She exchanged a glance of mild concern with her companion, Agatha Sommers. The pretty, thirty-year-old widow displayed an outward expression of tranquillity in the face of their worsening crisis, but the pinched whiteness around her mouth and the tiny quiver along the muscle of her jaw belied her seeming serenity. Hope thanked heavens for Agatha's good sense in hiding her true feelings. If she had lost her composure, poor Martha would become positively unmanageable in her terror.

Sensing Hope's plea for assistance, Agatha reached out and squeezed the maid's hand. "I am certain that all will be well."

"That's right." Despite the small clutch of fear in her own stomach, Hope smiled kindly at her abigail. "Please, Martha, do make yourself comfortable. I shouldn't wish you to catch a chill."

"I ain't cold, my lady, I'm scared!" Just then, the girl screamed as the coach lurched sideways, straightened, then plowed on. "We'll be killed!"

"No, we won't!" Hope said sharply, her own fright momentarily oversetting her deliberate self-possession. Swallowing against the great lump in her throat, she managed to soften her voice. "Remember, we must trust John Coachman."

"You don't know him like I do," Martha sniveled. "Sometimes he has things on his mind besides his business!"

Hope would have chuckled if the situation had not been so grim. "Well, I doubt if that is the case now."

"Certainly not," Agatha agreed. "John will be very cautious."

The carriage slid again and, this time, drew to a stop. Martha squealed.

"Hush!" Hope opened the window, admitting a bitter gust of flurries and frigid air. John Coachman, his handsome face half-concealed by his heavy wool muffler, appeared outside.

"We're going to have to seek shelter, Lady Hope," he

said gruffly. "I can't see where I'm going, and it's getting terrible slick."

Martha sobbed.

Hope reached out to pat the girl's knees. "Have you noticed any landmarks, John? Do you have any idea where we are?"

"I'd say we're near to Amberton Hall, my lady." He glanced with concern toward the weeping maid, then returned his attention to his mistress.

His quick gaze was not wasted on Hope. Contrary to Martha's complaint against him, she had suspected a growing *tendre* between her abigail and the young coachman. But this was no time to think of gentle matters. John was expecting her to make some sort of decision.

"We shall go to Amberton," she said. "Do you think you will be able to see the gates?"

"I hope so, my lady."

"Martha, Mrs. Sommers, and I will assist you. We shall watch from the window, and if we see the drive first, we'll pound on the roof. Good luck, John. I am sure you're almost frozen stiff."

"It's all right, Lady Hope," he muttered and hunched off into the swirling snow.

Hope withdrew a handkerchief from her reticule and passed it to her abigail. "Dry your eyes now, Martha. We must help John Coachman. Between the four of us, I am certain that we shall soon be safe, sound, and sitting before a cozy fire at Amberton Hall, with a cup of good, warm tea in our hands!"

"I hope so," the girl replied, echoing the coachman.

Hope closed the glass while Martha dabbed at her face and blew noisily into the fine lawn cloth. "I am confident that we will make it!" Hope said with bravado.

As the coach pitched forward, the women pressed against the window and peered searchingly into the blustery night. "I can't see anything," the abigail moaned.

"Perhaps it's because you're sitting backwards," Hope encouraged, but with the snow dashing against the pane, she, herself, could recognize little. She prayed that John was better situated. How far could it be?

The coachman saw the entrance to the Amberton estate before his passengers did, and with only a small skid, he turned into the lane. Hope exhaled with relief as they passed between the great, gray stone pillars. She smiled triumphantly at Martha. "There! We've made it!"

"Can you see the house, my lady?"

"No, not yet. I do recall that it's a rather long drive, but we're safe now. Even if the carriage should bog down in the drifts, I am certain that we could even find our way on foot if necessary. There are huge oak trees on either side of the lane to mark the way. So you see? Everything is going to be all right." She settled back into her seat. "We shall be most comfortable at Amberton Hall. The housekeeper is ever so amiable! She'll have us warm and fed in no time at all."

Hope had visited the Amberton estate only once before. Shortly after she had inherited Shadyside Park from her father and moved into the neighborhood, curiosity had driven her to see the legendary manor house, the centuries-old seat of the volatile marquesses of Amberton. None of the family had been in residence, but Mrs. Dawes, the housekeeper, a pleasant, motherly sort of woman, had been pleased to show her through the state rooms. Indeed, the servant was accustomed to doing so, for the Hall was a prominent feature in many guidebooks, and numerous summer travelers stopped by to view it. Hope felt a rush of excitement at the thought of staying, at least for the night, in such a fascinating dwelling.

She knew from local gossip that the present marquess, a renowned rake and libertine, preferred to seek his pleasure elsewhere and seldom came to the district. Currently he was likely in attendance at one of the wild house parties so favored by members of his dissolute set. He would never know, nor would he care, that he was the absentee host of his young neighbor on a snowy winter night.

Hope had first seen the excessively handsome, utterly

dangerous Lord Amberton during her first season in London. He, of course, had not noticed the pretty young ingenue. His interest was fixed solely on the dashing, beautiful woman on his arm, who was rumored to be his mistress. Hope and her friends had been ecstatically entranced by his wicked dark eyes, the arrogant curl of his lips, and his shocking reputation. Whenever he had appeared at a ball or rout, he had provided them with giggles and gossip for several days thereafter. Each one of the young ladies had imagined herself in the place of the scandalous Lady Marsh, and had speculated upon what might have happened after she had left the ball with him. How innocent they had been, Hope thought with a silent laugh. Their visions had been of heart-stopping romance and sweet, loving kisses. Now, at the age of twenty-four, Hope had a better idea of what would have gone on. Her friends would know for sure. All of them were married.

So far, however, there had been no husband for Lady Hope. Over the years, she had received many offers, but none of them had stirred her enough to accept. Her father hadn't pressured her. She was his darling daughter, and he wanted her to be perfectly happy with her choice. But now that he was gone, her brother was not so complacent. Gerald deplored her spinsterhood and her insistence on living alone, but Hope had stubbornly refused to reside with him and his ever-increasing family. They needed their privacy, and she needed hers. She enjoyed visiting them, as she had just done, but she must live her own life, and so must they. She sighed. Perhaps she would meet a wonderful gentleman this season and set her brother's mind at ease. Surely there was someone, somewhere, for her. She dreamed of a husband and family, but the man must be perfect. She would relinquish her carefully guarded heart and her independence for nothing less!

"My lady, are we there?" Martha asked from her cocoon of blankets, as the coach pulled to a halt.

"Yes, thank God, I think we are!" Hope exclaimed, leaning forward to look out.

Agatha smiled with relief. "Soon we'll be having the most welcome, hot cup of tea in all England!"

The storm had increased its velocity, but between gusts, Hope could see the vague, murky outline of Amberton Hall. Over the whistling wind, she heard John Coachman beating on the front door and shouting to the servants within. At last there appeared a shaft of light on the deeply drifted portico, and she saw John sprinting back to the carriage.

"Hold tight to me, my lady!" he cried as he hurried to help them out.

"What did they say?" Hope shrilled.

"I didn't wait to find out. It's something fierce out here!" John bellowed. "Please, ma'am, move quickly!"

Hope clung resolutely to one of his arms, while Agatha gripped his other and Martha grasped his coattails. With the gale whipping her cloak and tearing the pins from her silky blond hair, Hope struggled through the deep snow, in step with her companions. Praise God that they had reached a safe haven when they did, or surely they would have become stranded! With breathless relief, she nearly fell into the vast hall, her eyes teary from the wintry blast.

"I'll fetch the baggage!" John still shouted, his voice incongruous in the relative quietude.

Hope nodded, pressing her hands to her stinging cheeks. Praise God, indeed! They could have died out there! She blinked frantically and was finally able to see the ashen-faced butler and two wide-eyed footmen.

"Oh, miss," the elderly retainer gasped without preamble. "You can't stay here!"

She speechlessly stared at him.

"We cannot possibly accommodate females!"

Hope battled to gather her wits. "I am Lady Hope Blissfield," she announced sternly, as if this reply would be all that was necessary. What was wrong with the man? Did he think that they were thieves? Surely he could see that she and Agatha were proper ladies, and that it was impossible for them to continue on in the storm!

"My lady." He gained enough aplomb to bow respectfully, then lost it again, frenziedly wringing his hands. "You must go elsewhere! You . . . it . . . it isn't a good time to visit here!"

"Isn't a good time?" Hope shrieked. "This is not a social call! What is wrong with you? Haven't you looked outside? We are in desperate straits!"

He stared helplessly at the snow billowing through the open door. "It . . . It just isn't a good time," he repeated inanely. "Please, my lady, you must leave at once."

"Hope?" Agatha calmly put in. "Perhaps this man knows of a cottage or a farmhouse where we might be welcomed."

"No! We shall travel no further. Indeed, we cannot!" Hope lost the remaining shreds of her patience. She stamped her small, booted foot. "I have never heard such foolishness as this! I refuse to move from this hall!"

As if to punctuate her statement, John Coachman bustled in from the cold and tossed the lightest of their baggage onto the floor. Hope imperiously jerked her finger at one of the footmen. "Help my coachman. Now!"

The young man glanced uneasily at his superior and then at the lady. Apparently deciding that the butler was the least of the two evils, he scampered after John.

Hope pointed to the other. "You! Summon the housekeeper!"

He didn't even pause before he leapt to obey her.

"Please, my lady," the flustered butler began again, "you do not understand. You must go on to another house!"

"I shall do no such thing!" Hope snapped, slamming the door herself as John and the footman entered with her trunk and the last of the baggage. "Perhaps you do not care whether I, my friend, and my servants live or die, but I assure you that I do! I will not set foot from this house!"

"But . . ."

"I'll hear no more about it! And you, sir, will make us welcome!"

Somewhere down the hall, a door banged open, accompanied by the discord of raucous male laughter.

"Oh, no." The butler winced.

"What in the hell is going on here?" demanded a deep, slightly slurred voice.

Hope whirled. Shock written plainly on her face, her eyes met those of the very devastating, very intoxicated marquess of Amberton. *"Oh, my,"* she breathed.

"I tried to tell you," the butler murmured weakly.

Colin Amberton cautiously took his time surveying the scene in his front hall. Ever since luncheon, he and his friends had been imbibing quite freely of spirits, but he had always had a good head for the stuff and had drunk numerous multiple-bottle men under the table. Insofar as he could remember, alcohol had never caused him to conjure up fantastical illusions. Yet what else could this be? There was a woman—a rosy-cheeked, lovely *young lady,* to be exact—standing amidst her baggage and snapping orders to his servants. Another woman, older but still most attractive, stood beside her, eyeing him coolly. A tiny, more plainly dressed girl, probably their abigail, ducked behind them. Well-bred females at Amberton Hall! Impossible!

He had only a slight recollection of his mother, who had died in childbirth with his younger brother. Later, his aunt, his mother's childless, widowed sister, had arrived to assist in the upbringing of the Amberton progeny. She had scarcely lasted a quarter year before the old marquess's wild ways had set her on the run. After that, no lady of Quality had spent a single night under the vast roof. Only the portraits of ladies in the gallery, staring down at the onlooker with aristocratic sneers, lent a feminine touch of class to the scandalous goings-on within.

In confusion, Colin leaned against the doorjamb. The finely molded wood was as hard as ever, highly polished, and *real.* Therefore, this vision must be *real* as well. There were, indeed, two flesh-and-blood ladies at Amberton

Hall. And judging from the expression on the younger one's face, she was just as surprised to see him as he was to see her.

"Who are you?" he lazily inquired.

The female bristled, recovering quickly from her shock. "How terribly rude!"

Colin ambled forward. "Rude? *Me?* My dear madam, or miss, or whatever you may be, *you* are the one who is behaving in an uncivil manner! Here you are, a stranger, bursting uninvited into my home . . ." He paused to flick a glance of high contempt over the baggage. ". . . invading my privacy, screeching like an alewife at my servants, and apparently intending to take up residence. Yet you dare to call *me* rude?"

"I do!" she said vehemently. "And I am neither 'madam' nor 'miss.' I am *Lady* Hope Blissfield, and I am not your *dear!*"

"Ah . . ." He inclined his head in acknowledgment of her challenge. "Well then, Lady Hope Blissfield, would you also care to enlighten me on the reason that you are moving into Amberton Hall? It is my home, you know, and I like to think that I am somehow entitled to exercise some measure of control over it."

He shifted his attention to the elder female, who suddenly looked rather frightened. "Or perhaps you, madam, might be so kind as to explain."

"Leave her out of this," commanded the little vixen. "You shall deal with me!"

"Indeed?"

He was feeling steadier with every step, and the fog was clearing from his mind. The closer he came to her, the more he became aware that she was indeed what she seemed, a very proper, pretty young lady. Gad, this could turn into a dangerously delicate situation.

She looked up at him through the longest golden-brown eyelashes that he had ever seen. As he neared her, she stepped backward, struck her heel against her trunk, and sat down hard on top of it. Artfully, she arranged her skirts as if seating herself had been her intention all along.

Colin grinned and made a mock bow. "A graceful recovery! Allow me to introduce myself . . ."

"I am aware of who you are," she murmured, fussing with her cloak.

"Oh? Have we met?"

"No, my lord, but you were pointed out to me in London."

"I see." He tried and failed to place her, but that was not surprising for he seldom took notice of innocent ladies her age. "So! If you are acquainted with my identity, you must also be aware that this is my home and not a hostelry."

"Do not be absurd," she bristled. "Of course I am!"

"Excellent! Then you will lose no time in being on your way. You do not strike me as the type of ladies who would care to cast themselves into the midst of a bachelor party."

Her aggressive demeanor fled as her eyes widened. Colin could see that those lovely orbs were a luminous shade of brown, like well-polished oak with warm golden overtones. At present, they were turned on him with a rather helpless expression, but he had no doubt that they could easily burn once more with fury if he chose to reignite her ire.

In or out of a pet, Lady Hope Blissfield was deucedly attractive. Even though the *ton* would have preferred blue eyes with that rich, guinea-gold hair, she had the dainty facial features that were so highly desired by those arbiters of fashion. She was most petite. Though he was not an extremely tall man, the top of her head would barely come up to the hollow of his shoulder. Colin wondered if her legs were as neat and trim as the ankles he had glimpsed when she had tumbled to her seat on the trunk.

He ceased tallying her charms. Strangely enough, he found that he'd like to further their acquaintance, but he realized that the lady was not the kind of female to encourage dalliance. Besides, there was the possibility of a husband or a fiance lurking in the wings. Even the womanizing marquess of Amberton had a certain code of ethics which prevented him from the practice of cuckolding. He'd best speed her on her way.

"Mitchell," he informed his butler, "please see that the ladies' baggage is returned at once to their coach."

Hope, scarlet-cheeked from the marquess's leisurely perusal of her, leapt to her feet. "How dare you send me to my death?"

"I'm sure you exaggerate the situation," he said calmly. "Be reasonable, my lady. There is an inn not far from here. If you are seeking lodgings, you will be made quite comfortable there."

"My house is not a great distance away either! Don't you think I would have gone there if I could?" she cried.

Despite her bravado, Hope felt a stab of fear. What was wrong with the residents of Amberton Hall? Did they never look out a window? She was horrified at the thought of spending the night in the same house as the decadent marquess and his cronies, but she was even more terrified of the storm.

She would not leave. Lord Amberton would have to throw her out bodily, whereupon she would lie down and expire on his doorstep. That would teach His Haughty Lordship!

She heard Martha begin to sob. "See what you have done, my lord? You have frightened my abigail out of her wits!"

The muscles rippled along his jawline. "I don't know what you want from me," he said coldly, "but it will not work."

Hope squared her shoulders and faced him defiantly. "I seek only safe refuge for myself, my friend, and my servants. Are you too foxed to realize that there is a blizzard raging outside?"

"I am not foxed!"

"I can smell the alcohol on your breath," she accused severely.

"So? I had a drink while playing billiards."

"More than one, my lord." She lifted her chin. "You have had so much that the spirits have affected your judgment. You are so disguised that you are unable to discern a fierce storm from fair weather!"

"Damn!" He started toward the door. "I'll show you, Lady Temperance! To think that a man must suffer criticism for having a drink in his own home!"

When Hope realized that he merely meant to peek out the sidelight, she darted forward. The *nerve* of the man! He wouldn't have just a view of the blizzard. She'd give him the full blast of it! She jerked open the door.

Snow gusted into the hall, coating the marquess from head to toe. Icy wind blew his coat open and rattled the crystal of the chandelier. Clumsily, he reeled aside.

"There!" said Hope, smugly. "Would *you* like to travel in such weather?"

"My God," Lord Amberton meekly replied.

2

Colin stared at the avenging queen of ice standing across from him. The young lady was right. The gentle, picturesque snowfall he had noticed earlier in the afternoon had become a violent storm. Neither beast nor fowl could be safe in such a blizzard, let along a group of delicate females. The women were very fortunate to have reached the security of Amberton Hall. In fact, he was extremely lucky that they had not enacted him a scene of weeping, swooning hysterics. He offered Lady Hope Blissfield a lopsided, somewhat apologetic grin.

She glared at him in return. "You see?"

He nodded ruefully.

"Then there will be no more talk of our leaving?" she demanded.

Colin shook his head, gathering his thoughts. "No, but you must realize that this is not the best of circumstances. Storm or no, your reputations may suffer damage. There are those who would say that you should have risked your pretty necks with the elements, rather than have sought shelter amidst a party of bachelors."

She confidently lifted her chin. "We shall manage our reputations. That matter is of no concern to you."

"Oh, but it is," he said somberly. "I do not relish having an irate husband calling on me."

"My companion is a widow," she assured him, "and I am unmarried."

"Angry fathers, brothers, or fiances then."

She faltered a bit. "I . . . I hope that Gerald does not hear of this. He wouldn't like it, but I cannot think of how he could blame you for it, my lord."

"Gerald?' he queried.

"My brother. The earl of Blissfield."

Colin mentally reviewed his list of acquaintances, but could remember no Lord Blissfield. "Well, Lady Hope, if he does get wind of it, don't expect me to come to your rescue. It was *your* choice to come here. I won't be dragged to the altar to save your little hide from social ostracism. And if your brother thinks differently, it will be a case of pistols for two and breakfast for one. The problem is on *your* head. You alone will suffer the outcome."

She eyed him defiantly. "How dare you entertain the notion that *I* would consent to marry *you?*"

"Wouldn't you?" Colin asked wickedly. He knew of few young ladies who would refuse his suit, especially those who had remained on the marriage mart for more than one season, as Lady Hope obviously had done. Despite his reputation for philandering, there were his wealth, title, and looks to be considered.

"No, I would not wish to wed you!" Lady Hope passionately denied. "I should *never, ever* wish to marry a rake, a libertine, and . . . and . . . such an arrogant wastrel as yourself!"

He sighed dramatically. "Then I need have no fears on that score."

"No, you need not!"

"It is nothing personal, you know. I simply have no desire to marry anyone," he couldn't help teasing. Especially to wed such a shrew as Lady Hope, he silently added to himself.

"I understand," she replied, tight-lipped.

"Now that that is settled, what am I to do with you?" he mused.

A movement caught his eye. He glanced down the hall and saw his group of friends standing in the doorway of the billiard room and watching the scene with obvious pleasure. Hell, he'd have to deal with them too! To a man, they were gentlemen most of the time. But today all of them had been drinking steadily and probably would continue to do so, at least until he could drum it through their heads to behave with circumspection. He doubted if the events of the evening had sobered them as much as it had him. If they wished to avoid parson's mousetrap, they would have to be very, very careful.

"My lord." Mrs. Dawes, his housekeeper, stepped forward. "If I may suggest . . . Perhaps the young lady might be best situated in the Garden Suite tonight, and her companion in the room next."

He considered. The Garden Suite was a set of rooms once occupied by Queen Elizabeth. Considered state rooms, they were seldom used. In fact, the past generations of Ambertons had viewed the chamber as a sort of Tudor shrine, preserving the original furniture, trappings, and arrangement. His mother had modernized the attached sitting and dressing rooms, but that was all.

There were more up-to-date and comfortable rooms at the hall, but this suite, and the room next door to it, had one definite advantage. They were located just across the hall from his chamber. He would be nearby if there was trouble and the ladies needed assistance.

"An excellent choice, Mrs. Dawes," he agreed. "Will you see to it at once?"

"Yes, my lord."

He returned his attention to Lady Hope. "The Garden Suite is most historical. You must ask my housekeeper about it."

"Thank you, Lord Amberton." There was a flash of excitement in her soft, brown eyes. "I hope to enjoy it, for I do intend to keep to my room."

"That would be the wisest course. Furthermore, there are locks on the doors. I suggest that you ladies use them."

She inclined her head, raising an expressive eyebrow. "Never fear."

"Then I shall leave you in the capable hands of Mrs. Dawes." He motioned the footmen to carry the baggage upstairs. "I bid you good evening, Lady Hope. Madam."

"Good night, my lord." They turned to follow the housekeeper.

Colin walked slowly down the hall toward the suddenly vacant doorway of the billiard room. Ladies at Amberton Hall! Until they left, their presence would drastically tone down any masculine revels. Well, there was no point in bemoaning the fact. If the women were snowbound, so were they all. He and his male guests would simply have to make the best of a bad and probably boring time.

He entered the room and crossed to the table. "I believe it's my play."

Sir Roger Torwin blocked him. "The game is finished." He grinned. "No one is interested anymore."

"We had a wager," Colin protested.

Torwin lifted an expressive shoulder. "Called off. Who are they?"

"They?" he replied innocently.

"Such innocence!" Sir Roger rolled his eyes heavenward. "We took a peek into the hall, Colin. You know we did. You saw us. Now do tell. No secrets! Who are the fair charmers?"

Colin shrugged, chalking the cue stick. "Only ladies seeking shelter from the storm. Have you looked out the window? It's terrible out there!"

"Changing the subject?" Sir Roger leered knowingly.

"One of them must be Colin's latest fancy piece," the Viscount Bridgewater decided, "and he doesn't wish us to know about it and cause him competition."

"Who else could it be?" drawled Sir Roger, pulling back the undercurtain to peer out. "Yes, it's becoming rather bitter. Good thing you'll have her to warm your bed, Amberton. But must you deprive us of a chance at the other one? Very selfish, I must say!"

"Neither of the women is the sort of female you have in mind." Colin hit the ball with more force than necessary and watched it careen ineffectively off the board. "The ladies are neighbors of mine."

"Then why aren't they in their own homes instead of here?" the earl of Kelwin queried suspiciously.

"They were detained by the weather, as I told you." Colin laid down the stick and strolled to the crackling fire. Merely thinking of the blizzard outside, and the cold sample of it that he had received when Lady Hope opened the door, gave him a chill. "The ladies had been traveling and were unable to reach their home. The storm drove them to the nearest haven."

"A Banbury tale if I ever heard one!" Bridgewater laughed.

"You're off the mark," Colin told him with finality.

"Neither of them is your mistress?"

"No! I swear it!"

"Then they're fair game for us all," Sir Roger said cheerfully. "Think of it! Two lone females and four handsome, charming, *appreciative* gentlemen, imprisoned together by a snowstorm! Which one of us will win their favors? I'll wager a pony that . . ."

"No, you will not," Colin interrupted. "They are *ladies,* not objects for your amusement. Each of you will mind his manners."

"Devil a bit, Amberton!" Bridgewater snorted. "From a distance, they appeared most fetching. Won't you even permit us to exhibit our appreciation? If we must rein in on our masculine merriment, can't we, at least, make them the honored recipients of our flattery? What's wrong with a bit of flirtation?"

The marquess groaned. "Good God, Jamie, what a speech."

Bridgewater bowed.

"I doubt that any of you will have the opportunity to make yourselves known. The ladies intend to keep to their rooms."

"Most unfortunate!" Sir Roger shook his head. "But if they change their minds? Come now, Colin, you should be the first to admit that Jamie is right. There's nothing wrong with passing the time with a bit of flirtation."

"I suppose not." He shrugged. "But remember that my reputation is at stake here."

"What reputation?" Kelwin chuckled.

"Dammit!" He threw up his hands in surrender. "All of you know what I'm talking about!"

His friends merely grinned.

Colin let it go at that. Even in their varying degrees of sobriety, they must be aware of the delicacy of the situation. In the event that the ladies did show themselves, his colleagues would behave as gentlemen. With their airs of practiced gallantry and worldliness, they might not be the type of beaux that the women were accustomed to, but surely they would conduct themselves properly.

"You never did tell us their names," Sir Roger prompted.

"The younger one is Lady Hope Blissfield. I did not catch the name of the other lady."

"Ah, a mystery!" the baronet savored, and uncorked a bottle of port to fill their glasses. "Gentlemen, I shall propose a toast. To the beauteous Lady Hope and to the delectable Mystery Lady! May they reign in splendor over our little gathering!"

Colin winced. He was going to have his hands full with this tangle. He picked up his glass and brought it to his lips. Lady Hope may have deplored his uncertain state of sobriety, but if ever a man needed a drink, that moment was now. Solemnly, he swigged it down and prayed that his feminine guests were settled and locked in for the night.

After bidding good night to Agatha, Hope was not too weary to gaze with pleasure at her surroundings. She remembered the Garden Suite. Mrs. Dawes had shown her this chamber during her previous visit to Amberton Hall. She recalled that it had been the chamber of Queen Elizabeth during the monarch's tour of the district so long ago. She was surprised that she had been assigned such historic quarters and said as much to the housekeeper.

Mrs. Dawes smiled enigmatically. "I trust you will enjoy it, my lady."

"I know I shall. It is a great honor to sleep in the same room, even in the same bed as a queen!"

She drifted across the chamber to the huge, magnificent tester and appreciatively touched the hangings with her fingertip. "The fabrics must be so very fragile."

"Indeed so, but they are of such extraordinary quality that, to my knowledge, they've been repaired only once. That was in my mother's time."

"Your mother was housekeeper here?"

"Yes, my lady. And so was my grandmother before her. 'Tis a tradition in my family."

"Goodness, you must know a great deal about the Ambertons and their home," Hope said with interest.

"I do. I first came to work here when I was twelve years old. I had just become housekeeper when the marquess's mother came here as a bride, poor lady."

Poor lady? Hope's curiosity was pricked. "What happened to her?"

"Lady Amberton died giving birth to his lordship's younger brother." She sadly shook her head. "She was here for such a short time. Before and after her, the hall has had no real mistress. Lord Amberton's grandmother preferred to live in London."

"What a pity! The house seems like such a lovely place."

"Yes. Well, we do our best." Mrs. Dawes directed the footman to take Hope's trunk to an adjoining room. "We keep this chamber exactly as it was when Queen Elizabeth was here, but the dressing and sitting rooms are quite modern. I think you'll find them comfortable. Shall I order a bath?"

"Yes. I would appreciate it very much."

"I shall see to it immediately, along with tea and supper. Will there be anything else?"

"Not that I can think of." Hope smiled in anticipation of the comfort. "Thank you for your kindness. I do believe that Lord Amberton was set to toss me out, or at best to lodge me in the cellars."

"That was naughty of his lordship, but he does love to tease," she murmured uneasily.

"I don't consider him to have been funning with me, Mrs. Dawes," Hope said firmly.

"He probably got carried away. He was such a mischievous little boy."

"And now he is a roguish man and a depraved rake." She knew she shouldn't be discussing the marquess with his employee, but she still smarted too much from their encounter.

"Oh, no, my lady," the housekeeper loyally defended. "He only wants taming."

"T'would be impossible."

She staunchly shook her head. "Not for the right lady. Lord Amberton truly has a kind heart. With proper handling, he would make the best of husbands!"

Hope choked back a laugh and ended the debate. "Since you know him far better than I, you probably have the right of it, Mrs. Dawes."

The housekeeper speculatively looked her over. "A good wife would be the making of him, Lady Hope." She curtsied. "I'll be seeing to your comfort now."

"Thank you."

When Mrs. Dawes left, Hope wandered into the sitting room. It was a small but pleasant salon with a cheerful, floral chintz sofa and matching chairs. At present, it was chilly, but soon it would be warm from the flames licking up from the newly laid fire.

She went to the window and stared out into the bleak night. She was safe at least from the elements, but the marquess was a different story. Was she secure from him and his friends? She had seen several gentlemen lounging in a doorway and regarding her and Agatha with undisguised interested. She was glad that the rooms were equipped with sturdy locks.

What would her friends think of her adventure? When she went to London for the Season, she would swear them to secrecy and tell them the entire story. How shocked they would be!

On the other hand, it might be more fun to keep mum about the entire episode. Having made her acquaintance, Lord Amberton might actually ask her to dance with him. Then wouldn't her friends be curious?

The thought of waltzing with the marquess left Hope slightly breathless. My goodness! Up close, he was even more handsome than she had dreamed a man could be! For the sake of her own well-being, she must remember how odious he had been. The best of husbands? Ha! If Mrs. Dawes really and truly believed that, she was far wide of the mark.

"Lady Hope?" Martha interrupted her reverie. "Your bath is ready."

"So soon? I must have been woolgathering."

Her abigail nodded, laughing. "There's also a nice hot cup of tea for you while you soak."

"Are we in heaven?" Hope quipped as she sought the dressing room and allowed Martha to help her out of her clothes.

"I'd think so, my lady, after what we've been through."

She was glad to see a smile on the girl's face. Slipping into the deliciously warm water, Hope sipped her tea and relaxed in luxury. The bath made her so drowsy that she could scarcely stay awake to do justice to her simple supper. When Martha prepared to go to the servants' hall for her own meal, Hope dismissed her for the night.

"Do you want me to look in on you before I go to bed?" the abigail asked.

"No. I intend to fall sound asleep as soon as my head touches the pillow!"

"Very well then, my lady. Good night."

"Sleep well, Martha."

Hope closed the door behind her and turned the key in the lock. Crossing the room, she climbed into the big Tudor bed, noting with relief that the servants had exchanged the valuable, ancient counterpane for a modern serviceable one. Yawning, she buried herself under the covers and stretched luxuriously. The mattress was slightly lumpy and not as comfortable as it had looked, but she was too slumberous to care. She was safe from the storm in the bed of a queen. How could she complain?

Lying quietly, Hope listened to the howling of the wind and the tapping of a frozen branch against her window. It was a night for ghostly rambles. She could almost picture the dead Elizabeth floating around the room in spectral splendor. Could Amberton Hall be haunted? Nonsense! She was far too practical to believe in such fantasy. Still, though feeling foolish for doing so, she left the candle burning.

Hope came wildly awake. What sort of noise had that been? Her heart pounded so forcibly that she could feel it in her throat. Had it been a dream? Had she imagined it? She took several deep breaths. There *had* been a sound. But ancient houses did a great deal of creaking and groaning, didn't they?

The room was dark, eerily illuminated by only the glow from the coals in the fireplace. The candle had guttered out long enough ago that she could smell no scent of snuffed wax. The branch still chattered against the window pane, and the wind whined. Could the storm have awakened her? No, she'd grown accustomed to its fury. The noise had been of something heavier and more resounding.

A loud thump on her door startled her. This was not the sound a ghostly queen would make. It was a more earthly disturbance. Merciful heavens, was someone trying to enter her chamber? Almost afraid to breathe, she tightly drew her knees up to her chest. Thank God the lock was stout and the door strong. Surely it would keep her safe from any of Amberton's drunken revelers.

The bump echoed again, along with a muffled oath.

"Dammit, Bridgewater!" Hope overheard. "Can't you stand up and walk straight?"

"'Course I can! I ain't so very tipsy!"

"Then do it!"

"I will, Roger," the answering voice slurred. "Just let me get my bearings."

There was a heavy rustling sound against the panel. The doorknob rattled. Hope's anger ignited. She could picture exactly what was going on in the hall. One of Lord Amberton's inebriated guests was attempting to make his way to bed and had fallen outside her door.

"That's not your room," his exasperated companion complained. "Come on!"

"What the hell?" A third voice joined in. "Is this what I get for retiring early?"

"I'm trying to get him to bed, Colin, and he's half-seas over!"

"Well get him away from there."

"I'm trying! If he wasn't such a big son of a . . ."

"My mama was a Lanscomb, and I'll not have you insult her," the reveler drawled. "I'll have to call you out, Roger."

"Shut up, Jamie," the marquess ordered. "Torwin, get that arm. I'll take his other. Heave!"

"Confound it, Amberton, I'm in the midst of challenging Roger . . ."

"You can't do that till morning."

"Why not?"

"Against the law," Lord Amberton stated, chuckling.

"Oh. Didn't know that! Why didn't you say so? All right then . . . tomorrow . . ."

Hope pressed her lips together in a fine line of displeasure. She wasn't opposed to gentlemen enjoying a drink, but this was outside of enough! After all, she too was a guest, albeit an uninvited one, and she had her rights to a peaceful night's sleep. Angrily, she left her bed and marched across the room. Without a thought to her dishabille, she turned the key and wrenched open the door.

"What a disgusting . . ."

Those were all the words she managed. Suddenly deprived of their means of support, the three men reeled into her room, knocked Hope to the floor, and fell on top of her.

"Dammit!" cried the marquess. "I knew that your being here would become a disaster!"

Hope struggled beneath the weighty heap of masculinity and entangled limbs. Merciful heavens! Why hadn't she considered that the gentlemen might be leaning against the door? Worse still, why hadn't she thought of her state of undress? What a fool! She'd been so consumed with her own righteous anger that she hadn't even paused to don her dressing robe!

A bare leg grazed her own. Squealing, she drew up her knee to kick.

"God!" a male voice gasped as she made contact.

"Get off me!" Hope cried, flailing with her elbows.

"Ow! Right in m' ribs!"

The ponderous weight was removed. Hope quickly sat up, drawing her night rail over her bare feet. Her face burned with mortification. Thank God for the darkness! With only the firelight and the candle glow from the sconces in the hall, the horrible scene was poorly illuminated. Perhaps the gentlemen wouldn't remember how she looked in her bed gown. She hazarded a glance.

One very large gentleman was lying on his back beside her, grinning inanely at the ceiling. Another was stretched out on his side, laughing hysterically. Over her stood the marquess.

"Get up!" he snapped, extending a hand to her.

"At least you could ascertain whether I am all right or not," she said irritably, letting him lift her to her feet.

"At present, I don't care," he said, tight-lipped. "Ninnyhammer! Look what you have caused!"

"I? It appears to me that you and your foxed friends are to blame!" Hope accused, and gaped at Lord Amberton. Apparently he had retired some time before his friends had come upstairs, for he was clad only in his nightshirt and dressing robe, a glimpse of his bare lower legs and feet shockingly displayed for all to see.

"Just look at you," he lectured. "If you give no thought for your own reputation, at least you could have a care for mine."

"You disgusting libertine!" she cried. "Look at me? Are you not aware of your own appearance, sir?"

The marquess blushed scarlet. He looked down at himself. "I . . . I . . ." Angrily he rounded on his friends. "Roger, cease your merriment and get Jamie out of here!"

Grinning, the man picked himself up and bowed elegantly to Hope. "My apologies, my lady." He lifted his crony's legs and pulled him bodily out of the room and down the hall.

Lord Amberton's jaw clenched. "I, too, must apologize," he began.

"Just get out of here!" she gasped. "Please leave before anyone else comes along and sees us!"

A look of sheer terror crossed his face. "Indeed." Habitually, he began a bow, realized the incongruity of it, and fled.

Hope quickly secured the door and rushed to her bed, pressing her face into the pillow. How perfectly mortifying! Why, oh why had she allowed her anger to overcome her good sense? What if someone heard of the scandalous episode? She could only pray that the men had been so disguised that they would have no memory of what had happened. But the marquess had seemed rather sober. Oh, dear! At her earliest possible opportunity, she must beseech him to keep his knowledge to himself.

It was much, much later before she fell into a deeply troubled sleep.

3

Hope awakened to the click of a key in the lock. Hurtling from her uneasy sleep, she sat up in bed and drew the covers tightly around her. The door opened slowly and quietly, only to reveal a neatly uniformed chambermaid carrying a basket of kindling. Hope sighed with relief, but she mentally noted that if a key to her chamber was available to the servants, it would be at hand for others as well.

The girl closed the door behind her, caught her eye, and bobbed a curtsy. "Mrs. Dawes didn't want me to wake you with tapping, Lady Hope, so she gave me her key. I'm sorry if I bothered you."

"It's all right." Hope smiled wearily. "I wasn't sleeping well, anyway."

"I'll be done in a flash." She hurried to the hearth and knelt down, picking up the poker to level the remaining coals and charred wood. "'Tis terrible cold in here, almost as cold as his lordship's room sometimes is in the mornings. Most nights *he* sleeps with the window part open!"

"I'll wager that he did not do so last night," Hope said dryly.

"No, my lady." She giggled. "I was to his room first. It was closed up right and tight, an' his lordship was all cuddled down under a mountain o' blankets."

"How is the weather?" Hope asked, uncomfortable at discussing Lord Amberton's nocturnal arrangements.

"'Tis awful! The wind ain't so bad, but it's still snowing hard."

Her spirits sank. That brief report indicated her spending another night, probably longer, at Amberton Hall. But there was no sense giving in to self-pity. She couldn't change the weather, and she couldn't magically cause the marquess and his friends to disappear. She could, however, improve her lot. She was resolved to speak with Lord Amberton at the earliest possible opportunity. Last night's incident would be hushed up, and there would be no more scandal, not if she had anything to do with it!

She watched the maid lay kindling on the embers and pump the bellows, bringing the wood to a quick flame. "What time does the marquess arise?" she asked.

The girl sat back on her heels and puckered her face with thought. "It depends, my lady. He might have been stirring a little when I left, but it's early for him. I could go listen at the door, or find out if he's rung for his man."

"No, I do not wish to take you from your duties. Have you had your breakfast?"

"It'll be ready when I finish the fires." She added several logs and again worked the bellows.

"Has my abigail breakfasted?" Hope queried.

"We all eat at the same time. Shall I call her?"

"No, I want her to enjoy her meal. We had a very difficult time yesterday."

"Do you want some tea, my lady? Or anything?" the maid begged. "I'll gladly fetch it for you."

"It's time for your breakfast," Hope said kindly. "I can wait."

"Oh, no, Lady Hope!" she cried. "I'll bring you whatever you want! Just name it! 'Tis something fine to serve a lady. I've never done it before."

"Thank you." Hope smiled warmly. "I would dearly love a cup of tea."

"I'll bring it right now!"

"But your fires . . ." she protested.

"Mary's tending Mrs. Sommers's. The rest of mine're just for his lordship's friends. They sleep so late they won't know if they're cold or not!" She chuckled and hurried from the room.

Hope slid from the high bed without using the steps and donned her velvet dressing robe. It was cold in the chamber, but the maid's cheerful fire would soon take off the chill. Poor girl! Of course she'd never had the opportunity to serve a lady. She probably never would, unless Lord Amberton changed his wicked ways.

She walked briskly to the window and pulled back the curtains. The girl was right about the weather. The wind had ceased, but it continued to be terrible outside. Great flakes of snow fell swiftly from the leaden skies, adding to the previous day's accumulation. There could be no travel, even on foot, in such a storm. Still, there was a beauty to it. She settled herself in the window seat and gazed out.

The Garden Suite overlooked the rear lawn of Amberton Hall. Directly below it was a walled garden laid out in an Elizabethan knot. In the summer, it would be a most pleasurable spot to while away the hours. Even now, swathed in pristine white, it had a certain quiet peace. Hope could almost picture the lords and ladies of past generations strolling there, perhaps exchanging stolen kisses or secret tokens of regard. Somewhere in time, there must have been incidents of love, instead of scandal, at this magnificent house.

The maid returned, bringing her tea.

"May I have it here?" Hope asked. "I am enjoying the view."

"Yes, my lady." The girl pulled up a small table and set the tray onto it. "'Tis very pretty, if you don't have to go out in it."

"How true. I don't suppose we shall be leaving today."

" 'Twould be impossible!"

"I daresay. Well, I shall have to make the best of it."

She inhaled the aroma of the rich brew. "Thank you. What is your name?"

"'Tis Flora, my lady." She folded a blanket and placed it over Hope's knees.

"Thank you, Flora. I shall tell Mrs. Dawes how well you have served me."

"I'm happy to do it." She curtsied and turned to leave, then hesitated. "Lady Hope? You asked about Lord Amberton. He's called his man. He doesn't take long for his toilette, so he should be in the dining room soon."

"I see. Tell me, do any of the other guests share the meal?"

"Oh, no, my lady." She laughed heartily. "They don't get up till noon."

"Very well then. I believe I shall have my breakfast downstairs. Do you know if Mrs. Sommers has risen?"

"Still sound asleep." Flora curtsied again. "I'll send your abigail to you. She'd almost be finished by now.

Hope nodded. Sipping her tea, she stared outside, but she didn't think of the snowy vista. She concentrated on her imminent conversation with Lord Amberton. He wasn't going to enjoy hearing what she had to say. Not by half! She girded herself for an unpleasant confrontation.

"Good morning, my lord." Hope walked briskly into the dining room. She had chosen her attire with care, dressing in a simple woolen gown of tawny gold, with long sleeves and a high neckline. Her hair was arranged in a soft knot at the nape of her neck. There was nothing in her appearance to incite scandalous behavior.

The marquess hurriedly closed his book and rose, his oddly colored, deep-violet eyes reflecting his amazement at her invasion. "Good morning, my lady."

She studied him briefly. Lord Amberton did not look the worse for wear from his previous day's revels. His dark hair was artfully arranged *à la* Apollo. His bottle-green superfine coat and buff pantaloons were neat, conservative, and immaculate. Only the fine lines at the corners of his mouth and eyes told of his past excesses. In fact, he seemed disgustingly refreshed for a man who should be suffering from an unsettled stomach and a headache.

"Won't you be seated?" he invited, and pulled out a chair adjacent to his place at the head of the table.

"Thank you." She sank down, blinking away a sudden vision of how he had looked in his nightclothes. A giddy laugh welled up in her throat.

He returned to his seat. "Tea?"

"Yes, please."

Stifling that awful urge to giggle, Hope watched him pour. His hands were quite unusual for those of a man. They were long and graceful with slender, elegant fingers. She idly wondered if he had ever played a musical instrument. Those hands would move ever so beautifully across the keyboard of a pianoforte.

"Lady Hope, I am surprised to see you outside of your room."

"Indeed?"

He inclined his head. "I thought you wished to avoid me and my friends." His eyes twinkled. "Of course, I should have realized, by the events of last night, that I am wrong. I believe that you do encourage our company."

Hope flushed with mortification. How dare he insinuate that she might wish to be a part of future escapades! She swallowed a retort as a footman entered to serve her.

"Thank you," she told the servant, "but I shall help myself."

She could feel Lord Amberton watching her as she filled her plate at the buffet, but her hunger defeated her resentment. My, how famished she was! Setting aside the notion that a lady should eat only dainty amounts in front of a gentleman, she took a small helping of almost every offering and returned to the table.

"A healthy appetite," the marquess observed.

There he was! Deriding her again! What a despicable man! Pursing her lips, she cut her slice of rosy ham. She would not allow him to spoil her meal.

"One seldom sees a lady truly enjoying her food," he prodded.

"Do you actually believe that?" Hope smiled sweetly. "If so, you must be quite inexperienced in the matter, my lord."

"You're right, my lady. My expertise lies in other areas."

Once again, Hope felt a blush suffuse her cheeks. She lifted her chin and looked toward the window, which was still heavily draped. "It continues to snow."

"A misfortune." He returned to his breakfast. "You will not be able to leave today," he said between bites.

"Regrettably not. I wish to speak with you about that."

"May we finish our meal first? I sense that you are going to cause me indigestion."

"A wise thought, my lord."

They ate in silence. Hope cleaned her plate, but she didn't particularly enjoy her food. The ham, bacon, and browned potatoes were entirely too greasy, the eggs undercooked, and the toast was burnt on the edges. She must speak with Mrs. Dawes about it. But no, she couldn't do that! Amberton Hall might not have a mistress, but it was certainly not her place, as a guest, to correct its management. Goodness! How Lord Amberton would laugh! She laid down her fork.

The marquess, too, crossed his utensils. Hope couldn't help noticing that he had eaten little, merely pushing the food around on his plate. He refilled their tea cups.

"Well, Lady Hope, now I am ready for anything."

She nodded curtly. "About the incident last night . . . There must be nothing said about it. *Ever!*"

"I agree wholeheartedly."

"I have no idea how much your friends will recollect, but they must be sworn to secrecy."

"I shall do so," he promised.

"Thank you." Hope sighed with relief. "You may not recall how very distressing the incident was."

He grinned. "I remember how fetching you looked in your nightgown."

"Lord Amberton!" she gasped. "I must request that we do not discuss this further! May I remind you that, last night, you yourself were certainly displeased with what transpired?"

"In retrospect, I find that the event did have its moments of humor . . . and titillation."

"My lord!" Hope cried heatedly. "I am warning you . . ."

"Very well," he answered amiably. "End of topic."

"Next," she went on, matter of factly, "I have come to the conclusion that, despite the reason, I and my friend are just as much guests in this house as anyone else. Since the snow shows no sign of ceasing, we shall be here longer than one night. I see no reason why we should be forced to remain in our rooms. It would become most boring."

"I'm sure it would." His violet eyes sparkled. "You wish to be entertained. What do you want to do, my lady? Join us at billiards? Cards? Or do you prefer more scintillating sport?"

She felt herself blushing again. Vexatious man! He was baiting her. It was as if he thoroughly enjoyed her discomfort. She lifted her nose and sniffed deprecatingly.

"Certainly not, my lord! I can find my own amusement!"

"Such as?"

"I have a great fascination with Amberton Hall," she said hesitantly. "I would love to examine its treasures."

"Please make yourself at home, Lady Hope," he agreed. "I have no objection. If you need a guide, please ask Mitchell or Mrs. Dawes."

"Thank you!" She could scarcely wait to begin. "But I won't take them from their work. If it is all right with you, I shall simply wander about on my own"

He nodded. "So long as you avoid my friends."

"I shall! I hope they will stay away from me, too."

"I intend to warn them. But Lady Hope, your explorations will not occupy you for very long."

"I could spend days doing it," she breathed.

"I doubt that," he said wryly. "When you tire of your pursuit, Amberton Hall has an excellent library, nothing very new, but you might find something you would like to read. Also, there is a pianoforte in the drawing room, if you enjoy playing music. I can't vouch for the tuning though."

"Do you play?" she asked curiously.

He laughed. "The majority of my life is spent in play."

"I was referring to the pianoforte," she snapped, "and you know it! Now I have one more request."

"Continue."

"The drinking must stop," she said firmly.

A muscle twitched at the corner of his mouth. "Lady Hope, may I remind you that *you* are the one who thrust herself into the midst of *my* house party, however good the reason may have been. I understand your situation; I have granted your requests; I am taking measures to ensure your well-being. But I will not *completely* overset the festivities because of you."

"You will severely limit the flow of alcohol," Hope informed him stubbornly.

His geniality ceased abruptly. "Ha! What are you? A reforming Methodist? A Quaker? It's no wonder that you've reached the age you have without nabbing a husband."

"How dare you?" she cried. "I'll have you know that I've had offers!"

"Why didn't you accept any of them?"

"They were boring men! Not that it is any of your business."

"No wonder they were dull," he mused. "You're afraid of a *real* man. He might take a drink of brandy, or wager on a horse race." His eyes narrowed mischievously. "He might even kiss your luscious little lips."

"Oh!" She ground her teeth.

Lord Amberton stood and walked toward the door. "Enjoy your tour of my home, Lady Hope, and don't concern yourself with worries about your virtue. I assure you, you are so bristly and managerial that no man in his right mind would wish to touch you."

Hope's first impulse was to provide him with the most blistering setdown in history, but she refused to give in to it. In all probability, she would be under his roof for several days. She must not allow him to overset her so. It would only provide him with vast amusement. Instead, she would concentrate on delighting in the wonderful architecture and furnishings of Amberton Hall.

She prayed, however, that he would take her suggestion on drinking to heart. Overindulgence might be a way of life for these raffish, multiple-bottle men. But in this situation, it could only bring about a high probability of scandal.

On his way to the library, Colin informed Mitchell that he wished to see his friends as soon as they left their rooms. Despite what he had said to Lady Hope, the revels at Amberton Hall must be curtailed. Last night, the fellows may have been too far in their cups to pay him heed. This morning, they would be sober and must agree to be attentive and agreeable to the feminine guests. If they were not, someone was going to end up becoming the lady's husband. That thought should put a damper on any high spirits. Who among them would wish to marry such a shrewish prude?

He sat down behind his desk and leafed through the stack of correspondence that had been growing, unattended, for the past few days. Most of the letters were invitations to house parties. Several were bills. Two were written in the careless hand of his former mistress, who apparently did not wish to believe that he had given her her congé. All of the missives seemed frivolous in comparison to his present dilemma. He tossed them aside.

Lady Hope Blissfield. For all her bravado, she was but a babe when it came to dealing with hardened bachelors like himself and most of his friends. They knew women just as well as he did and could see through their tricks and games. Lady Hope was no different from any of her sex. She wanted something. In her case, innocent though she must be, she probably wanted a husband. Trying to reform a rake would be quite a challenge to the little vixen. Why else had she opened her door last night? She'd planned to compromise one of them and to proceed to make his life miserable. He hoped that his friends would take due notice. Now that she was on the prowl in his home, everyone was fair game.

He didn't think for a moment that she was really interested in Amberton Hall, unless it was to become the mistress of it. Oh, probably she was curious to make a brief tour of the residence, but that wouldn't occupy her for as long as she wished to pretend. She was merely using it as an excuse to be seen and approached. He must keep track of her activities.

He glanced at the clock. It was still early for his friends to make an appearance. Had the lady begun her ridiculous 'tour'? Grinning to himself, he decided to spy on her. He left the library and went in search of the wily lady.

Colin didn't have far to go. He could hear her clear voice coming from the open door to the Blue and Gold Drawing Room. What on earth was she saying?

"One does not wipe a painting with a cloth. That rubs in the dirt."

Captivated, he drew silently closer.

"I am certain that Mrs. Dawes would agree. It must be done like this."

He leaned against the doorjamb to watch. Lady Hope and a very young maid were standing before the hearth, gazing up at the portrait of his great-grandfather. With an expert flick of a feather duster, the lady dislodged dust from the lower edge of the frame.

"And one must work one's way down," Lady Hope instructed. "You see? Now we have dirt on top of the mantel which you had already cleaned. Work down and in. Do the sides of the room first, working your way to the middle. That is the most efficient way to clean."

"Yes, m'lady." The maid stared at her with awe.

"Have you ever cleaned this room?" she asked.

The girl shook her head. "I'm a kitchen maid. The regular maid that does this is sick today."

"I see. Do you like this work?"

"Oh, yes, m'lady! 'Tis better than the kitchen!"

"Then you must learn to do it properly, so that you may advance. And remember, you must be very careful. Amberton Hall is filled with priceless treasures. It is a privilege and a great responsibility to care for them."

"Yes, m'lady. There's lots of pretties in here." The little maid glanced around the room and caught sight of Colin. With a small shriek, she dropped an awkward curtsy.

Lady Hope turned. "My lord?"

He straightened and strolled in. "A most enlightening lesson." He nodded to the servant. "Leave us for a moment."

With visible relief, she scurried away.

Lady Hope laughed. "I do believe she's afraid of you."

Colin shrugged, grinning. "I don't remember ever seeing her before."

"She is a kitchen maid doing double duty because one of the downstairs maids is ill. You probably have a small staff, my lord, since you are seldom in residence. When there is illness at a time like this, with guests to attend, resources may become quite strained."

"Chiding me, Lady Hope?"

"Not at all," she said honestly. "I was merely stating a fact. Contrary to your opinion, I do not wish a constant quarrel with you."

"Good." He couldn't think, for the life of him, what reason he could use for seeking her out. "I'm surprised that you know so much about cleaning," he wondered idly.

Her reply was brittle. "I suppose you now suspect me of being a maid in disguise."

"Impossible, Lady Hope! Not with your air of command. But come now, I don't wish a fight with you either. I was simply expressing an interest."

"Well, in that case . . ." She smiled, a becoming little

flush staining her cheeks. "All properly brought-up ladies are taught to manage a household." She laid the duster on a table and sat down. "Did you not know that, my lord?"

"I thought it was the job of others."

"No. I suppose it has been—here at Amberton, at least—but I will assure you that a capable mistress of a home is knowledgeable about all facets of its management. Before she died, my mama taught me all she knew about the subject. Didn't your papa teach you how to run an estate?"

"All he taught me to do was drink liquor, play cards, and seduce women," he answered waspishly.

Colin was shocked by his own bitter viciousness, but what he said was true. The previous Lord Amberton had been a lamentable wastrel. Slightly embarrassed by his own admission, he turned away from her and kicked a log in the fireplace, sending a burst of sparks up the chimney.

He drew a deep breath. "Lady Hope, I doubt that my father himself knew how to run an estate."

"I'm sorry," she murmured.

"Why? It is the Amberton heritage!" He laughed mockingly. "Luckily, we've always had excellent stewards."

"And you accept that?" she asked incredulously.

"Certainly. Am I not an Amberton, following in the footsteps of my forebears?"

Lady Hope exhaled with a small *whew.* "Somehow I do not think you are satisfied with that."

"No? Why shouldn't I be? I lead a life of pleasure, my lady. I have stewards to oversee my estates and a man-of-business to handle my investments. I seldom need to bother with any of it. I am free to pursue my own amusement."

"Is it enough?" she asked quietly.

Colin found himself drumming his fingers on the mantelpiece. This conversation was decidedly uncomfortable. She was forcing him to throw wide many windows of his life that were better left unopened. He dropped his hand to his side and swung around.

"I am doing what is expected of me." He saw the vivid disagreement in her eyes. "You don't approve, do you?"

She shook her head. "No, my lord, I do not. Nor do I think that *you* are satisfied with it."

"No?" He smiled cynically.

"No." She remained solemn. "No one wishes to be useless."

He laughed again. "But, Lady Hope, I am of great use to some!"

"No doubt you refer to your mistresses," she said primly, ignoring all decorum.

He lifted an eyebrow. "I did have that in mind, among other things."

"Such as?" she challenged.

"I provide grist for the gossip mongers and entertainment for my friends."

"What do you provide for yourself?"

Excitement? Stimulation? Suddenly Colin found himself at a loss for words. It was past time that their talk had ended.

"Have you experienced the pride of accomplishment?" she pounded on. "Of responsibility?"

"This is outside of enough," he flared. "I don't believe I have ever met a lady with such a frank tongue in her head."

Lady Hope had the grace to look contrite. "I apologize, Lord Amberton. It is one of my weaknesses. That, and my . . . impulsiveness."

He seized on her concession. "You mean you *do* admit to having some?"

"I'm sure I do." She rose hastily. "If you will excuse me, sir, I shall go to my room for a while."

"But you haven't finished your tour."

She looked out at the falling snow. "It seems that I shall have a great deal of time to do so."

Colin watched her walk from the room, her hips gracefully moving the soft wool of her dress. What a fine derriere she had! He would like to fondle . . . He caught hold of his fantasies. No, no, no! She was a *lady.* Damn it all, it was dangerous even to contemplate ideas like *that.*

4

"Oh, Hope." Having heard the story of the young lady's morning foray into the company of Lord Amberton, Agatha Sommers, seated at the table in Hope's sitting room with her breakfast before her, sighed and sipped her tea. "You should never have left your room."

"I gave the subject considerable thought."

The widow raised a skeptical eyebrow.

"Well, I did. *Honestly,* Agatha, I truly did! And I decided that we too are guests in this house, no matter what the circumstances of our presence. As such, we are entitled to amuse ourselves as we see fit." Hope sank down on the softly cushioned window seat and curled her legs beneath her. "It is unfair that we should be imprisoned in our rooms like common criminals."

Agatha glanced pointedly around the luxuriously furnished room. "Hardly like common criminals," she said wryly. "And truly, our seclusion is for our own safety. These men are hardened, unsavory rakes."

"Fustian! They may be perfectly scandalous, but by birth they are gentlemen. Now that they have sobered up overnight, they will mind their manners. Lord Amberton will direct them to do so."

"Goodness, he is the worst of the lot! It is like asking a fox to guard the chickens." She slowly shook her head.

"I must strongly insist that you remain confined to your room."

Hope laughed. "I shan't do it, Agatha. Indeed, I doubt you expect me to heed what you say! When I am determined, you know you are unable to exercise the slightest amount of influence over me."

Agatha frowned worriedly. "Please, Hope, you have always listened to reason. You must be rational about this. We are cast into a veritable den of iniquity! We must be circumspect. If Lord Blissfield, your brother, discovers that I have permitted you to associate with these . . . these reprobates, he will fire me!"

"He cannot do that," Hope said firmly. "You are my employee and, most of all, my friend. Besides, Gerald will never know. No one will."

"You are wrong!" Agatha cried. "When these gentlemen return to London, they will become intoxicated at their clubs and tell the story to every member present! Word will spread to the entire *ton*. As it is, we shall be lucky to maintain our reputations. Society may eventually forgive us, because of our predicament, but if tales of our socializing with these rogues leaks out, we shall be ruined!"

"Ha! Who believes a man who is foxed?" she scoffed. "I refuse to hide in my room and be bored beyond belief. Lord Amberton has given me permission to explore the premises and to make use of his library. I intend to do so."

"Please do not," Agatha begged. "If you wish reading material, I shall fetch it. I am too drab and unattractive to ignite the gentlemen's lust, but you are not. The very thought of you entering that nest of debauchery makes me shiver."

"Eat your breakfast," Hope said shortly, eyeing her companion and appreciating what the other lady apparently did not.

Agatha Sommers was actually quite lovely. Her dark eyes were heavily lashed and held a hint of mystery. Her shining brown hair, coiled in a neat knot on her swanlike neck, was thick and lustrous. Her face was finely boned and perfectly oval. Her body was slender and willowy. Hope envied the lady's statuesque appearance and was continually surprised that Agatha had never remarried.

The widow ate a piece of toast and laid her utensils on her plate.

"You should eat more of that," Hope commented. "You've scarcely had enough to keep a bird alive."

"I cannot. This food is so greasy it makes me nauseous."

"It certainly is poor," she agreed wholeheartedly. "I am appalled to find that the country seat of a marquess boasts such a lamentable cuisine. I happened to notice that Lord Amberton merely played in his food too. Obviously it was not to his liking. I do believe that I shall complain to Mrs. Dawes about the cook."

"Hope, you cannot!" Agatha gasped. "You are not the mistress of this house!"

"Then I shall inform Lord Amberton." She nodded sharply. "Yes, that is what I shall do. It seems that we will be in residence for some time. We may as well make our visit as enjoyable as possible."

"Oh, please do not," the widow pleaded. "We should remain as unobtrusive as we can. We must not incite his ire. After all, we are remaining here in his largess."

"We are not charity cases," Hope proclaimed archly. "We have rights as guests."

"Guests do not make issue over their meals or accommodations. Or entertainment, for that matter!" Agatha wailed. "Hope, I've never seen you like this. Why are you forsaking your good manners? You know better!"

"Yes, I do, but . . ." She lifted a shoulder in a half-shrug. "This is such a wonderful house. It deserves better. Do you believe that houses have souls, Agatha? If they do, then Amberton Hall merits perfection."

Her companion eyed her suspiciously. "You are speaking fustian. It isn't this mansion you're concerned with. It's Lord Amberton. Why must you challenge him?"

Hope smiled wickedly. "It's exciting, I suppose, though he can be terribly irritating."

"He can also be terribly dangerous! He is a rake of the first order. He is beyond redemption. You cannot be ignorant of the Amberton reputation! They say he has mistresses by the dozens. He drinks. He gambles. He is without honor."

"Ha! I can handle him! I have already been successful in getting my way."

"Only because he has allowed it!" Agatha shrilled. "Hope, he comes from a long line of scoundrels. You are playing with fire!"

"I shall not even be singed." She lifted her pert chin, a devilish glint in her eyes. "He shall learn some lessons from me. Oh, yes, so he shall!"

Her friend moaned. "Is there nothing I can do to bring you to your senses? Don't you realize what he could do to you?"

Both of the ladies startled as the door to the outer chamber burst open and, just as abruptly, slammed shut. Martha ran into the sitting room, clutching Hope's newly ironed dress so tightly that it was compressed into a small, sure-to-be wrinkled bundle. With an oath that was shrieked out in a mixture of anger and distress, she flung it onto a chair. Tears trickled down her cheeks. Frantically, she wiped them with the back of her hand.

"What is it?" Hope cried.

The abigail sniffled, swallowing with difficulty.

"What has happened?" she entreated more soothingly.

"That Mr. Torwin!" Martha shrilled loudly. "That thatchgallows!"

"Quietly," her mistress implored. "Who is Mr. Torwin? Tell me, what did he do?"

"He's a guest of Lord Amberton, and he leered at me! That's what he did! An' then he gave me a wink!"

"What!" She sat up straight, dropping her feet to the floor. "Sit down, Martha, and fully describe what happened."

The girl plopped into the chair atop Hope's ruined gown and wiped her eyes on her sleeve. "I went downstairs to iron your dress, my lady. When I came back up, that Mr. Torwin and another man were coming down the hall."

"How do you know Torwin's name?" Hope queried.

"The other man called him that."

"Very well, what happened next?"

"When I saw 'em coming, I got way to the side of the hall, but that Mr. Torwin gave me that nasty smirk and told the other gentleman that I was a lovesome wench. Then he winked at me. He told his friend that he'd like to see me later, Lady Hope."

"Oh, he did, did he?" She set her jaw.

"What will I do, my lady?" the girl whimpered. "I'm afraid t' leave the room!"

"Do not be afraid. I shall tend to the matter." She rose, her body stiff with anger. "If anyone is confined to a room, it will be that blackguard, Torwin!"

"It ain't fair," Martha wept. "Just because I'm a servant don't give gentlemen the right to treat me like a bit o' muslin, does it, Lady Hope?"

"No, it does not." Hope patted her shoulder.

"It wasn't my fault! I got way out of his path!"

"You are not to blame," she declared. "Nothing about it was your fault."

"What are you going to do, my lady?" the abigail asked timidly.

"I shall confront him. Never again will he play his shabby games with you!"

"Be careful, my lady. He . . ."

"I am not afraid of him." Hope strode toward the door. "Stay in the room until I return."

"Hope!" Agatha leaped after her, catching her arm. "You must not go! Aren't you aware of the possible consequences?"

Hope shrugged free. "I will not allow my servants to be accosted," she muttered coldly.

"You cannot say that Martha was precisely *accosted.* It

was a mere flirtation. It is in the nature of many gentlemen to trifle with any female in sight. I am sure he meant nothing by it." Agatha turned to address the abigail. "You need not fear Torwin, Martha. I am certain that nothing will come of it."

Two huge tears rolled down the maid's cheeks. "I'm afraid of 'im, I am."

"I won't stand for it," Hope growled. "I will not have my servants intimidated."

"Oh, please," her companion entreated. "Let us remain sequestered! Martha can sleep on the sofa. Your dresses do not need ironing, for no one will see you. Lord Amberton's servants can bring us our meals. There is no need for any of us to venture from our rooms."

"Right is right, and wrong is wrong," Hope stubbornly persisted. "I shall see that justice is done. Please comfort Martha, Agatha. I shall return presently."

Still clutching Hope's arm, Agatha made one final appeal. "My dear friend, do not think you can defend us all."

Hope tilted her head questioningly.

"You took up arms because my breakfast was ill-prepared," the widow said softly, "and yet I'll wager you ate your own and remained silent about it. The same is true of Martha's little incident. If it had happened to you, you would have bristled, I'm sure, but there it would have ended. There is no need for you to confront the man. We shall soon be gone from here."

"Look out the window, Agatha. You will see that we shall be remaining here for longer than I care to imagine. Therefore, I shall settle this matter. The man deserves his comeuppance."

Agatha leaned close to her ear. "But the transgression was not so terribly serious. Poor Martha is so very skittish and imaginative," she whispered.

Favoring her with a long, combative look, Hope stalked from the room and down the hall. Her heels clicking sharply on the treads, she descended the stairs. The poor breakfast, indeed, was of no great consequence, and she didn't intend to discuss that subject at present. But nothing, absolutely nothing, angered her more than a member of the upper class taking advantage of one of the lower orders. She simply wouldn't stand for it.

"Where are Lord Amberton and his frivolous friends?" she irately demanded of a footman in the hall.

Fear flashed through his eyes. "In . . . in the library, my lady."

"Show me the way!"

The footman ran before her. He paused to scratch on the door, but Hope swept past him and opened it herself. Head high, she paused in the transom as startled eyes turned toward her.

"Lady Hope!" With shock on his face, Lord Amberton started toward her.

She ignored him. "Which one of you is Torwin?"

"I am Sir Roger Torwin." A tall, slender gentleman stepped forward.

Hope marched across the room to where he stood.

"My lady?" With confusion, he began his bow.

"I'm warning you, sir," she hissed. "You will stay away from my servants, or you will answer to me! I will not abide your villainous games!"

"W—what?" he stammered. "What did I do?"

"You winked and leered at my personal maid. You uttered suggestive comments about her to your comrade. In short, you frightened her out of her wits!" She shook her finger under his nose. "I won't have it! Do I make myself clear?"

"Oh, for God's sake." Recovering from his befuddlement, Sir Roger bit his lip to keep from laughing.

Hope ground her teeth. "Do not think you can make merry about your foul deed! I will cause you to be very sorry for it, sir. And that goes for each one of you," she coldly addressed the assembly. "Those who do not conduct themselves as gentlemen will pay!"

"What is the meaning of this?" demanded Lord Amberton, regaining his wits.

"I wish I knew," Sir Roger muttered, backing away. "I didn't touch the girl. I merely appreciated her comeliness. You know how it is, Colin, I . . ."

"This man," Hope interjected, pointing an accusing finger at Torwin, "completely overset my maid!"

"Did he really?" The marquess grinned.

"Yes, he did! And it isn't amusing!"

"Come now, Lady Hope," Lord Amberton soothed. "Roger's crime seems minimal. He simply expressed admiration of a pretty face. Your abigail should be flattered to have attracted the notice of a man of his caliber."

"That's right," Sir Roger grumbled. "After all, she's only a servant."

Hope gasped. She tried to utter a caustic reply, but her rage made any semblance of coherence impossible. Clenching her fists, she started toward the baronet once more.

Lord Amberton was quicker than she. He neatly stepped between the two adversaries, permitting Sir Roger to duck out the door. He lifted a hand, locking his sparkling violet eyes with her smoldering brown ones.

"Allow me to settle this, Lady Hope," he said calmly.

"I do not need you to fight my battles!"

He ignored her, shifting his gaze to his engrossed colleagues. "Gentlemen, though I'm sure this is vastly amusing, I must ask you to leave us."

"Are you sure, Colin?" One of them snickered as they obeyed his request. "Looks like you have a tigress by the tail! You might need our assistance."

"I shall most likely survive."

Hope whirled, striding to the window and standing with her back to him. She felt weak all over from her explosion of temper. She almost wished that she could have hit Sir Roger for his denigration of poor Martha, but it was probably better that Lord Amberton had intervened. Still, she would not back down. The baronet was in the wrong, not she.

"Lady Hope, are you composed enough to listen to reason?" the marquess asked.

"To reason, yes!" she snapped, turning. "To absurd excuses, no!"

"Whew, what a shrew." Lord Amberton shook his head.

"If you think I am shrewish to defend the rights of powerless serving girls, then you are right. That is what I am, and I am proud of it!"

"Don't you think you're exaggerating a bit?"

"No!"

He sighed, moving to the sideboard. "I believe we could both use a drink."

"That is all you think about," she observed disparagingly. "Drinking!"

"In times of trial, I consider it helpful." Refusing to rise to her bait, he poured himself a glass of brandy and for her, a measure of wine. "I must apologize for serving you port, Lady Hope. There are no ladies' drinks available at the moment and I did not wish to call a servant."

"I don't want anything!"

"Please? It will ease your distress." He pressed the goblet into her hand. "For me?"

Hope stared into his beautiful, oddly colored eyes with their absurdly long, dark lashes. No man should possess such an irresistible attribute. It was patently unfair!

"Very well," she capitulated, "but do not expect the spirits to cause me to change my position."

"Never! Let us sit down?" He presented his arm.

Hope allowed him to seat her on the sofa. She was rather dismayed when he sat down beside her. Pretending to straighten her skirt, she edged away.

Unable to suppress a smirk, Lord Amberton quickly took a slip of his brandy. "My lady, I am certain that Roger was merely engaging in a small flirtation, a momentary thing which would have gone no further. He meant no harm. Perhaps your abigail is overly excitable?"

"Martha is cool-headed," Hope stated, feeling slightly guilty for the fib. "But that is not the point. It incenses me to see those who are privileged taking advantage of those who are not."

"I agree," he said reasonably. "You may assure your maid that she is safe. None of my friends would force themselves on any female. They are not debauchers."

"Then why did you tell us to lock our rooms?" Hope fired back.

"Prudence, my lady."

"Humph!" She sipped the fruity, full-bodied wine, marveling at its superb quality. The marquess might be a multiple-bottle man, but he was not indifferent to what he drank from those vessels. He was a true connoisseur.

"You see," he went on to explain, "most men of my acquaintance like to flirt. So do the ladies, for that matter. Don't you agree?"

"No! Certainly not!"

He leaned back his head and gazed at the ceiling. "Really, Lady Hope, haven't you ever engaged in flirtation?"

"Never in my life have I tried to lure a man," she said airily.

"You're wrong." He chuckled. "You do it all the time."

"I absolutely do not!" She stiffened, but couldn't help eyeing him curiously. "What makes you think so?"

"The way you walk, for instance."

"How do I walk? I walk just like anyone else. Explain yourself!"

His laughter faded to a lazy grin. "I don't believe you want me to get into that subject. You'd take offense."

"I promise I will not," she prodded. "Tell me."

"Suffice it to say that your . . . uh . . . derriere moves in a most fascinating manner."

Heat surged to Hope's cheeks. "I . . . I can't help it!"

"I wouldn't want you to. I find it immensely charming."

Hope nearly choked on her mouthful of port. Oh, how could this be happening to her? How could she be sitting here on Lord Amberton's sofa, discussing her bottom with him? It was scandalous!

"You asked me," he reminded her.

"You infamous rake!" Setting aside her glass, she leapt to her feet. "You odious lecher!"

He leaned back his head and rolled his eyes.

"You deliberately directed the conversation in a manner to insult me!" Hope railed, hands on her hips.

"An insult? My lady! I was paying you a compliment."

"Oh . . . oh . . ." Words would not come. Flustered, she started toward the door, then remembering her controversial derriere, she turned and sidled out sideways to the echoes of Lord Amberton's laughter.

What a vexatious man! But he could be reasonable too. Why couldn't he be that way always?

After finishing his drink and regaining possession of his aplomb, Colin departed the library and found his friends in the billiard room. He waived a turn to play and lounged back in a chair, sipping a glass of brandy and regaling the gentlemen with tales of his morning encounters with Lady Hope. "So far, these are her rules." He chuckled. "We shall be sworn to secrecy about her and her companion's presence here. We shall avoid the ladies as much as possible and not disturb them. Furthermore, we will limit our partaking of spirits."

The gentlemen laughed.

"You are already aware of the fourth rule, that of not taking liberties with the servants. Really, Roger, you know that I don't permit familiarity with the serving girls, anyway."

"I'm sorry, Colin. The whole thing was exaggerated, but the girl's a comely wench, and, well, one never knows." He grunted sarcastically. "I do now. Lady Hope is a formidable crusader. I do believe she was prepared to hit me."

"What a magnificent vixen!" Lord Bridgewater agreed. "I'd like to see someone tame her. In fact, I'd like to be the man to do it. Limit our drinking! The very idea! What is she? Some sort of temperance advocate?"

"Actually she's right," Lord Kelwin said quietly. "The

ladies are in an uncomfortable situation. We should try to make it as easy for them as we can."

"And ruin our fun?" Bridgewater protested.

Kelwin shrugged. "We can have fun when they are gone."

'Thank you, Andrew," Colin told the earl. "I'm glad to have an ally. Much as I hate to curb my love of brandy, I'm afraid it's the only answer. I'm just hoping that we'll soon have a break in the weather."

"As much as I enjoy seeing their pretty faces, I suppose that the ladies should stay in their rooms," sadly commented Sir Roger. "After all, this is a bachelor gathering."

"Yes, indeed," Colin concurred, "but Lady Hope won't accept it. She claims to be a guest and not a prisoner."

"*Make* her do it, Amberton," the baronet grumbled. "This is your house party. She wasn't invited, and it wasn't designed for her pleasure."

"I don't think I'll go that far. Let us get by in the best way we can and avoid confrontation. I'll admit that I'm challenged by fencing with her, but it's best not to raise her hackles. Surely this circumstance won't last much longer, and she'll soon be on her way."

Viscount Bridgewater grinned. "I can understand your feelings, Colin. She is a luscious little baggage just begging for a man to tame her. Watch your step, though. The task of making her submissive to male superiority would take a lifetime . . . and a trip down the aisle."

"Good God, Jamie! The nonsense you come up with!" Colin rose, refilled his glass, and strolled to the window. "Everyone in this room knows that I will never marry."

"Do we?" Lord Kelwin asked. "With your brother's death last summer, you're the last male of the line."

"That's right," he murmured, "but it doesn't change my decision."

Sir Roger laughed. "Give him a few more years and we'll see what he has to say on that score. We're all of us going to end up leg-shackled. It's our duty!"

"It isn't mine," the marquess affirmed.

"You're really serious, aren't you?" The smile collapsed on the baronet's lips. "But Colin, what would happen to your title? Your entailments?"

"They'd go back to the Crown, I assume."

"You can't let that happen," Jamie Bridgewater said with shock. "Good God, man, haven't you been schooled like the rest of us on our family responsibility?"

"What would it matter to me? I'd be dead." He forced a smile. "Truly, gentlemen, can you picture me as a husband and father, dandling a baby on my knee?"

"God forbid that sight, but you don't have to touch your infants." Sir Roger's face distorted with aversion. "All you have to do is sire 'em."

His words and expression brought on a shout of laughter from his friends.

"I'm serious!" he insisted. "All of us have enough blunt to pay a servant to give our brats the attention they need. When I marry, I intend to go my own way, and my wife can go hers, after she's given me legitimate heirs that is."

"What a warped idea," said Drew Kelwin.

"What's wrong with it?" Roger demanded. "Tell us, Kelwin. You're a widower. You have two children. You've had the experience of it."

"I like spending time with my twin daughters. Now that they're getting a little bit older, I'm beginning to have fun with them." He flushed slightly. "And at the risk of sounding sentimental, I enjoyed the companionship of my wife."

Bridgewater whistled low. "This is serious talk."

"Yes, it is. *Too* serious for a bachelor party," Sir Roger lamented, picking up a cue stick. "Let's have a game, fellows, and take our minds off this subject. Good Lord, Kelwin makes marriage sound so good that I'm almost ready to run out and propose to Lady Hope!"

"She'd make mincemeat of you, friend," Jamie warned. "She'd serve you up on a platter, and you certainly wouldn't be accompanied by wine!"

"More like vinegar," said Sir Roger. "I wish she'd leave."

So did Colin. Tuning out the chorus of jesting, he turned to the window. Pulling back the undercurtain, he peered through the glass. The wind had diminished. The flakes weren't as large. But the snow continued to fall steadily from the leaden skies, promising a lengthy period before the roads were clear enough for travel.

"Marriage isn't so bad," Lord Kelwin intoned, sauntering up beside him. "It's a matter of finding the right woman."

Colin's lip curled cynically. "From what I gather, my forebears had no trouble with that. It's just that though the lady was right for the Amberton, the Amberton was not right for the lady."

Dropping the drapery, he swung back to the festivities.

5

Following her unsettling confrontation in the library with Lord Amberton and his friends, Hope was more than willing to allow Agatha's pleas for their privacy to prevail. The two ladies had requested that a simple luncheon, consisting mainly of soggy meat pies and cold, limp vegetables, be served in Hope's sitting room. After pushing the food about on their plates and eating little of it, they'd spent the rest of the afternoon in dreary conversation and uninspiring needlework.

When Agatha began planning to have their supper sent up as well, Hope put an end to the idea. No, no, and no! She could not bear another minute of confinement! They would take their meal in the dining room just like any other guests. Not surprisingly, Agatha didn't like the notion, but, after extracting a promise that Hope would mind her manners *and* her tongue, the widow reluctantly agreed. So together the ladies descended the stairs to whatever fate might await them.

Hope was rather surprised by her friend's appearance. She had expected Agatha to dress drably and unattractively in order to ward off any unwanted male attention, but although she remained prim in her attire, the widow was perfectly lovely in her soft blue woolen gown. She even wore the small diamond earrings that Hope had given her for Christmas.

"You look so nice tonight," Hope told her.

"Thank you." Agatha blushed with pleasure. "So, of course, do you."

Hope glanced down at her unadorned, deep pink dress. "I hope that my garb is not too plain. I certainly do not wish to draw Lord Amberton's scorn and ridicule! But I decided that dressing formally for dinner would not be expected under these circumstances."

"No, probably not."

"Perhaps we should have asked Mrs. Dawes though." She hesitated, suddenly seized with uncertainty.

The widow halted on the next step down. "There really isn't time now. Besides, you haven't a care for what these gentlemen think of us, do you?" she asked practically.

Hope fiercely shook her head. "Definitely not, but . . ."

"If Lord Amberton makes a derogatory comment," Agatha interjected; "you need only pretend that you didn't hear it. It's just as simple as that." Agatha continued downward.

"No, it isn't simple at all," Hope muttered, catching up. "I do so like to give him tit for tat."

"But you're not going to do that anyway." Agatha smiled sweetly. "Remember? You did promise to hold your tongue."

Hope sighed.

Mitchell met them at the bottom of the stairs. "Good evening ladies," he intoned, respectfully bowing. "The gentlemen have already assembled in the library to await the meal."

"They're having drinks, no doubt," Hope uttered disparagingly.

The dignified butler's carefully schooled face confirmed nothing, but he seemed to stiffen a little, as if waiting for a storm to strike.

"May we wait in the drawing room?" Agatha hurriedly put in.

"Of course, madam. This way please." He ushered them to the Blue and Gold Room and offered them sherry, which Agatha declined and Hope accepted.

After he left, Agatha gazed with outright awe at their surroundings. "My, but this is lovely. If all of Amberton Hall is as magnificent as this, it must be a veritable palace!"

Hope nodded eagerly, her small pique forgotten in her enthusiasm for the beautiful home. "It's just full of treasures. You should accompany me in my explorations."

"Perhaps," she said doubtfully. "I truly don't know if you should poke and pry like that."

"Lord Amberton gave me his complete permission."

Her companion wavered. "Well, it would help pass the time. But still . . ."

"Please join me, Agatha! We'll take care to avoid the gentlemen. I promise!"

"We can't, however, escape reminders of them, can we?" Agatha looked pointedly at the portrait over the mantel. "He must be an Amberton. He greatly resembles the marquess. Goodness! They are a handsome family, aren't they?"

"Too handsome for their own good," Hope snorted. "Totally dangerous and entirely depraved."

Her companion giggled unexpectedly. "Notice that wicked glint in his eyes. It's as if he knows how we look without our undergarments."

"Agatha!" Hope cried with mock horror. "I cannot believe that you would note such a thing, let alone voice it!"

Agatha's whole expression twinkled uncharacteristically with daring, mischievous merriment. She bit her upper lip in a failed attempt at stemming her levity. "Oh dear, I am becoming quite corrupt! Decadence must be in the very air of Amberton Hall."

"Or in the anticipation of the company we will keep at dinner. Is there such a thing as a *lady* rake?"

"I don't know," Agatha tittered. "Wouldn't we shock the *ton* if we suddenly became very raffish and brazen?"

Both ladies burst into peels of laughter.

"Yes, the aura of impurity just might rub off on us. I wonder if we shall learn to disrobe gentlemen with our newly acquired, lascivious gazes?" Hope chortled, rising and approaching the painting to salute it with her wine. "How would you like it, sir, whichever Amberton you may be, if we stripped you of your unmentionables?"

"He's my great-grandfather," stated Lord Amberton from the doorway.

Hope startled, nearly dropping her glass. Her cheeks, her neck, her entire body burned with mortification. Slowly she turned to face him.

"My lord," she said breathlessly, "I was not aware of your presence!"

"Obviously." A lazy grin played at the corners of his mouth. "But here I am. Here *we* are, in fact. In a valiant effort to appear civilized, my friends and I have decided to join you."

Hope glanced quickly at Agatha to gauge her state of well-being. Her poor companion's reaction to the embarrassment was just the opposite of her own. Instead of being hotly flushed, the widow seemed drained of every ounce of blood she possessed, but she was gallantly battling to regain some semblance of poise as she favored the marquess with a brittle smile.

"How kind of you, my lord," Agatha managed to murmur.

Lord Amberton bowed politely to her and entered the room, followed by his snickering friends. He made a straight line to Lady Hope. Violet eyes glittering with the same naughty spark as those of his ancestor, he bent his head toward Hope's ear.

"In answer to the question you put to my forebear, the old reprobate would probably like it fine, my lady," he whispered.

"Oh!" she mumbled nervously, hurriedly taking a sip of sherry.

"You see, the Ambertons have always enjoyed the ravishing attentions of beautiful ladies. But he is only paint and canvas. You would receive a more appreciative response from an Amberton of flesh and blood."

Hope wished that a hole would open in the floor and swallow her up forever. "I am appalled by your effrontery, sir," she tried to say severely, lifting her chin. "We shall not discuss this further."

He chuckled. "You're right. We shan't, for the excitement of the topic is causing me to forget my duties as a host! I must make introductions." Stepping away from her, he began to perform the task.

Hope, of course, had earlier become acquainted with Sir Roger Torwin and was dismayed when the baronet strolled up to her.

"Well, Lady Hope, quite the pert, little hypocrite, I see."

"I don't know what you are talking about," she coldly replied.

"Your wine, of course," he retorted. "Amberton has instructed us on all your rigid rules, especially the one concerning the imbibing of alcoholic beverages. I now observe that you do not practice what you preach. Somehow, I am not surprised."

"You mistake the matter, Sir Roger," Hope rallied. "I have nothing against a person taking an occasional drink. I do, however, deplore the overindulgence of spirits. The practice is unhealthy, disgusting, and can be perilous."

Lord Bridgewater joined them, catching her last sentence. "What activity is so disagreeable?"

"Drinking," Sir Roger answered flatly.

"Drinking? How strange of you to say so, Rog! I thought you engaged in a lot of it," he quipped.

"It's *her* opinion, you dolt," the baronet growled.

"Oh, I see," he drawled, taking a step closer. "It's the opinion of the most opinionated, but breathtakingly luscious, Lady Hope. But, hark! Perhaps she is changing her mind! Is that not a glass of sherry I see in your hand, my dear?"

"I'm sorry it was ever offered to me. And I am not your

dear!" Hope set her glass on the mantel with a decidedly firm click. "It is obvious that none of you can tell the difference between what is permissible and what is not."

Bridgewater shrugged negligently. "I, too, have my doubts as to whether any of us can. That even includes you, madam, and your companion."

She gritted her teeth. "In that, sir, you are wrong."

"Am I?" An unholy glow of amusement lit up his handsome face. "I seem to recall—pardon my pun—your *mention* of *un*mentionables."

"Eavesdropper!" Hope snapped. "You expect me to deny it, don't you, my lord? Well, I will not! I shall, however, inform you that my jest was not meant for the ears of the opposite sex."

"I realize that." He nodded reasonably, but a smile still tugged at the corners of his mouth. "In the same vein, our partaking of spirits and, yes, revelry, is not meant to be witnessed by you and your chaperon. Why don't you keep to your room, Lady Hope, and cease attempting to ruin our party?"

"I am a guest too!" she claimed defiantly.

"But an uninvited one, though I must say that you are a marvelous delight to look upon. If you don't wish to be cooped up in the nether regions, why not shed your prickles and join in our fun? You might just enjoy yourself, and I do assure you that none of us would ever reveal your naughty little secret."

"Odious beast!" Hope glanced about for an escape route, but flight was impossible. The fire was at her back. Sir Roger and Lord Bridgewater were standing too close to afford her easy passage. Unless she literally pushed them out of her way, she was trapped.

Helplessly gazing past the two, she managed to catch Lord Amberton's attention as he conversed with Agatha and Lord Kelwin. Thankfully, he must have recognized the look of desperation in her eyes and decided to play the role of her champion. Detaching himself from the others, he came to her aid.

"What's this?" he asked genially. "Are my friends distressing you, my lady?"

"We were praising her beauty," Bridgewater claimed. "I swear, Colin, I have never seen a *femme* more stunning! Her neck is so swanlike; her nose, so splendidly chiseled. Good God, I could lose myself in her eyes. And her hair . . ."

"Cut line, Jamie!" The marquess held up his hands in protest, while Hope groaned irritably. "Please do not commence one of your orations, or our dinner will grow cold before you are finished! I'm sure that Lady Hope has captured the general gist of your appreciation. And now, if I may steal her from you?" Without waiting for a reply, he neatly drew her away from them, tucking her hand through his arm.

"Thank you," Hope muttered.

"It's quite all right. I was growing jealous of their monopoly anyway," he purred.

"Nonsense!"

Lord Amberton laughed. "Jamie's correct, you know. You are an extremely attractive woman."

"Now it is your turn to cut line," Hope warned him. "And furthermore, he wasn't . . ."

Abruptly Mitchell appeared in the doorway and announced the meal. The marquess guided her from the room and turned down the hall. Peeking over her shoulder, Hope saw that Agatha was being escorted by Lord Kelwin and was actually smiling up at him.

"He wasn't what?" Lord Amberton queried, returning to the previous subject.

"Lord Bridgewater and Sir Roger were not being complimentary. They were being disrespectful and cruel!"

He lifted an eyebrow. "Indeed? It sounded like flattery to me."

"My lord, you did not hear it all. They were making fun of my requests and my standards of conduct. They even questioned my very status as a lady!"

"They did? Then they were absolutely in the wrong! The veriest corkbrain would realize that you are a lady."

"I appreciate that, my lord," she told him earnestly. "Your level of intelligence must be a great deal higher than that of your friends."

"Apparently so. After all, your father was an earl. That circumstance positively makes you a lady," he proclaimed.

"That's not what I meant! I . . ." She saw the twitching of a smile on his lips. "Knave! You are fully aware of what I implied!"

He laughed.

"Very well!" Hope bristled. "If that is the way it's to be, I shall not speak with you or any of your colleagues for the duration of my stay at Amberton Hall!"

"I doubt that, Lady Hope," he mirthfully declared. "I doubt it very much. I have an idea that keeping a still tongue in your head would be a total impossibility for you."

"Just wait and see," she warned and, dropping his arm, preceded him into the dining room.

"At all our meals, I prefer to maintain informality," Colin explained to the ladies when all had taken their places at the table. "Under the circumstances, it would be ridiculous to observe the usual social customs."

Lady Hope gave no indication that she had even heard him, but Mrs. Sommers inclined her head in agreement. "That is very true, my lord. Informality will be much more pleasant."

"I've always detested formal dining," added Sir Roger. "Whoever came up with the rule that one had to spend an equal amount of time conversing with the person on each side of one? I always seem to end up with at least one antidote seated beside me and find myself bored beyond all measure."

"So do I," agreed Jamie Bridgewater, "and in this case, it's you, Rog. I'd much prefer to talk with Lady Hope."

The others laughed, but Lady Hope remained stiff-faced.

"So you see, Sir Roger?" Mrs. Sommers ventured rather timidly. "If there were no rules, you yourself might be the one who is neglected at a very large party where your host or hostess might not be aware of your predicament."

"Exactly!" seconded Lord Kelwin, eyeing her with something like reverence.

"Balderdash!" insisted Sir Roger jovially. "I can fend for myself."

"He'd be the first to complain," Kelwin told the widow.

While Mitchell and his footman served up the soup course, Colin peered down his table of assembled guests. Lady Hope sat on his right, with Mrs. Sommers on his left. Next to the earl's daughter was Jamie Bridgewater. Beside her companion was Drew Kelwin. Sir Roger had seated himself below Jamie. It was the most unlikely group of diners ever convened. Colin prayed that they could get through this meal and the subsequent ones, which would probably be many, without disaster.

Their first whole day together had passed, and the snow continued to fall, showing no sign of abating. Even when it did, it would be a long time before the roads would be passable. There was a possibility, though, that he and his friends might be able to chance traveling while the conditions were still too treacherous for the ladies. He would feel no guilt about leaving Lady Hope and Mrs. Sommers without a host. They would be only too glad to witness the departure of the gentlemen.

With a sigh, Colin dipped his spoon into his bowl. Matters would improve if the males would completely ignore the females, but that was well-nigh impossible unless the ladies would keep to their rooms. He and his comrades were red-blooded, virile men who greatly appreciated women. They couldn't disregard such comely creatures as Lady Hope and Mrs. Sommers, when the two thrust themselves right under their noses. Besides, he found it was too much fun to flirt and fence with the volatile Lady Hope.

Giving up any thoughts of exhorting the gentlemen, and himself for that matter, to overlook the ladies, he sipped the broth. The situation with the females was not the only objectionable thing at Amberton Hall. So was the food. The soup was greasy and gritty. There was even a sliver of onion skin floating in his serving. Colin couldn't understand what had happened.

The cuisine at Amberton Hall had always been one of the few good things about being at home. In the past, it had been unquestionably delectable; now it was undeniably atrocious. It was either greasy, dry, cold, undercooked, overcooked, or a nasty mixture of several of those attributes. Colin wondered if he'd angered the cook by arriving unexpectedly to host a house party of ravenous gentlemen. That might well be. Cooks were known to be cantankerous, weren't they? Perhaps he should speak with Mitchell, or Mrs. Dawes, or better still with Cook herself. He might be able to charm his way into forgiveness.

From the corner of his eye, he saw Lady Hope lay down her spoon with a faint expression of distaste. The meals at her house were probably perfect. They wouldn't dare to be otherwise!

"Is something wrong, my lady?" he couldn't help prodding.

She pretended not to hear him, and he remembered her oath of silence.

"Hope?" her companion prompted anxiously.

"I haven't much of an appetite tonight, Agatha," the lady directed.

"Too much sherry?" teased Bridgewater.

A muscle quivered and hardened along Lady Hope's fine jawline.

Colin grinned with appreciation. The little beauty might have vowed not to speak, but it was hardly necessary. Her expressions and postures were thoroughly eloquent. He tried to predict how long she would last and concluded that Lady Hope couldn't keep her mouth shut for long.

The meal lumbered onward with course after course,

each seemingly worse than the one preceding it. Due to their snowbound isolation, there could not be much variation on the food served, but couldn't what they had be nicely prepared? At least the joint and the middle of the slices of bread were edible, though the beef was dry and tasteless. Surreptitiously, Colin motioned to Mitchell.

"Is Cook angry with me?" he asked quietly.

"Of course not, my lord!" The butler was shocked. "Like the rest of us, she is always glad when you come home."

"I see."

Mitchell glanced down the table at the huge amount of food that would be returned to the kitchen. "Cook is old, sir," he said gently.

Colin nodded. "That will be all, Mitchell."

Old? What did that have to do with cooking ability? She should be more experienced and even better at the job. But if that was the only explanation, Colin supposed he'd just have to live with the problem. Cook had been at Amberton Hall all her life, and he certainly wasn't going to fire her.

Colin watched Lady Hope gracefully turn down a dessert of crusty, sagging cake. One after one, his guests followed suit. It was embarrassing, but there was nothing he could do about it. The meal had ended. The food had been horrible, and without any participation from Lady Hope, the conversation had been dull.

Mrs. Sommers rose. "We shall leave you gentlemen to your port."

The marquess and his friends stood. "You'll join us for tea or coffee in the drawing room afterwards?" Colin asked.

"Please excuse us from that, my lord," the widow said pleasantly. "It has been a long day."

"Of course, but . . ." He thoughtfully eyed Lady Hope, who also had risen from her chair.

Proudly holding her head aloft, she curtsied minutely and swept out of the room with her companion hastening after her.

"Well, what do you think of that?" Jamie Bridgewater inquired. "What did you do to her, Colin?"

"Ruffled her feathers, I suppose."

"See that you don't do it again! I was looking forward to her spice," he complained.

"You and Roger had a hand in it too, Jamie." He signaled Mitchell to serve the wine. "She is aggravated with us and has taken a vow of silence."

Bridgewater grinned. "So straighten it out."

"Me? Why me?"Colin objected.

"You're the host."

"Yes," Sir Roger concurred. "Smooth it over, Colin. It was a dead bore without her pithy tongue."

"I doubt if I'll have to," he admitted ruefully. "We'll commit some transgression, and we'll hear from her soon enough. Before this farce is ended, she shall probably appreciate her choice to leave us alone!"

Closing the dining room door behind them, Hope marched past Agatha and headed toward the stairway. Her companion caught up with her just as she swung around the newel post. Luckily, Agatha didn't try to slow her, for Hope was of no mind to proceed decorously.

"What on earth has gotten into you?" Agatha gasped. "You purposefully ignored the gentlemen's questions."

"Didn't I promise you that I would hold my tongue?"

"You know that is not what I meant! You were rude, Hope. It isn't like you."

"If I was ill-mannered, they deserved it." Swiftly she related the conversation that precipitated her total silence. "They questioned my very position in life!"

"That may be," Agatha admonished, "but you should let it pass over your head. You are too gently bred to behave like you did."

They entered Hope's chamber, bolted the door, and advanced to the sitting room.

"Every remark that they make to me is couched in

thorns," Hope complained, collapsing into a chair. "They deliberately try to overset me."

"Might it be that they think *you* deserve it?" Agatha asked softly. "The rules you lay down, the justice you attempt to mete out . . . And didn't you admit that you enjoy fencing with Lord Amberton? How can you expect him not to return your parry?"

Hope was forced to smile self-consciously at this logic. "Well, I suppose you could be right."

Agatha exhaled with relief. "Either directly or indirectly, you have challenged all of them, and they are reacting to that."

"I almost wish I hadn't. They are unfortunately worthy adversaries! But my standards are correct, and I intend to uphold them," she vaunted.

"Then be prepared for the barbs."

Hope sighed. "Agatha? Do you believe that I am in the right?"

"I believe that we should have remained in our rooms from the very first moment. However, we wouldn't have met . . ." Eyes wistful, she turned to stare at the fire.

"Yes?" Hope urged, sensing something strange in her friend's mood.

"It's nothing." Agatha blushed furiously.

"Tell me! What were you going to say?"

"It's silly, really, and you must make nothing of it," she shyly related. "I simply found Lord Kelwin's company to be quite pleasant. He doesn't seem so rakish as the others."

"Lord Kelwin," Hope mused.

"Now there's an end to it!" Matter of factly, Agatha stood up. "It might be early, but I'm going to go to bed. The day's events have exhausted me more than I can say. I suggest that you seek your rest too."

"Perhaps I will, but I'll give Martha time to finish her supper before I ring for her."

"I can help you undress," her companion offered.

"No, I wouldn't think of asking you! You are weary. Be

off with you!" Hope rose, laughingly shooing her friend to the door.

"Very well. Good night. And bar the door!"

"I shall." She squeezed Agatha's hand. "Sleep well."

Securing the lock, Hope wandered back to the sitting room. What a day! It seemed like ages since she had greeted Lord Amberton over breakfast. Like Agatha said, it had been fatiguing. She was just too tired to think of it all.

There was one thing, however, she couldn't dismiss. Her stomach was rumbling in objection to its emptiness. With all her other concerns, she had banished the notion of finding out what was wrong in the kitchen. At dinner, she had overheard Lord Amberton's soft conversation with Mitchell. Perhaps tomorrow she would investigate Amberton Hall's culinary facilities. After all, the marquess had given her his permission to explore at will.

The thought of improving the food renewed her spirit. She could scarcely wait until she delved into the matter. Without prolonging the time it would take for Martha to attend her, Hope began to make ready for bed. The more quickly she slept, the faster the next day would come. Food! No one, not even a devilish rake, could ridicule her for arranging a tasty meal.

6

In spite of her weariness, Hope had a poor night's sleep. She was disturbed very late by the noisy bedtime procession of Lord Amberton and his friends. Apparently, they had not heeded her edict concerning their drinking, for they sounded as if they'd once again partaken to excess. But more distracting than that, she was absolutely starving. Those hunger pangs made her more restless than anything else and confirmed her determination to do something about the cuisine. She rose, eager to commence her culinary reforms.

Hope did not hesitate to take breakfast in the dining room. Lord Amberton had retired far too late to be up and about as early as she. Therefore, she was so astounded to see him sitting at the table that she forgot she had vowed never to speak to him again.

"My lord!" she gasped. "I cannot understand why you are here! I certainly never expected it."

He looked up blearily from the open book beside his place and failed to rise respectfully. "As I have informed you in the past, this is my house. I do suppose I have the right to sit in my dining room and eat my breakfast."

"You don't look so well," she chided.

"Please leave off, Lady Hope," he begged. "I have a ferocious headache."

"Such a shame." She waved away Mitchell's assistance and filled her own plate from the sideboard. "If you had followed my advice, you would have greeted the morning with pleasure."

Lord Amberton grunted.

Hope sat down at the table and eyed her meal. She was so hungry that she could eat almost anything, but this serving would tell the tale. It was just possible that the cook had had an off day and that everything would be right from now on. Toying with her eggs, she prayed that was so. Taking a deep breath, she tentatively nibbled a bite.

The eggs were almost worse than they were the day before! They were greasy and salty and rubbery. She pushed them aside and cut a bite of ham. Cured and seasoned before Cook got her hands on it, it was edible, though slightly overfried.

Mitchell must have seen her dismay for he bent over her shoulder. "Is everything all right, my lady?'

How could he ask such a question? Had the man no taste buds? Surely the Amberton servants received much the same food as the master.

She opened her mouth to complain, but thought better of it. There was no point in forewarning the kitchen of her displeasure. She could accomplish more with surprise tactics. But in the meantime, she might as well punish Lord Amberton for his overimbibing by forcing him into a conversation. She smiled with anticipation.

"I am not so hungry, Mitchell," she said sweetly. It was no lie. She would have to be a whole lot hungrier to eat those awful eggs.

The butler nodded, satisfied. "Coffee or tea, my lady?"

"Tea, please. And Mitchell?"

"Yes, my lady?"

"Could you open the draperies?" she requested. "It is so dark and dismal in here. One should meet the morning with good cheer."

"Indeed, ma'am." He poured her beverage and moved to accomplish the task.

"Must we?" Lord Amberton winced as light flooded the room.

Gnawing on a piece of charred toast, Hope ignored his doleful question. The dining room did have a lovely view from its long row of windows. The vista swept across a hedge-enclosed side lawn to a rolling field beyond. Unfortunately she could not see for any great distance. The sifting snow obliterated any possibility of that.

"Still it snows," she observed.

Lord Amberton groaned.

"I have never, in all my born days, seen such a storm," she mused. "It should go down in the record books."

The marquess growled unintelligibly.

"It might be interesting to keep written notes about the weather," she wickedly went on. "Don't you think so, my lord?"

"I give up." He snapped shut his book. "I see that you have broken your vow of silence and are determined to talk."

"Oh, that . . ." She shrugged. "Do forgive me, Lord Amberton. I am accustomed to conversation at the dining table. Agatha and I usually discuss our daily plans over breakfast. And my father, and now my brother after him, always indulged in morning chats. Discourse just seems to start the day off right!"

"Not for me it doesn't," he grumbled. "Not today."

"Informal meals should be a time of comfortable togetherness," she went on. "At Blissfield Hall, we find great camaraderie in our mealtime discussions. You should try it, sir."

"Um."

"At Blissfield Hall, no books or newspapers are permitted at table," she scolded saucily. "We take pleasure in each other."

Lord Amberton rolled his eyes. "Far be it for me to criticize the sainted Lords Blissfield, but since I frequently dine alone, I am in the habit of taking pleasure in myself."

"But you are not alone today," she lightly reminded him.

"Believe me, Lady Hope, I am well aware of it!" His clouded violet eyes narrowed dangerously. "But if I were truly to be permitted to take pleasure in you, I would not do so in the dining room, under the eyes of my staff. I would choose a more secluded location."

Behind him, Mitchell cringed. The footman bit back a grin and turned, shoulders shaking, to flee the room. In brief seconds, the butler followed, coughing.

Hope flushed hotly. "How dare you?" she hissed.

The marquess pressed onward. "The type of conversation which you describe, my lady, implies a degree of intimacy. To my abject disappointment, I doubt that you and I will ever achieve that level of communication. Unless, of course, you have second thoughts on the matter? Remember that I am your servant, always willing to please."

Her mouth dropped open to this suggestive dialogue. Even when he was under the weather, he was quick-witted. She suddenly realized that if she berated him as soundly as he deserved, he would probably trap her with accusations of lack of innocence. In fact, that was probably his gambit. Well, he wouldn't catch her! Wishing she could give him a rich setdown, she demurred.

"I do not think it requires such deep knowledge of the other's *character* for two people to chat about the weather, or about one's plans for the day," she countered artlessly, sipping her tea.

He grinned appreciatively. "Rather mundane topics for the comfortable togetherness you seem to recommend," he persisted.

"Not really. This snowstorm is such an unusual and awe-inspiring occurrence that it must be foremost in everyone's mind, despite the nature of their relationship."

"Very well, Lady Hope," he conceded, draining his cup and reaching for the bell to recall Mitchell. "You are correct. I have never seen such weather either. I am greatly discommoded by it."

"Had you planned to leave the hall, my lord?" she queried.

"No, but I certainly hoped you'd be gone by now."

"So had I," she said with heartfelt fervor, crossing her knife and fork on her plate so that the distasteful mess could be removed.

"I had intended to hunt," he reflected. "I wish I had done so before the storm. The venison would have been a welcome change."

Hope wrinkled her nose. "More likely it would have been tough and gamy. Wild meat requires great finesse in cooking to make it palatable."

They suspended the conversation while Mitchell served the beverages and the footman removed the plates.

"Must you disagree with everything I say?" Lord Amberton goaded when the servants had finished.

She negligently lifted a shoulder. "I am merely stating facts."

He eyed her suspiciously. "Then why do I have the distinct impression that complaints are forthcoming?"

She flicked a glance at him. There was that glitter of wariness in his violet eyes, but his tone of voice was amiable. Perhaps he really was fishing for her opinion of the food. Lord Amberton was a man-about-town. Even if she hadn't witnessed his quiet comment to Mitchell last night, she would be certain that he knew that the hall's cuisine fell far below average. He might be desiring a feminine point of view on what to do about it. On the other hand, he could merely be picking a quarrel to spice up their discourse. Whatever his motive, she decided to take her chances.

"You must be aware, my lord," she succinctly informed him, "that the food here is barely tolerable."

"Aha! I knew you had criticism up your sleeve!" he gleefully cried. "You didn't want a friendly chat. You wished to provoke me!"

Hope pursed her lips. "That breakfast was enough to provoke anyone without my assistance."

"God almighty, I have never been acquainted with such a persnickety guest!" He laughed. "I do believe that you are the most outspoken, opinionated, and dictatorial female I have ever met, Lady Hope. You should be grateful that I took you in, but no, you make complaints and lay down regulations."

"My *requests* are for the good of the group," she snapped. "Goodness, I should have realized that you did not want my advice on what to do about the food. You only wished to fence with me! And here I was, in spite of the storm, attempting to be in good spirits this morning."

"Poor little lady," he mourned mockingly. "She was cheerful, and the bad, old marquess ruined it all. Such a dreadful man!"

"You jaded wastrel! Disgusting, obnoxious beast!" she shrilled.

"Now, now, my dear." He chuckled. "You know you derive the greatest pleasure in crossing swords with me." He laid down his napkin and rose. "I've won our little duel this morning. Won't you allow me the victory? After all, yesterday I was kind enough to listen to all your rules and homilies. And today I set aside my book and ignored my headache for you. Shouldn't I receive some reward for my thoughtfulness?"

"Victory! Reward!" Hope snorted. "It looks to me like you are in retreat."

"I consider my reward to be the solitude of my library. I am withdrawing to enjoy it." He made a taunting bow. "Good day, *petite.*"

"Shut up," said Hope as the door closed behind him.

Damn and blast! Could he never be serious? The gentleman was incapable of carrying on a normal conversation.

Setting her jaw, she stared across the table and through the window. He might disregard the displeasing meals at Amberton Hall, but she would not! His support would have eased the interview with the cook, but she could prevail without him.

From the looks of the weather, she would be snowbound

far longer than she wished to contemplate. So be it! She would not suffer herself to go hungry. As soon as the kitchen was cleared up from breakfast, she would pay Cook a visit and set matters to rights. If the feat could not be accomplished, she and Agatha would prepare their own meals.

Hope smiled with the righteous anticipation of a crusader. Her appearance backstairs would no doubt be unsettling to the servants. With any luck at all, a disgruntled Cook would cut up Lord Amberton's peace by clapping him over the head with a rolling pin.

"May I serve you anything else, my lady?" Mitchell worriedly broke into her reverie.

"No, thank you." Eyes sparkling, she got up and left the room, intent on her mission.

"Oh my, I detect trouble on the wind," the butler muttered to his footman, staring anxiously after her. "The lady has something on her mind. I fear that things will not be the same here. Perhaps never."

"She's a handful, that she is," the servant ventured. "Some man should turn her over his knee. She's a shrew."

Mitchell stared unhappily at the sideboard full of barely touched food. "She's also right," he murmured. "I wish something could be done about Cook, but unless Lord Amberton steps in, our hands are tied. After all the years she's been here, I'm not going to fire her and neither is Mrs. Dawes."

Avidly watching the clock, Hope allowed an hour to pass before making her way through a veritable rabbit warren of halls to reach the service area of the great house. Allowing her nose to be her guide, she stopped before a door from which emanated an acrid scent of burnt bread. Quietly throwing it open, she paused to take note of her surroundings before any of the occupants saw her.

Amberton Hall's kitchen was a dreary place. The whitewashed walls were dingy with age, smoke, and grease from the steam. Masses of iron and copper pots, pans, and skillets hung from the ancient rafters. The cabinets and work tables were dented and bowed from centuries of use. Apparently all cooking was done on the mammoth open fireplace and brick bake ovens. There were no modern improvements like the innovative Rumford stove in Hope's home. The whole facility looked like an unhappy survivor of the Middle Ages. Hope could scarcely believe her eyes.

The inhabitants of this anachronism were unaware of their visitor. A small boy turned a spit upon which was a row of chickens roasting over scorchingly high flames. In the corner, a girl was peeling apples. At a bleached oak table, another maiden poured vinegar into a huge pot. With her back to Hope, a gigantic, gray-headed woman was stirring the contents of a cracked bowl. If they were oblivious to Hope, they were also inattentive to the thread of smoke that seeped from one of the ovens.

Hope cleared her throat. "Hello?"

The servants startled. The boy fell to his backside on the hearth. The girl dropped an apple, which rolled bruisingly across the flagged floor. The other lass lost hold of her spoon and plunged her hand into the concoction to retrieve it. Only the immense older woman retained her assurance as she slowly revolved around to face the caller.

"Something is burning," Hope announced flatly and advanced into the room.

"Oh!" The servant at the table let go of her spoon again and darted forward to pick up a pad and open the oven. Pungent smoke billowed forth. She hastily jerked a tray of buns from within, slinging several to the floor as she did so. Bending down, she began to pick up the fallen rolls and return them to the pan.

"No!" Hope cried.

The girl faltered, staring first at the buns and then at the lady.

"They fell on the floor. They are soiled," Hope firmly told her.

"Oh, no, ma'am." She smiled bashfully. "I cleaned this floor m'self this very morning."

"No matter how spotless it appears, it is not fitting to eat from it. Dropped food must be discarded." She picked up one of the rolls and turned it over. "Moreover, these are burned."

"I can scrape their bottoms, ma'am," the maid persisted. "They'll be fine."

"I cannot allow these to be served." Realizing that with such an announcement, she was proclaiming herself the mistress of Amberton Hall, Hope lifted her chin and met the gaze of each member of the kitchen staff.

As she expected, they gaped at her, then at each other, and finally the younger employees cast sidelong glances at the older woman. She knew they were assuming that she was Lord Amberton's fiancee. She must put a period to it before the inevitable spate of gossip circulated through the mansion.

"I am Lady Hope Blissfield," she informed them. "Since there is no mistress of this house, I shall perform those duties during my residence here."

The expressions of speculation left their faces, but not the looks of surprise. Though they may not have entertained lady guests at Amberton Hall before, the servants obviously knew that such an assumption was not in the proper way of things. She could only wish that she would appear strong enough to have her way in spite of conventions.

Turning back to the oven, Hope stuck her hand inside. "It is entirely too hot to bake a suitable bread. Let it cool before you put in the rest, and then watch them very closely."

"Yes, ma'am." The girl curtsied.

"My lady, I am the cook."

The moment had come to face the ruler of the kitchen, who would certainly not welcome this interference. Up close, Hope could see that the old servant was practically a giantess, towering over her like a gargantuan. She fought intimidation.

"Lord Amberton has never complained of my cooking. He likes it," Cook intoned in a low, deep voice.

"Is that why he scarcely touches his plate?"

"He eats a lot," Cook refuted.

Hope was not about to get into a sparring match with the obdurate old virago. "You have your opinion; I have mine. Nevertheless, it appears that I shall be dwelling here for some time. I will direct the meals."

Cook pressed her lips together in an unmovable line. "I been cookin' at Amberton Hall all my life, an' my mother before me. I know what m'lord likes. I don't need advice."

Hope struggled for a comeback. "Nevertheless, I have several recipes that I wish to have prepared."

"Can't read."

"Then I shall stay here and direct matters."

"This is my kitchen," the amazon rumbled. "Stay abovestairs where you belong, my lady."

Hope drew herself up to her greatest height, which only brought her to the monumental bosom of the woman. "No."

Cook began to tremble. "Get out!"

"I shall not go away, and I shall not abide your impertinence!" Hope snapped. "You go too far. You will be sorry!"

"Not me, my lady. 'Tis you who'll be in trouble! M'lord won't have your meddling in m'business!"

"We'll see about that." Hope pushed past her and went to the work table, beckoning the girl who had been laboring there. "What is this?" she asked peremptorily, indicating the mess in the pot.

Quavering, the servant came forward. "S-sauced potatoes, ma'am."

Hope dipped the spoon and tasted, blanching at the sourness of the mixture. "You have used too much vinegar. Fetch sugar. We'll see if we can make it right. Otherwise, we'll have to throw it out."

Cook followed, looming large across the table. "Go away!"

Hope ignored her. The servant girl, apparently deciding that the lady was to be obeyed instead of the cook, complied with her instructions. She appeared with a cone of sugar and began grating it, while Hope added and sampled until it was just right.

"Now," she said with satisfaction. "Try it."

The maid tasted, her lips curving into a wide smile. "'Tis good, my lady!"

She nodded with satisfaction. "Always remember to taste while you are mixing, especially when you do not follow a written receipt. What is your name?"

"Daphne, ma'am." She leaned toward Hope's ear. "I can read a little bit."

"Would you like me to write down some recipes for you?"

The girl eagerly bobbed her head.

"We don't need nothing like that," Cook said. "M'lord likes the way I do it."

"No, he does not," Hope disputed. "The food here is inedible."

"It ain't!" The old woman picked up a rolling pin and shook it. "I ain't never seen the likes of this! You get out of here right now!"

Hope eyed the culinary weapon and the angry retainer. It was probably best to make a retreat. But the battle had not been lost. Now that she had broken the ice, she'd speak with Mitchell and Mrs. Dawes about the situation. It was too late for them to come up with a way to prevent her involvement. And she and Agatha would write down every receipt they could remember for Daphne.

The cuisine at Amberton Hall would improve. Her will would prevail over Cook's. At least, today's luncheon potatoes would be good.

She dusted her hands and strolled to the door. "I'll be back!" she tossed over her shoulder as she departed. "Never doubt it a minute."

From across his desk, Colin unhappily eyed his three servants. Mrs. Dawes looked stiffly uncomfortable. Mitchell had taken refuge behind his sober mask of dignity. Cook was angrily shaking her rolling pin.

"I won't have her meddling!" the old retainer screeched. "Not in my kitchen!"

"No, Cook," Colin soothed. "I'm sure Lady Hope did

not mean to insult. She is probably longing for some of her favorite foods."

"She don't belong backstairs!"

"The lady is accustomed to managing her own household. She realizes that you have been saddled with unexpected mouths to feed and, no doubt, thought to lend her assistance. I'm sure she means well and did not wish to hurt your feelings."

"She said my cookin' was no good!"

Colin exchanged glances with Mitchell and Mrs. Dawes.

"I'll just quit cooking," she raged. "That's what I'll do!"

"No," he said hastily, "you mustn't do that. There is no one to take your place."

"It'll serve her right! Let her do it all!"

Colin groaned. Lady Hope, of course, was correct in her judgment of the meals. The food was abominable. But he couldn't do without Cook. No matter how poor the cuisine, it was all they had.

"I've cooked for you all my life, she railed, close to tears. "You used to come to the kitchen to snabble macaroons when you was a little boy. You liked my cooking."

"Yes, I remember. How could I ever forget your macaroons?" he murmured, recalling how soggy they were when he'd eaten some last week. "I don't want you to quit, Cook."

"Then keep her out of my kitchen, m'lord!"

"Don't fret, Cook." He rose, signaling that the meeting was ended. "I'll speak with Lady Hope."

"You speak loud, m'lord. It'll take a great big bellow to get through that thick head o' hers!" Cook snapped the rolling pin onto the desk. "Shake that at her! Pop her on the backside! That's what that young lady needs."

That was probably true, Colin thought as Cook curtsied awkwardly and whirled out of the room with Mrs. Dawes following. He sank back down into his chair and tented his hands, resting his chin on them and staring into space. The interview with Lady Hope would not be a pleasant one.

"Brandy, sir?" Mitchell chanced.

"No." He didn't want to meet with the lady with alcohol

on his breath. That would open up a further field for battle. This one was bad enough. "What do you think of it, Mitchell?"

"If you do not wish a drink, my lord, it is solely your affair."

"No, no, I'm speaking of this situation. What do you think of Lady Hope?"

The butler seemed to retreat even further behind his mask of dignity. "I'm sure I couldn't say, sir."

"Come now, my man," Colin prodded. "I know that you and the other members of the staff must have opinions of her. I'd like to hear what is being said."

"Is that an order?" Mitchell asked politely.

"No." Colin sighed. "You've known me from birth. I wouldn't presume to give you an order. It was simply a request."

The old retainer permitted himself a small, fleeting smile. "Lady Hope is accustomed to getting her way, and her opinions are most definite."

Knowing that the servants were as well informed about the lady as he was, because of their uncanny web of gossip, Colin waited for more, but nothing seemed to be forthcoming.

"Is that all?" he finally queried.

Once again that ghost of a smile crossed the butler's lips. "The lady's views, my lord, may not be welcomed by those they affect, but they are often correct."

Colin eyed him uncomfortably. Many of those views involved himself. He was certain that the people of Amberton had loved him as a boy. What did they think of him now? This, however, was not the time to assess his popularity. He must address the issue at hand. Lady Hope might take it into her head to return to the kitchen before luncheon.

"Thank you, Mitchell." He took a deep breath. "And now, would you please send for Lady Hope?"

7

Nerves jangling, Hope presented herself in the library. She had few doubts about the reason why Lord Amberton had requested an audience with her. At best, Cook had probably voiced her complaints about Hope's visit to the kitchen. At worst, someone had reported her claim to be the temporary mistress of Amberton Hall. In either case, she had the feeling that the marquess was going to be rather irritated with her. When she saw his frown, she was certain of it. Mentally preparing herself for battle, she curtsied prettily.

"You wished to see me, my lord?" she asked innocently.

"Yes," he said shortly, rising and motioning to a chair that had been drawn up behind the desk to face his. "Won't you sit down?"

Hope seated herself on the edge of the chair, anxiously fussing with her skirts. Lord Amberton, too, sat down, his back as stiff as a ramrod, as if he were barely holding back his temper. She cast him a doleful glance.

"Why?" he asked without preamble.

Hope retreated to ignorance. "Why what, my lord?"

"Why did you interfere in the kitchen?"

In Hope's mind, aggression was always the best defense. "How can you ask a question like that?" she replied in wonderment. "I went to the kitchen in an effort to improve the cuisine. It certainly does need it, my lord!"

"Oh it does, does it?"

"You know it does! It is barely edible," she answered fervently. "I cannot eat it, and you yourself scarcely touch your food. Also, I overheard your conversation with Mitchell last night."

"If you noticed all that, and knew I was aware of the problem, why didn't you come to me?" he queried, slightly peevishly.

She smiled in what she hoped was a caring and concerned manner. "I did not wish to take you away from more important matters, my lord."

"Oh, ho!" Lord Amberton hooted. "You won't tempt me to believe that fustian! I know for a fact that you consider my activities to be trivial and useless. *Important matters,* indeed! Given your agile mind, I would expect you to come up with something better than that, Lady Hope."

"I am trying to avoid making you angry," Hope snapped, giving up on her sweet and gentle approach.

"That is a fruitless fantasy, madam, because I already *am* angry. Go on, Miss Frank-tongued Busybody! Let us have the truth of the issue."

"Very well, Lord Amberton. You asked for it! I did not come to you about the cuisine because I knew you would do nothing about it," she accused. "This beautiful house deserves better; your guests deserve better; I know I deserve better; and so do you! How can you put up with such abominable meals?"

"And how can you assume that I would do nothing about it?" he pried.

"Because you are a man."

His anger seemed to lessen somewhat. His eyes glittered roguishly as if a suggestive remark had crossed his mind, but he did not voice it. "What does my sex have to do with something like this?"

"Gentlemen are not adept at household management," she airily told him.

"I must disagree."

Hope snorted. "I am not surprised. Though you have already accused me of constantly disagreeing with you, I find that you, in turn, generally dispute everything I say. You are a pot who is calling the kettle black."

"That isn't true!" He sat up even straighter. "But as to your previous proclamation, I see no reason why a man cannot run a house just as well as a woman. There's nothing to it. The staff does all the work."

"Ha! I might have expected you to have such a thought! My lord, you are wrong. Do you remember our conversation in the drawing room yesterday?"

He grinned. "Yes. About the unmentionables."

"I am not referring to *that,*" Hope faltered, blushing furiously. "I am speaking of the cleaning of the room. Oh, it is just like you to bring up that other! Gad, you are such an impossible libertine."

"At least I do not pretend to be something I'm not," he laughingly told her. "Yes, Lady Hope, I am a rake, but you are not a cook. Why are you feigning that role?"

"I know how to cook," she said in no uncertain terms. "I can cook better than that old termagant in the kitchen."

"Indeed?"

"Indeed!"

He shrugged. "Unfortunately you will not be able to prove it. I am forbidding you to go to the kitchen, my lady. If you attempt to enter it again, I'll have you evicted."

Hope trembled with irritation. "You'd toss me out? In this weather?" She dramatically waved her arm toward the window and nearly smacked him in the face.

Lord Amberton dodged. "Please, my lady, let us not be so demonstrative! I almost lost my nose on that gesture. Unless you truly did intend to hit me?"

"If I'd had that intention, I wouldn't have missed!" she said sharply.

His eyes glowed with merriment. "I always thought I had a rather nice nose," he mused. "Don't you agree?"

"Your nose is fine, my lord, but . . ."

"Thank you. I appreciate the compliment. Furthermore, I am astonished to find that we agree on something! Perhaps we should confine our conversation to my nose for the duration of your visit."

"Stop this nonsense." Hope folded her hands in her lap. "We have not finished our discussion of the cuisine."

"Oh, yes, we have. We have decided that you are not allowed to go into the kitchen."

"You decided. Not me!" Unable to sit for a moment longer, she got up and began to pace the floor. "I can do something about it. If you would approve my actions and encourage Cook to pay me heed. I can reverse this mess."

"Do you see this?" He picked up the rolling pin from his desk.

Hope eyed him warily. She had been so intent on his facial expression that she hadn't noticed that threatening culinary weapon. What on earth was he doing with that?

"My irate cook left it with me, along with the suggestion that I use it on your bottom, my lady."

"Such impertinence!" she gasped.

"I tend to agree with her." He chuckled. "But I would prefer to use my hand. A good spanking would benefit you immensely, Lady Hope."

"How dare you!" She glared. Such nerve! Here she was, attempting to help in a matter that greatly affected his comfort. And what did she get? Threats of violence!

"Oh, I would definitely *dare,* my lady." His violet eyes twinkled. "But much as I would like to be the administrator of such discipline, I will not indulge in the whim at this time. I will merely reiterate that you are to stay out of the kitchen, else I may change my mind."

"I am Lady Hope Blissfield! I have my rights! I am the daughter of an earl and, by birth if nothing else, I do possess a respected position in society. You cannot lay a hand on me!" she told him severely.

He laughed. "Pulling rank on me, my dear? All right, I am the *marquess* of Amberton. And this is *my* house, *my* estate, and *my kitchen!*"

"Here you are again!" she blazed. "Treating me like a child!"

"And here *you* are again, acting like one."

"Only because of *your* attitude." She scowled at him. "You are behaving like a selfish little boy who will not share his toys."

"My kitchen and my cook are not your playthings, Lady Hope." He smiled wickedly. "You, on the other hand, could be *mine,* if you would redirect your passion to pleasure, instead of to self-righteousness."

"You disgusting lecher! I shall pretend that I did not hear that remark."

"Just as well, I suppose. If you took me up on it, I'd really be in the suds." He grinned, tenting his hands and resting his chin on them. "It would be like welcoming a hedgehog to my bed."

"There will be no more talk of seduction," she admonished him. Good heavens, how could she be carrying on such a discourse? A proper young lady would already have swooned away. Perhaps Sir Roger and Lord Bridgewater were correct. Perhaps she really wasn't a lady in the true sense of the word.

"My, my, another rule, Lady Hope. One which concerns seduction?" Lord Amberton asked teasingly.

"Yes!" she shrilled.

"Then I must inform the others of this latest development. We cannot leave them in ignorance of any new regulations."

"You will say nothing about it," she warned. "And in the future, you will treat me with the respect that is my due. I cannot believe that you have the audacity to speak to me about debauchery!"

He lifted an eyebrow. "Isn't that what you expect of a rake and a libertine? I am merely fulfilling my role."

Hope's temper eased somewhat, as she considered his statement. Once more, she wondered if he was simply playing a part that others had cast for him. There were many layers to Lord Amberton's character. Which one of them was truly him? She had witnessed him behaving reasonably and had glimpsed his concern for others. Was he merely hiding behind a frivolous facade?

Against her better judgment, she sat down again. "My lord, why don't you change your way of life?"

"Oh, no, not more moralizing!" he groaned.

"I am serious. You could become a valuable member of society."

"Enough, Lady Hope. I'm not going to listen to this." He removed a gold watch from his pocket and consulted it. "It's almost time for luncheon, anyway."

"Who cares?" she said with disappointment. "It won't be worth eating. I could have done some good in that kitchen."

He shook his head. "Given Cook's mood, you would have only succeeded in making her quit. Her cooking might be poor, but it is cooking nonetheless. We need her. Besides, she is an old retainer."

Hope wavered a bit. "Can't you cajole her into accepting advice? Lord Amberton, while we are bound to the house, the meals are especially important. They provide us a break in the day and should be something which we all eagerly anticipate."

He shook his head. "I won't delve into it."

Sensing that his vexation on the topic had diffused and that he might listen to reason, Hope pressed onward in a final attempt to score a victory. "I will do it for you. All you need do is to charm Cook into accepting my assistance. I know you could accomplish that."

"Can't we just muddle through this dilemma without adding more problems to it?" he begged.

"Spoken just like a man!" she announced triumphantly. "Avoiding the issue!'

"Avoiding this domestic issue, yes! Lady Hope, I spend little time at Amberton Hall. I don't know what is wrong with the cuisine. It used to be quite good. But whatever it is, I see no point in stirring up trouble. Mitchell and Mrs.

Dawes offer no comment about the situation. If they are satisfied, so am I. I doubt we'll starve."

Sensing a chance to win, she exuberantly hopped onto the desk, perching above him. "But wouldn't you rather be eating good food?"

"Yes, of course, but . . ."

"I can assure it!"

"No. And there's an end to it." His eyes wandered downward to her exposed ankles.

"I can't talk you into letting me try?" Hope, following his gaze, unsuccessfully tried to shrink her legs up beneath her skirt.

"No."

Frustrated and self-conscious, she slid to her feet. "What you need, Lord Amberton, is a wife to take care of you."

He laughed. "That's the last thing I need! Go along with you now. I'll see you at lunch."

"Yes, I suppose you shall. For what it's worth," she said morbidly, then brightened, remembering the portion of the meal that she'd salvaged. "Ah well, I suppose there may be at least one dish worth eating."

"That's the spirit!"

"Yes, isn't it?" She sauntered lightly to the door. Knowing what she did, she would take an extra large helping of potatoes, and she would be sure to advise Agatha to do the same. The dish she'd helped prepare would be delicious.

In her seat at the table, Hope waited anxiously for the potatoes to be served. First the chickens were presented incongruously on a silver platter and set before Lord Amberton to be carved. Briefly she closed her eyes at the very sight of them.

Yes, Cook and her kitchen boy had certainly succeeded in ruining them. The skin of the fowls was a deep brown and hard as old, ill-kept leather. The wing tips were black, and so were the protruding ends of the drumsticks. At least they weren't *under*cooked and slimy, Hope thought bitterly. But the meat was sure to be dry, tough, and tasteless.

The marquess picked up the meat fork and carving knife. He tried to stick the fork properly into the bird, but the utensil would not pierce the stiff skin with decorum. A soft titter from his guests accompanied his efforts. Flushing, he irritably moved the handle of the implement into his fist and stabbed it viciously into the breast meat.

Hope bit her upper lip to contain her mirth. She watched him try to slice the fowl, but the knife merely slid back and forth across the bird, making scarcely a mark on the impenetrable exterior. A look of determination settled on Lord Amberton's face. He clamped his teeth together and sawed harder.

The snickers of his guests increased in volume. The marquess's blush deepened to scarlet. Hope let loose her giggle.

"God damn it!" he cried, whacking savagely.

Agatha gasped, shocked by the mealtime profanity. Simultaneously, the chicken, as if it had had enough abuse, shot off the platter and onto the floor. The guests roared with laughter. Lord Amberton was taken aback. He stared helplessly at the company and then at the hen, while Mitchell gravely picked up the bird by its leg and carried it, at arm's length, out of the room. Grimly the marquess turned his attention to the next victim on the platter. Minus the meat fork which had departed in the breast of the previous subject, he grasped the fowl by the drumstick.

Feeling sorry for him, but unable to keep the smile from her lips, Hope lightly laid her hand on his arm. "My lord, I believe I can speak for all of us in saying that we shall pass on the chicken this meal."

The gentlemen burst forth with another round of hilarity.

"That's right, Colin!" Sir Roger chortled. "We've chickened out!"

Lord Amberton clenched his jaw. "I'm sorry," he muttered.

"I am sure that there will be sufficient offerings to

satisfy our appetites," Hope said. "Now, *that's the spirit,* isn't it, my lord?"

"You're enjoying this to the utmost, aren't you?" he growled, and motioned to the nearby footman. "Take these birds and get them the hell out of here."

Agatha wailed again.

"I apologize for offending you, Mrs. Sommers," the marquess meekly told her. "I am annoyed, and I am frustrated. I am not myself."

"You are forgiven, of course," the widow tightly declared. "I know you will refrain from further outburst."

"Yes, ma'am. I am properly chastened."

"That'll be the day," Hope murmured.

Lord Amberton sent her a scorching glance, but did not attempt to cross verbal swords.

When the offensive chickens had been removed from the table, the Amberton staff set about serving the rest of the luncheon. Knowing that the demise of the fowl would divert attention from her seeming greediness, Hope took an even greater helping of potatoes than she had previously planned. She was happy to see that Agatha followed suit. Their meal might be one-sided, but it would be tasty. She was right. Her first bite informed her that her travail in the kitchen had not been in vain.

From the corner of her eye, she glimpsed Lord Amberton eating a forkful of her concoction. Curiously cocking his head to one side, he chewed solemnly. He quickly took another morsel.

Hope smiled. He liked it! Her own dish was the best food on the table. She caught her companion's eye. Agatha nodded approvingly.

"I say, Colin!" Lord Bridgewater expounded. "These potatoes are superb. Your cook may have her failings, but she has certainly outdone herself on this offering."

"That's true," agreed Sir Roger between mouthfuls. "It's unusual, but it's delicious."

Hope caught the marquess's thoughtful gaze as he glanced from her face to her plateful of potatoes and back again to meet her eyes. He knew, she decided, that she'd had something to do with this particular creation.

She smiled sweetly. "Very outstanding. How lucky I am that I took a large helping."

"As did Mrs. Sommers," the marquess noted suspiciously.

"The two of us are quite partial to potatoes, my lord," Agatha said, regaining her pleasant demeanor.

"Yes," Hope concurred. "Please send our compliments to the cook."

"Vixen," he muttered under his breath.

"Well, I am glad that the ladies have taken aplenty," Sir Roger enthused, "for truthfully I would fight anyone, so as to have as many servings as I can get! Delectable! Utterly sublime!"

Lord Kelwin added the highest compliment. "Colin, perhaps your cook could write down the receipt so that I could give it to mine."

"Yes, Lord Amberton," Hope devilishly seconded. "Please ask her to do so. I, too, would like to serve this dish in my own home."

"I'll see what I can do." he brusquely promised. "You must remember, however, that those who prepare food can be frightfully contrary. Veritable hedgehogs!"

Hope nearly choked at that reminder of their brazen affray that morning. "Perhaps I could go to the kitchen and speak with Cook," she countered. "Sometimes a woman's touch can overcome the worst of evils."

"Oh, no, my dear lady." He almost simpered. "I wouldn't dream of allowing you to set your pretty foot into the service area."

Drat! she thought. He'd neatly slithered away from that one. Well, she'd just have to come up with another ruse. She'd get control of that kitchen, or she'd expire in the effort!

She observed that every scrap of her dish was eaten, while most of the other offerings were sent back untouched. Ha! That should prove something to his lordship!

Following luncheon, she drew him aside as they left the dining room. "Lord Amberton, did you enjoy your potatoes?"

"You know I did," he acknowledged uncomfortably.

"Do you know who directed their preparation?" she demanded.

"I have a good idea of it." He tried to squirm away, but she bodily blocked his escape.

"Well, then, won't you permit me to make further improvements in the cuisine?"

"No, Lady Hope, I will not. I *can't!*" he protested. "I've explained the situation to you. It's beyond control! Why can't you see it my way?"

"Balderdash!" She threw up her hands in frustration. "What I do see, and can scarcely believe, is that you're afraid of your own servants."

"I am not!"

"Well, so it appears to me! Listen here . . ." she commanded.

"No, *you* listen here! You run your house, and I'll run mine. That, my dear Miss Meddler, is my final say," he cautioned. "This subject is closed. Forever! I will hear no more of it."

"Gad, but you are a hardheaded man." Turning on her heel, she started toward the front hall and the stairway, then paused and looked back over her shoulder. "You have such a lovely home, Lord Amberton. It is too bad that you are so incompetent at managing it."

He started after her. "I swear I'm going to throttle your pretty neck!"

Laughing breezily, Hope scampered away to her chamber.

"He still refuses to permit me to straighten out that mess in his kitchen," Hope told Agatha, gaining the safety of her bedroom and enfolding herself into the window seat.

Her companion picked up her needlework and settled

herself for an afternoon's sewing. "He does have a point. With all the other troubles besetting us, we don't need to ask for more."

"You can't possibly agree with Lord Amberton!" she cried with astonishment.

"I fear that I do. Hope, you said yourself that the cook was cantankerous. If she refused to lift a finger, we'd really be in a tangle. Amberton Hall is short-staffed. The marquess cannot afford to lose the help of a single one."

"But Cook is not earning her keep!"

"That may be, but in this case, even inept hands are better than none at all."

Hope chewed the inside of her lower lip. "If he wanted to, Lord Amberton could sweet-talk her into compliance. The man could charm the tusks off a wild boar. Why won't he try?"

"From your description of the woman, I doubt if it would work. She's old, and she's been here too long for her to fall for anything like that. You know how these senior retainers can be! She probably sees him as a little boy."

"Most likely, you're right, but, oh, how I long for an entire meal of the quality we are accustomed to." Hope sighed and looked out the window. "It's still snowing, Agatha. Will it never stop? Will we be here all winter?"

The widow shrugged. "So much the more reason to avoid confrontation with Cook. If she were to quit, I don't know what we'd do."

"You and I would manage the kitchen."

"We couldn't! It's not just a matter of cooking for Lord Amberton, ourselves, and his guests. There are the servants to be considered. How could we cook for everyone in this household? We haven't the experience."

"We could figure it out," Hope said stubbornly.

"No." Agatha firmly shook her head. "My dear friend, I have never denied doing anything you asked of me, but I do refuse to take on that burden. It would be a travesty. I won't do it, even if you fire me over it."

"I would never fire you!"

"Then you will promise not to interfere with Cook?"

"Oh, all right. I'll stay away from the kitchen . . ." She suddenly brightened. "I'll stay away from the kitchen while Cook is present there. But Agatha! Do you know what we could do?"

Her companion moaned. "I am afraid to ask."

"After everyone is in bed, we can slip down to the kitchen and fix ourselves something good to eat!" she enthused. "Isn't that a marvelous idea?"

"No."

"But why not?" Hope cried.

"In the first place, we'd run the risk of being caught by some reveling gentleman," Agatha declared. "Secondly, Cook would be sure to see the signs of our invasion. Thirdly, how do we know that some of the staff does not bed down on pallets in the kitchen?"

"This is a big house. There wouldn't be the need for anyone to sleep there." Hope mulled over the idea. "If we stay awake, we can definitely hear the gentlemen going to bed. Even so, we could go down the servants' stairway to avoid the tiniest possibility of apprehension. As far as Cook is concerned, we can wash our dishes and clean up all evidence of our invasion."

Agatha worriedly shook her head. "I can't. I'm afraid of it."

"But aren't you absolutely starving to death?" she wailed.

"Not really. I don't eat as much as you do, Hope. If I get too terribly hungry, I shall eat what is served."

Hope wrinkled her nose. "Well, I won't. I just might try my idea."

Her companion closed her eyes as if she could shut out the entire matter by doing so. "You know I wish you wouldn't."

"Yes, but I shall be very cautious," she assured her. "I love my food and I *can't* go on this way much longer!"

* * *

That evening, after a miserable meal, Hope waited impatiently for the gentlemen to retire. When it became obvious that they were keeping very long hours, she stretched out across the bed to ease her weariness. The next thing she knew, it was late in the morning. Though at some point in the night, she had become conscious enough, or cold enough, to worm her way under the covers, she had slept fully dressed, rumpling her gown and creating extra work for Martha. Worst of all, she had not only missed her midnight feast, but she had slumbered through the regular breakfast as well. She was forced to tide herself over till luncheon with a tray of tepid tea and cold, charred toast.

At least there was one bright note to the day. Although the sky remained leaden, the snow had ceased.

Hope was not so naive as to believe that they could leave immediately. Many days would pass before the roads were safe for travel. Still, the promise of an imminent departure for home was uplifting. The vision of her dining room table heavily laden with delicious fare possessed a far greater attraction than she had ever conceived. Stomach growling, she tidied herself for a lunch that she knew would not be worthy of the china upon which it was served.

8

Colin picked indifferently at his soggy chicken pie and noticed that his guests, with the exception of Lady Hope, exhibited no more enthusiasm for the repast than he did. The lady, however, put away a credible amount of the doughy concoction. He wondered if she actually liked it or if, in truth, she was terribly hungry. Due to her past performance, he decided on the latter. Where food was concerned, she was far too persnickety to enjoy the sodden mess.

With a sigh, he acknowledged to himself that he was going to be forced to have a word with Cook. He wasn't looking forward to the confrontation. In fact, he didn't know quite how to go about it. Mitchell or Mrs. Dawes should have broached the subject with Cook, but it was obvious by their attitudes and actions that they wanted no part of the matter. They'd probably grown accustomed to the unappetizing cuisine.

Colin, himself, was finally getting hungry. If the amount of brandy and wine he consumed hadn't quelled his appetite thus far, he'd be as famished as Lady Hope. If he didn't do something about the meals, he was going to find himself in a permanent state of tipsiness.

It was a tempting idea to place the dilemma in Lady Hope's hands, but he could not do that. As a guest, it was not her place to involve herself in his household problems. More than that, he didn't like admitting to her that he could use her help. No, he'd have to resolve the difficulty himself. After luncheon, he determined to go to the kitchen to size up the situation.

Dreading his errand, he was easily diverted as he passed the small, infrequently used Rose Salon. Pausing, he remembered that he had mentioned the pianoforte to Lady Hope. If the instrument were not too badly out of tune, it could provide an excellent means of occupying the ladies. Although it would be just his luck that the neglected pianoforte would be dreadfully off-key. With a groan of anticipated disappointment, he opened the door and went in.

The unheated Rose Salon was frigid. Sheets of ice had even coated the inside of the windows, creating a frosty opaque barrier to the view. The delicate French furniture was covered with a light layer of dust. The satin draperies had lost their sheen. Obviously, Mrs. Dawes merely shut the door in the winter and ignored the room, a fate not beneficial for a musical instrument.

Colin crossed the dusty rose Aubusson carpet and sat down at the pianoforte. It had been a long time since he had played. He and the instrument would probably match each other in incompetence.

His long fingers rippled across the keys. Out of a series of chords and scales, he developed a simple folk melody. That was not so bad. He wasn't as rusty as he'd expected, nor was the pianoforte so tuneless. Indeed, he was rather pleased.

He embarked on a dimly remembered selection from Bach. Though he struck several wrong notes, he managed to do a credible job on the piece. The vicar's wife, who had taught him to play, would not have been too terribly disappointed in her former pupil, he thought. Enjoying himself, he performed an easy minuet from a memory he did not know existed. When the last lilting chord floated through the air, he heard a small murmur from behind his back.

Glancing over his shoulder, Colin saw Lady Hope seated on a dainty settee just inside the door. A footman, bearing a basket of wood, bent over her. Shaking her finger in a scolding fashion, she directed the servant to the fireplace, then caught his eye.

"That was so beautiful, my lord," she said, blushing slightly. "Won't you continue?"

"I don't know how much more I can remember." He wasn't enthused about performing before an audience, especially when it was composed of the critical Lady Hope, but the magnetic lure of the keyboard overrode his reluctance. He managed to make it through "Greensleeves" and "The Ash Grove" without too many bobbles.

Lady Hope applauded exuberantly. "Bravo! Marvelous, my lord!"

He felt himself flushing. "I imagine that you are much more proficient."

"Oh, no." She firmly shook her head. "Like most girls, I was taught to play the pianoforte, but I merely strike the notes. I have never been able to project the feeling for the music that you do, my lord. Your rendition of "The Ash Grove" nearly made me weep."

"Balderdash," he scoffed.

"No, it's true," she said sincerely. "Please play another."

He did not wish to make her cry. A weeping Lady Hope was beyond the realms of his imagination, and he doubted that he could handle it. So he treated her to a lighthearted Morris dance, then sat back.

"I can't remember any more pieces, and my fingers are cold."

Lady Hope rose, motioning him to keep his seat, and came forward. "You must have sheet music somewhere."

"Yes, I suppose it's still there."

"And the fire will soon take the chill away." She nodded toward the crackling flames that the servant had started. "Perhaps we could find the music and have a hot cup of tea while the room is warming. Then would you play again for me? I do so enjoy it."

"You have a silver tongue, Lady Hope."

Her brown eyes danced with merriment. "May I take that as assent?"

"All right." He grinned, happy to postpone the confrontation with Cook.

"Excellent!" Clapping her hands, she rang for a servant to bring a tea tray.

"I am surprised that the pianoforte is not farther out of tune. And that I can remember anything at all about it," Colin admitted ruefully, idly executing a scale. "It's been years since I last played."

"With your talent," she breathed, "that is a crime, my lord. You play so beautifully. With practice, your performance would equal that of a professional concert pianist."

He laughed heartily. "Coming at it a bit strong, Lady Hope."

"I am not," she insisted.

It was rather awe-inspiring to receive actual compliments from Lady Hope, but Colin had had just about enough of it. He wasn't *that* accomplished. The lady's wits were scrambled.

He arched an eyebrow mischievously. "My lady, my performance in more primitive human achievement is far superior to my piano playing."

"Now do not come the rake with me," she admonished, setting her hands on her hips. "In fact, after hearing your music I am beginning to disbelieve the myth of your black reputation. Where is the sheet music?"

With a chuckle, he stood up and traipsed over to a small painted commode. "I used to keep it here."

How naive she was! he mused, squatting down. She had seized upon one tiny facet of his character and decided that he was not really the dyed-in-the-wool rake that he truly was. Poor Lady Hope! She may have had a number of London Seasons, but she was nearly as innocent as she was on the day she was born. She certainly had no knowledge of depraved men like himself.

She knelt beside him as he opened the cabinet doors. "When did you learn to play?"

"When I was a little boy, of course."

Lady Hope laughed lightly.

Colin smiled. "What's so amusing about that?"

"You . . . as a little boy. I can scarcely picture it. Were you cute?"

"Oh, for God's sake!" He rummaged in the cabinet and drew out a bundle of papers that, besides being well used, were singed on one corner. Hell! He'd forgotten about that ugly incident. Now Lady Hope would be full of questions.

"What . . ." she began as expected, but he forestalled her.

"Father didn't like my piano lessons. He thought they were effeminate," he explained shortly. "One day, he came upon me and my teacher at work. He flew into a rage, tossed the music in the fire, and hauled me away by the ear. Luckily, my instructor, Mrs. Barnes, was quick and unafraid of him. She rescued the music, stomped out the flames, and from then on, we carried out our lessons in secret."

He glanced sideways at Lady Hope. Her brown eyes were enormous, and her very kissable pink lips were parted in shock. For once, the *femme* was speechless.

Colin rose, taking her hand and lifting her to her feet. "Don't be so overset, my lady. It wasn't so bad."

"It was abominable!" she gasped. "Didn't he recognize what talent you had?"

"As I said, my father did not believe that playing the pianoforte was a manly exercise. I suppose he was right."

"He most certainly was not! He was a tyrant! An absolute monster!"

Colin shrugged. "Well, it's over and done with. It's buried in the past."

Her lovely eyes seemed to bore into his as if she searched to see his soul. It made him uncomfortable. He had thought he'd long outgrown that uneasy sense of vulnerability.

"It's over," he repeated.

"Is it, my lord?" she asked quietly.

"Yes." In an attempt at levity, he flicked her under the chin with his index finger. "Don't be so disturbed, Lady Hope. Just now, you look as if you could open my father's vault and despoil his remains."

"I would like to!" she vowed, still incensed. "If I ever have a child, I shall never permit such cruelty!"

"If ever?" Colin snatched the opportunity to divert attention from the unsettling topic of his childhood and his father. "My lady, can you truly be uncertain about having a husband and family some day?"

She lifted an expressive shoulder. "It is difficult to find the perfect mate, and I shall not settle for less. Do you not agree, my lord?"

"I don't know, and I don't intend to try."

They were interrupted by the arrival of the tea tray. Colin deposited the music on the pianoforte and joined Lady Hope beside the hearth. Pushing all the unhappy memories from his mind, he dropped into a chair and watched her pour the steaming, aromatic liquid. She was very graceful about it. Obviously she'd had much practice.

Ladies! They must spend hours perfecting the most mundane of skills. Such a thing would drive him out of his mind, but he was glad that she had done it. It was pleasant to observe how beautifully she carried out the commonplace task.

"Cream, my lord? Sugar?"

"Plain, please."

She handed him the cup and saucer and presented a plate of biscuits and cake. Colin shook his head, still half-mesmerized by her gentility. When Lady Hope wished to be sweet and dainty, she could charm him more than she'd ever guess. A lady at Amberton Hall! It was beyond belief.

Lady Hope set the plate on the tray and sat back with her tea. "You don't intend to try?"

He blinked, unsure of what she was speaking.

"I was taking up our conversation where we left off," she said. "You were implying that you did not plan to marry."

He stifled a groan and wished that he hadn't directed the discourse to this issue. "That's right," he told her, "I do not."

"Then apparently you have a brother to carry on the line."

"My brother died childless."

"But who . . ."

"You're right, Lady Hope." He chuckled, reading her mind. "Who will carry on? No one, that I know of."

"But the title will revert to the Crown! And Amberton Hall . . . is it entailed? What will happen to it?" she wailed as if she were truly worried.

"At that point in time, I doubt that I will care," he said cynically, his genial mood forgotten.

"For shame, my lord," she chided, sipping her tea. "You are teasing me. I know you will not neglect your responsibility."

"You're wrong. I'm absolutely serious."

Lady Hope made a small strangling sound. "Then Amberton Hall will never have a mistress! And it needs one so desperately!"

Colin raised an eyebrow. "Surely, after your proclamation about finding the perfect mate, you cannot expect me to wed for the sake of a house and a title."

"Touché, my lord." She looked slightly abashed, but recovered quickly. "I must say, however, that there are certain to be dozens of ladies from whom you could choose."

"One would assume as much."

"If you would but pursue acquaintance with *proper* females, I am positive that you could come up with a suitable candidate," she lectured. "You are committing a disservice to the ladies of England to dismiss them so readily."

"Oh I am, am I?" Colin had had enough, first from his friends and now from her, about this concept of filial duty. This had to do with *his* life and no one else's.

"Let me tell you this, Lady Hope. I rather thought I was doing the ladies of England a *service*. I wouldn't wish anyone to live in the hell that a marriage to an Amberton would be."

"Fustian!" she said archly. "Don't cut up stiff."

"I'm tired of this topic."

"Very well, Lord Amberton, I shall allow you to escape it."

"Allow?" he blared.

Her eyes twinkled with mischief.

"Brat," he said and held out his cup for more tea.

Lady Hope giggled and served him with a flourish.

Colin eyed her cautiously. The little vixen! She was a bundle of sweetness, bossiness, conviction, and mischief all packaged into one pretty, petite parcel. Whoever married her could never be bored, but the man would certainly have his hands full.

He saw her shiver slightly and set aside his tea to rise and stir up the fire. "You're cold. We should have taken refreshment in another room."

"But I like this one so well."

"Then I must reach deep into my soul and pull out some measure of chivalry." With a flourish, Colin removed his coat and draped it over her shoulders. "There. Is that better?"

"Yes, thank you." Blushing a bit, she snugged it around her. "But now you will chill."

"My vest is enough." He returned to his chair.

"Are you almost prepared to play again?" she asked hopefully.

"I am always ready for play," he drawled.

"Lord Amberton, behave yourself!"

Abruptly, the door burst open.

"Look at this, Roger!" Lord Bridgewater laughed. "We have stumbled upon a tête-à-tête!"

"My, what a domestic little display!" Sir Roger pronounced.

Colin moaned and sent Lady Hope a speaking look. He would not play the pianoforte now. Their musical interlude was at an end.

Lady Hope pursed her lips with disappointment. "Gentlemen, will you take tea?" she asked blandly.

"I would rather drink in your beauty." Bridgewater drew up a chair beside her.

"I, too." Sir Roger stood over her shoulder. "Colin is not being fair in monopolizing your charms like this."

"How true!" Jamie agreed. "I have been pining away for the very sight of you, Lady Hope."

"You saw me at lunch not so long ago," she dryly replied.

"I have been longing for your touch." Sir Roger whirled around to the front of her, fell to his knees, and lifted her fingers to his lips.

Lady Hope jerked her hand away and leapt to her feet. The hasty movement sent the baronet sprawling to his haunches. Regally, she stepped past him.

"If you will excuse me, gentlemen, I find that I am rather weary. I believe I shall seek my chamber." Without a backward glance, she walked from the room.

"Tsk-tsk," jecred Bridgewater. "She must be a one-man woman. She certainly knocked you on your backside, Roger."

Colin joined him in laughing at Sir Roger's downfall, but inwardly he was irritated. Why did they have to come along when they had? He'd been looking forward to playing more music and, strangely enough, for the most part, he'd been enjoying the lady's company.

"Ah well." The baronet picked himself up. "I shall return to the fray at a later date, surely with more success. She is still miffed at me over that abigail business."

"Perhaps she sees you as you are, old friend. A heartless, dallying shell of a man," Bridgewater quipped smoothly. "A despoiler of maidens, a leering lecher, a . . ."

"Shut up, Jamie," said Roger. "By God, I know I'm going to have to call you out someday."

"Choose swords, Rog. I know for a fact that you've never been pinked, and it's time you were." The viscount naughtily gazed at Colin. "Do you realize that the lady escaped with your new Weston coat?"

Roger chortled. "I once had a mistress who collected items of apparel as souvenirs from her various paramours."

"Oh? What did she get from you?" Bridgewater asked and, without waiting for a reply, queried, "What did you get in return? A case of the French pox?"

Colin stood. "This is going nowhere, and it's cold in here. Let us go to the billiard room and have a game of cards."

"And a glass of brandy," Jamie added.

Colin nodded and rose to depart, feeling a tiny twinge of guilt at the thought of the drinks he knew they'd consume. No matter, they were accustomed to it and would not show the effects until Lady Hope was tucked in for the night. She would know nothing about it.

Hope snapped shut the door of the Rose Salon a bit more loudly than necessary, and hurried toward the stairs before any other flirtatious bachelor came along to arrest her progress. Fiddlesticks! She had been having an interesting time with Lord Amberton. Why did his friends have to come along and ruin it?

Men! What absurd specimens of the species! It was shocking to witness how inclined they were toward panting and prattling after anyone in skirts. Didn't they realize how ridiculous they appeared?

Even Mitchell and those two footmen who were conferring in the front hall were not immune to absurd male behavior. They were staring at her as if she were a freak from a raree-show. What was wrong with them? Had their snowbound existence suddenly rendered them daft? Hope favored them with a hard glare and dashed up the steps.

No, she would never be able to understand men. With their flighty temperaments, how could they claim to be the wiser of the sexes? With a snort, she entered her chamber.

"Agatha, are you here?" she called and traipsed to the sitting room.

"Yes, how . . ." Agatha gaped.

"What is the matter?" Hope demanded. "First the servants gawk at me, and now so do you!"

"What . . . what are you wearing?"

Hope glanced downward. "Oh, for heaven's sake! I forgot to give him his coat before I left the room."

"W-what room?" the widow asked as if she didn't wish to hear the answer. "Whose coat?"

"Lord Amberton's."

Agatha wailed unintelligibly.

Hope began to laugh. "Lord Amberton's *coat,* not his room. I'm sorry I gave you a start."

Her companion visibly relaxed. "You certainly did. One never knows where your explorations might take you."

"Well, I wouldn't go into his chamber! You should know me better than that."

"I put nothing past you these days," Agatha retorted, but she smiled at her own suspicions. "Now do tell all."

Hope briefed her on the events that took place in the Rose Salon, including the recounting of the horrid tale of Lord Amberton's father.

"Poor little boy," the widow crooned. "No wonder he grew up to be as he is. He had no model of tenderness or proper gentlemanly behavior. He must have had a miserable childhood."

She nodded, slipping the marquess's coat from her shoulders and strolling to the window. Peering out at the wintry scene, she idly caressed the soft fabric. Oblivious as to how it would appear to her friend, she brought the garment to her nose and inhaled deeply of the interesting scent of cologne and man.

A small wrinkle of surprise on her brow, Agatha stared at her friend and wrung her hands.

After dinner, Agatha was still mulling over Hope's strange gesture while she sat in the far corner of the drawing room and watched her friend pour tea for Lord Amberton and his friends. She was pleased to see that Hope's mellow mood had continued on through a dreadful meal. The young lady was chatting cheerfully with the gentlemen and conducting herself in a perfectly proper manner. She seemed to be having such a pleasant time that Agatha was glad she'd agreed to remain downstairs for a time before retiring. In general, the company might not be the most desirable, but if it would relieve Hope's restlessness, she was fully in favor of it.

Hope's good behavior left Agatha free to pursue her needlework, which a servant had fetched at her request. She bent her head over the exquisite design she was creating on a new chair cover. Smiling to herself, she set an expert stitch.

"You seem lonely over here all by yourself," observed a deep, male voice.

Agatha jumped, pricking her finger. "Oh, dear! How clumsy of me!" She flushed, looking up into the handsome face of Lord Kelwin.

"It is I who must apologize for startling you." He quickly set down his cup and saucer and brought forth a fine linen handkerchief.

"Thank you, my lord." Agatha dabbed at the tiny red bead of blood. "Do not distress yourself. I am forever being all thumbs."

"Somehow I doubt that." He nodded pointedly at her beautiful stitchery. "May I join you?"

"If you wish," Agatha murmured, her heart beating uncomfortably hard.

"I *do* wish." With an elegant flip of the tails of his coat, he sat down in the chair beside her.

"I shall launder your handkerchief and return it to you,

my lord." She folded the article and laid it atop her sewing basket, glancing surreptitiously at him.

Most ladies would consider Lord Amberton to be the best-looking of all the gentlemen, but Agatha much preferred Lord Kelwin's friendly features and modest height. His hair was blond. Indeed, it was as golden as Hope's enviable tresses. His eyes were blue and kindly. While his finely sculpted cheekbones and chiseled nose bespoke his aristocratic heritage, his expression bore none of the lofty cynicism of a man like the marquess. He seemed down to earth and entirely approachable. Flattered that he had sought her company, Agatha picked up her needlework and smiled at him.

"Tell me, my lord, is being snowbound a new experience for you?"

"Yes, it is. And you?"

"Yes. I have never had such an adventure."

He smiled. "No doubt it is not the most pleasant occasion for you, being imprisoned with a batch of cads."

Agatha laughed ruefully. "It would certainly not be my choice of activities. It is rather scandalous, isn't it? But I don't think I would use the term *cads* for all of those present."

"Thank you, Mrs. Sommers. I hope you retain that opinion and that I fall under it." He leaned sideways to examine her handiwork. "Your sewing is quite lovely. What is it to be?"

"A chair cover, my lord." She spread out the piece of fabric so he could see it in its entirety.

"Very nice. My wife used to do needlework," he said reminiscently.

His wife! Agatha's heart sank, though she couldn't explain why. He was too far above her in birth and station to form an attachment for her. Besides, she had resigned herself to her widowed state.

"Your work, however, is far superior to hers," he added gallantly.

Agatha forced a smile. "Perhaps she is too busy to perfect her stitches."

"My wife has been dead these many years," he told her.

"Oh, I am sorry," she sympathized, pulse fluttering.

He waved off her condolences. "It happened a long time ago."

"But you have remained true to her memory."

"I wouldn't say that," he denied. "My single status is more a case of my inability to find an amiable mate. I liked marriage," he mused, "and I'm sure my children would like to have a mother."

Agatha started to ask him more about his home and children, but she caught herself in time. The conversation was already headed in a much too personal direction. Goodness, was she becoming influenced by Hope's tendency toward frank speech? Furthermore, it would be impertinent for a lowly companion to query an earl about his personal life, however interesting she might find it. Regretfully, she returned their discourse to the weather and their snowbound condition and kept a close eye on Lady Hope for signs of disturbance.

9

Noting the pleasant little coze of Agatha and Lord Kelwin, Hope arched a delicate eyebrow. It was strange to see her companion so obviously enjoying a conversation with a member of the opposite sex. And with an earl, no less! Hope remembered that Agatha had shyly mentioned the gentleman to her and, though she'd teased her about it, she hadn't expected anything to come of it.

Despite her attempts to draw Agatha into her social life, the woman had resisted. In private, the two of them might be bosom bows. In public, however, the widow considered herself to be some sort of glorified servant, which, of course, was what the *ton* had expected her to feel. So tonight, her apparent fascination with Kelwin was nothing short of bizarre.

Lord Amberton, seated beside Hope on the sofa, noticed the couple, too. "I see that Drew has made a conquest."

"A conquest?" Hope countered. "What an odd term you use for a simple chat, my lord!"

The marquess chuckled. "It's a flirtation if ever I saw one. Just look at all the blushes and flutterings."

"Agatha," she severely informed him, "does not flirt."

"No? I can see it from all the way across the room. She's charming him. You could take lessons in geniality from your companion, Lady Hope."

She bristled, irritated that he seemed to have forgotten, or chosen to ignore, the measure of compatibility they had experienced that afternoon in the Rose Salon.

"Yes," he went on, "instruction in the art of beguilement would benefit you immensely."

Hope pursed her lips, a small frown creasing her brow. "Allow me to inform you, sir, that I am quite capable of charming any gentleman, if I choose to do so."

"Indeed?" he queried doubtfully. "I find that hard to believe."

"You have my word on it." She nodded curtly.

His violet eyes clouded with mock disappointment. "Only your word? I was hoping for more."

"What do you want me to do? Flirt with you?" she demanded.

Lord Amberton lounged back languorously against the deep cushions. "It might be diverting," he drawled.

"Fustian!" she exclaimed. "I cannot picture your being amused by flirting with me. You are much too sardonic and cynical."

"On the contrary, I greatly enjoy a flirtation with an attractive lady."

Hope snorted. "Oh, yes, and I can imagine what *kind* of lady you are referring to!"

"Really? And what type is that?"

"A person such as Lady Marsh!" Hope blurted.

He grinned. "My one-time mistress?"

"You admit to it?" she gasped.

"Why not?" Those expressive eyes glowed with unholy mischief. "You seem to know about it anyway."

"But . . ." she stammered, then stiffly squared her shoulders. "I can scarcely believe that you seem prepared to discuss such matters before me. Sir, you are not behaving as a gentleman should!"

"Of course not. I would hate to disappoint you. And don't I recall that you are the one who first mentioned the Marsh? For shame, my *lady.*"

Mortified by her abominable frank tongue, Hope flushed

to the roots of her guinea gold hair. He was right. She was the one who had channeled the subject into this dangerous strait. But in all propriety, she shouldn't have been reminded of her cursed *faux pas.* Lord Amberton should have been a gentleman and overlooked it.

"You are an absolute scapegrace," she proclaimed.

"Why, Lady Hope, how you wound me! As per your rules, I have been struggling to be on my best behavior." He captured her hand, adroitly turned it over, and kissed her palm. "Gad, but you are attractive when your eyes are flashing fire at me."

"Lord Amberton!" She jerked free, but not before an unexpected tingle of pleasure surged through her body. "How dare you? Everyone is watching us!"

It was true. Every eye in the room was avidly trained on them. Lord Amberton's friends, who had been diverted by a game of cards, had ceased their play and were now watching the lively tableau with intense interest. Lord Kelwin had paused, mouth open in mid-sentence. Agatha was visibly disturbed.

Face burning, Hope straightened her skirts. "Now see what you have caused?"

Lord Bridgewater tossed his unplayed cards into the center of the table, picked up his empty teacup, and rose. "I am missing something."

His companion followed his lead. They deserted the card table and descended upon Hope. Dragging their chairs as close to her as humanly possible, they sat down.

Hope cursed inwardly. She hadn't been enjoying herself as she had in the Rose Salon, but it was infinitely more pleasant to limit her fencing to Lord Amberton than it was to expend the activity to include the others.

As she politely filled their empty cups, Hope desperately sought a witty reason to flee. Unfortunately, if she sought her chamber, Agatha would be obliged to depart as well. Up until she and the marquess had created their little scene, her friend had given all evidence of having a good time. Hope didn't want to ruin the widow's evening. Perhaps she could bear these trifling scamps for just a while longer.

"Well, gentlemen," she said genteelly, "how was your game?"

"Decidedly not as much fun as yours and Colin's," Sir Roger answered irreverently.

"Definitely not," agreed Lord Bridgewater. "Lady Hope, I am almost overwhelmed by jealousy. Here you are in another most fascinating rendezvous with Colin. Gad, I am overset! My heart is broken. Why have you singled him out for your favor? Why not me?"

Hope gaped at the impossible declaration.

Lord Amberton chuckled. "The answer is simple, Jamie. The lady knows quality when she sees it."

Hope gathered her wits. Though she deplored the foolish flirtation engaged in by most ladies of her set, she certainly knew how to do it, no matter what the marquess thought. Ha! She would show him, and she would save Agatha's evening, too, by giving all appearances of having a high time.

"Lord Bridgewater." She overtly fluttered her lashes. "It would seem that you deserted me in order to play cards. Perhaps it is truly *my* heart which is broken."

He dimpled appreciatively.

"And I never did get to kiss your hand," Sir Roger complained.

"Then we must remedy the situation." She extended that member to him, but resisted when he tried to turn it over and kiss her on the palm as Lord Amberton had. "Naughty boy! You shall do it properly or not at all."

"Colin got to . . ."

"Lord Amberton took me unawares. Now I am mindful of the tricks you gentlemen play. I shan't be trapped again." Coyly, she winked at him.

"Lady Hope, don't ignore me in favor of Roger," Lord Bridgewater grieved.

"Dear sir! Such is not my intention!" She batted her

lashes for all she was worth. "Do forgive me or I shall never have another moment's happiness!"

Lord Amberton groaned.

"What's that, Colin?" Sir Roger chortled. "Can it possibly be a moan of envy?"

"Of anguish, more like. I'm mired to the knees in a bog of lunacy."

"Poor Lord Amberton!" Hope patted his sleeve. "Such a sad state of affairs."

"Hope!" Agatha appeared, clutching her sewing basket, with a concerned Lord Kelwin at her side. "See how late it is. It is time we retired."

She glanced at the clock, surprised to see that her friend was right. She wished that Agatha had enjoyed her exchange with Lord Kelwin for just a while longer, but the widow seemed determined to seek her chamber. Hope rose.

"Chatting with you, gentlemen, has been most inspiring, but now I must bid you good night."

Everyone, except Lord Amberton, mounted a protest.

She airily lifted a hand. "Alas, I must seek my beauty rest." Favoring them with a minxish curtsy, she followed Agatha from the room.

"What were you about?" her companion cried as they started up the stairs. "Encouraging those rogues!"

"Oh, I was trying to buy further time for you to enjoy Lord Kelwin's company. At first, that is. Actually, in a way, it was rather fun to flirt with them."

"You were flirting with danger!" Agatha scolded. "Lord Amberton was jealous. I could see it in his eyes."

"Good for him. He is far too sure of his own invincibility. A good dose of envy is exactly what he needs."

"Such a thing is perilous. Whether they exhibit it or not, there's rivalry among those gentlemen. Goodness, I have never seen you behave so outrageously!"

Hope shrugged. "You know that I dislike the falsity of flirtation. I probably won't engage in it again for the duration of our visit."

Agatha sighed. "You just don't understand, do you? Those men were pursuing you like starving hunters on the trail of a delectable prey. They won't just stop tomorrow. In all probability, they will double their efforts to trifle with you."

"And I will double *mine* to avoid them."

They topped the steps and proceeded down the hall, pausing at the door to Hope's chamber.

"I am weary. I'm going on to bed," Agatha announced.

"To dream of Lord Kelwin?" she asked playfully.

"Lock your door," her friend stated, refusing to rise to the bait.

Hope laughed. "Lock yours, or a certain earl might be sorely tempted."

"Fustian!" Agatha sputtered.

She began to enter her chamber, then paused. "Agatha, do you really think he was jealous?"

"Good night."

With a giggle, Hope closed the door and turned to greet Martha, who was patiently waiting for her. "I believe that our Mrs. Sommers has attracted a gentleman."

"That's right fine, my lady." The abigail smiled brightly. "She needs a husband."

So do I, Hope thought. How nice it would be to have a dashing, handsome husband, a man like Lord Amberton. It was too bad that he possessed all those vexatious vices to make him ineligible, and that he wasn't interested in marriage.

With Martha's assistance, she readied herself for bed, reflecting on Agatha's warning. Had Lord Amberton really been jealous of her flirtation with his friends? The idea was quite pleasant, she decided as she slipped under the heavy covers.

Hope dozed, awakening shortly after one o'clock in the morning. She was absolutely ravenous, having scarcely touched that ghastly dinner. Tonight she would do it. She would make her secretive foray to the kitchen of

Amberton Hall and prepare herself a delicious repast. But staring unhappily at the clock, she knew that the gentlemen were probably still engaged in their usual late-night revels. Damn and blast! The very thought of tasty food was driving her mad with hunger. It wouldn't hurt to sneak to the top of the stairs to ascertain the situation.

Her mouth watering with anticipation, Hope slipped from the bed and into her dressing robe and slippers. She plunged her candle into the fire to light it. Hurriedly, she went to the door, softly turned the key, and opened it just a crack. The hall was dim and absolutely silent. Eagerly, she tiptoed to the stairway and stifled a cry of delight when she saw no light nor heard one single sound. The gentlemen must have retired unusually early. Oh, what wonderful luck!

Hope dispensed with the idea of using the servants' passages and skipped downstairs. On her way to the kitchen, she would select a book. She could entertain herself by reading while she indulged in her marvelous feast.

Feeling as free as a bird and as mischievous as an elf, she entered the library and lit extra candles. In the wee hours, Amberton Hall was hers. She could do whatever she wished. In fact, she would do this every night. She would never have to depend on those awful meals again. Happily she climbed upon the library ladder and began a quick search for something of interest.

She had only just begun when the door clicked. With a gasp, Hope whirled around, nearly toppling from her perch. She wildly swept back her hand to clutch the shelves, sending a rain of leather-bound volumes showering to the floor.

"What are you doing here?" she cried, righting herself.

"What am I . . . ? It's my house!" Lord Amberton, clothed as informally as herself, quietly entered the room and shut the door.

"But you are supposed to be in bed," she accused, eyeing him as if he were a recalcitrant schoolboy.

"So are you," he retorted irritably, glancing toward the bottle of brandy on the sideboard.

Hope followed the line of his gaze. "Ha! I might have known! You are sneaking around, looking for a drink."

"I'll have you know, madam, that I do not have to *sneak* around in *my own home!* Furthermore, I came here to select a book. I can't sleep." He favored her with a condescending glare. "Not that my actions are any affair of yours!"

"Be still," she hissed. "You're making too much noise. Servants will come to investigate."

"Oho! You consider me clamorous? What about that batch of books you knocked to the floor? You probably ruined their bindings."

"You make it sound deliberate!" she snapped, aggravatedly pushing back a drooping lock of hair. "Would you have preferred that I fall?"

"Hell, no. No doubt you'd have injured yourself so badly that you couldn't be moved for months." He strode toward the sideboard.

Hope leapt from the ladder and speedily blocked his way. "Don't touch that bottle! I know a far better remedy for sleeplessness."

He hotly studied her from her head to her toes, his gaze lingering on her pert breasts. "So do I," he finally managed, "and indeed we are dressed for it."

"Oh . . . *oh!*" Her entire body burned with mortification. She drew back her arm to hit him, then thought better of it and covered her movement by clasping her hands behind her back. Unfortunately the stance had the effect of poking her bosom out as if it were on display. She had never been so embarrassed in all her life.

Lord Amberton grinned. "Does this indicate a willingness to try my treatment?"

"No, it does not." Crossing her arms in front of her, she summoned up every ounce of her courage. "Select your book and go back to bed."

"I shall not. I am curious. I might just try your antidote to wakefulness."

"Just take your old brandy and go away," she returned. "You are too irritable, and you are probably half-seas over.

Coming in here and shouting at me as you did! It was your fault that I almost fell from the ladder."

"I am a long way from being foxed, madam. And I have good reason to be irritable upon finding you traipsing about the house in your nightclothes, especially after the brazen way you flirted with my friends."

"You requested flirtation."

"Not with them. But, Lady Hope, I am not irritable now," he cajoled. "Let me in on your great secret for slumber."

Ravenous, she had intended earlier to coax him to return to bed and engage in counting sheep, so that she might proceed to the kitchen for a satisfying repast. After this interchange, she doubted that the sheep would work, or that she could even get rid of him. She should, of course, dash to her bedroom, but hunger won out. At huge risk, she decided to reveal her cooking plan.

"Very well," she agreed. "Come with me."

"Where? To your bed?" he asked hopefully.

"Don't be ridiculous! I am a proper lady."

His eyes twinkled. "You're not dressed like one."

"Just come along." Picking up her candle, she led him from the room and through the hall, then walked briskly down the corridor to the service section of Amberton Hall. She opened the kitchen door.

"Oh, no," moaned Lord Amberton.

"Sit down." She pointed to the huge, scrubbed oak table with its collection of scarred chairs.

He obeyed. "What are you going to do?"

"I'm going to cook a meal."

He began to laugh.

"What is so funny?" Hope challenged.

"You." He chortled. "Cooking!"

"Just wait and see."

She went into the larder and immediately cast her gaze on a beautiful haunch of ham. The very sight of it made her stomach twist with anticipation. Oh, this was going to be so good! She wondered how much the marquess would eat. She knew she herself was desperately hungry, so she sliced a large amount. She would smuggle anything left over from it to her room for breakfast.

She returned to the kitchen, removed a legged frying pan from the wall, and placed the meat in it. The dying coals were perfect for her purposes. She knelt down, raked a small pile of them forward, and set the pan to cook.

"This is the most inefficient kitchen I have ever seen, my lord," she tossed over her shoulder. "If you possessed one of the new Rumford stoves, my task would be much easier."

"Lady Hope, I don't even know what a Rumford stove is." He chuckled. "And I don't care."

"Obviously. I'll wager, however, that your London house is equipped with one. Have you a French chef?" She glanced at him.

He nodded. "Of course."

"Then your kitchen, there, is up to date. No Frenchman would ply his trade under such primitive conditions as this."

Hope retrieved a half dozen eggs from the larder and a jug of milk. Unearthing a small bowl from a cabinet, she expertly cracked the eggs into it. She reached for the milk and caught Lord Amberton intently watching her.

"How lucky it is, my lord, that your chickens have continued to lay well, right through this bitter weather."

"Why shouldn't they?"

Hope laughed. "For heaven's sakes, Lord Amberton, don't you know that hens are not reliable in the winter?"

He smiled self-consciously. "No, I didn't. Curious, isn't it? I wonder why they aren't."

"It's quite simple." Hope raised an eyebrow. "How would you like to raise a brood of chicks in the snow?"

"I suppose you have a point," He tented his hands and rested his chin on them. "How do you know all these things?"

Hope added the milk, salt, and pepper and began to stir. "As I have mentioned previously, young ladies are taught to manage a household and all that affects it."

"I must disagree. I believe that you are more capable than most."

"Why, Lord Amberton! A compliment?"

"You are naive, though, about the important matters of life," he added impishly.

"Humph," she disdained. "I imagine those areas are best left undiscussed. Furthermore, I must maintain that a comfortable home life is *very* important."

She retrieved another frying pan and set butter to melt in it, then searched through an old food safe for a loaf of bread. "I'm not sure I can do much with this," she mused, scraping its charred crust, "but I shall try to make us some toast."

"Cook is going to be livid when she finds out about this," he stated when Hope had settled herself at the hearth.

"She won't find out," Hope said confidently.

"Why not?"

"We'll clean up our mess."

Delicious aromas filled the kitchen. Hope's stomach was reacting with vigor. She wondered how Lord Amberton's was responding.

In no time at all, she finished preparing the meal. To save dishwashing, she brought the two pans right to the table. In a cupboard she found two cracked plates and old table knives and forks. Putting the toast on their dishes, she set them on the table. All conversation ceased as they applied themselves to the food. Lord Amberton matched her bite for bite. How absurd! The poor man was starving in his own house. Finally satiated, Hope laid down her utensils and let him finish the remainder.

"My God, that was good," he said, wiping his mouth on his handkerchief.

"Thank you, my lord." She smiled with satisfaction, then sobered. "Something must be done about Cook, you know."

"Yes, yes." He eyed her, painfully.

"Look at us, a marquess and an earl's daughter, slinking downstairs in the middle of the night to fix our own meal."

"Lady Hope, I am full and contented. I'd rather not talk about unpleasant issues just now."

"Very well." She wasn't in the mood to fence with him.

Indeed, she was suddenly terribly sleepy. She stood up. "Let us clean up our mess and retire. You can help me."

"What?" he asked in wonderment.

She repeated herself.

He stared at her, shaking his head in disbelief. "Surely you don't expect me to wash dishes?"

"I expect you to help. You ate, didn't you?" She regarded him with feigned surprise. "And after all, doesn't this concern *your house, your kitchen,* and *your cook?"*

"Oh, just leave the damned things!" he grumbled.

"Aren't you afraid of Cook?"

"No!"

Hope laughed impishly.

He grinned, getting up from the table. "Brat."

They extinguished the candles and left the room, strolling companionably down the hall and up the stairs.

"This has been an interesting late-night venture," Lord Amberton said as they reached the doors to their chambers. "We could make it even more entertaining if you would but allow it."

Even in the dim light, she could see that his eyes were positively dancing with deviltry. "My lord, your attempts to seduce me are bound to fail. Why not save your breath to answer Cook's charges in the morning? I have the notion that you are going to get an earful."

"I'm not concerned, Lady Hope. I shall blame it all on you."

"Knave! I'll toss it right back in your lap."

"Ssh." He laid his index finger across her mouth; then, as if the touch had spurred him to greater intimacy, he cupped her face between his hands and gazed down at her intently.

Hope's heart pounded. He was going to kiss her, the scoundrel! But she was powerless to pull away.

"Thank you for an excellent meal, my dear."

"My lord . . ."

Gently he lowered his lips to hers.

To give herself credit, Hope put up a token resistance by placing her arms against his chest, but she was unable to bring herself to shove him away. Instead, with an apparent will of their own, her hands slipped upward and around his neck. She kissed him back.

It ended all too quickly. As if he had abruptly come to his senses, he lifted his head and caught her shoulders. He took a quick step backward, his expression revealing something of amazement.

"Good night," he said in a husky voice.

"Good night," she whispered, strangely unwilling to see him go.

But the beautiful spell was broken. Suddenly aware of the dangerous undercurrents, Hope fled into her room and secured the door. Breathless, she dashed to the bed and dived under the covers. Lord Amberton had kissed her . . . and she had allowed it. She had *liked* it!

The scandalousness of the whole night's business struck her full force. What a hussy she was! She had not only engaged in a secretive rendezvous with the greatest rake in the world, but she had done it while clad in her nightclothes. Merciful heavens! She was lucky to have escaped with only that final brief intimacy. How would she ever face him again? And, knowing what she'd allowed, how could she ever face anyone?

Hope closed her eyes as if to blot out the event. It must never happen again. Given the way she'd responded to him, he might have the idea that he could, in truth, seduce her.

With a worried moue, she rolled over. Never again must she permit herself to be alone with him. It shouldn't be difficult. During the day, there'd be servants about, and she could always beg Agatha's company. But there could be no more nighttime excursions to the kitchen. She might be ravenous by the time she left Amberton Hall, but that was the way it would have to be. Unhappily accepting her fate, Hope fell into a restless slumber.

10

It was barely daybreak when Hope was jolted from slumber by a loud, determined scratching at the door. She lay there momentarily, wondering whether to answer the summons or to feign sleep.

"My lady!" a voice hissed through the solid oak barrier.

Hope knew at once that it wasn't Agatha. But though the speaker's tone was deep and muffled, it did not seem to be masculine. Nor was it the accent of a member of the upper class.

She paused. Why would one of the servants be calling on her at this time of day? But she was too curious to ignore her visitor for long. She quickly slid from bed and donned her dressing gown and slippers as the scraping came again.

"Who's there?" She unlatched the door and threw it open. "Cook!"

"Shh." The big woman bustled past Hope, almost jostling her aside.

"You wanted to see me?" Fearfully, Hope eyed the servant's hands, half-expecting to see a meat cleaver poised and ready to crack her skull.

The cook nodded nervously. "You be alone, my lady?"

"Yes. Of course." Hope frowned at the insinuation.

"Good! I want to be private-like." She pointedly ogled the open door.

Hope hesitated. This curmudgeon bore an active dislike for her and could turn violent. If that happened, she would have to scream for help. But her odious inquisitiveness won over her reluctance. She closed the door and crossed the room to take a seat beside the cold fireplace.

"Will you sit down, Cook?"

"No! Not in front of a lady!"

"I truly don't mind, especially since it's so early in the morning," she said. And because I don't like you towering over me, she wished she could add.

"No thankee." The cook began to pace back and forth. "You don't like my cooking," she finally stated.

Hope was afraid to reply to that declaration.

"You don't like my cooking, an' you're right!" She halted, took a heavy breath, and resumed her march. "I used to be a good cook. I made the best breads and cakes of anyone round here. But now . . . now I just can't do it anymore! I ain't got any good help. They let things burn or they don't cook 'em enough. By the time I find out, it's too late and I have to serve 'em, anyway. What'll I do, m'lady?"

Tilting back her head, Hope thoughtfully gazed up at her. "Your kitchen staff is very young and inexperienced."

"That's right. People won't work for me long. They say I'm cranky," the servant grumbled.

Hope thought of the menacing rolling pin. "Perhaps you could soften your approach," she gently suggested.

"Well, I do lose my temper when things don't go right."

"I know."

Cook cringed and wrung her hands. "That was bad o' me, m'lady. I'm begging your pardon."

"You are forgiven. We're friends now, and I am going to help. But I must insist that you sit down. I'm getting a crick in my neck from looking up."

"I'm sorry, m'lady!" She whirled around and settled her bulk onto a fragile chair.

"When I was in the kitchen," Hope began, "I talked with that one girl. Daphne, was it?"

Cook nodded vigorously.

"She is young and uneducated, but she seems willing. With good instruction and more supervision, I believe she would make you a fine assistant. Perhaps the others would be the same."

"I ain't no teacher!" the servant gasped. "I can't read 'n' write!"

"You don't have to read or write to teach these people to cook," Hope explained patiently. "Just explain well. Go into detail. And watch them more closely. They need more careful overseeing."

The servant sorrowfully hung her head. "That's the trouble, m'lady."

"Supervising them? But they know that you are in charge of the kitchen! They will do as you say."

"I can't do it," she whined.

"Of course you can," Hope encouraged. "They won't think that you are cruel just because you give them directions, especially if you do it in a kind, but firm, manner."

"I can't oversee 'em. I . . . I can't see much of anything, m'lady." The huge woman burst into loud sobs. "I'm almost blind!"

"Oh, Cook!" Hope hurriedly left her chair, fetched a handkerchief from the chest of drawers, and knelt beside the servant. "I am so sorry. I wish I'd have known!"

"I didn't want no one to know," the servant blubbered. "Don't tell Lord Amberton, m'lady! I'm afraid he will send me away!"

"No, no, he would not do that." She patted Cook's shoulder. "You have been with the family for far too long for him to turn you off. He will give you retirement."

"I don't want no retirement. I wouldn't have anything to do. It'd kill me!" She blew noisily into the dainty cloth. "What'll I do?"

"Dry your tears and do not worry," Hope confidently told her. "I will manage everything."

Cook made an enormous snuffle and wiped her eyes. "What'll you do?"

"First of all, while I am in residence, I'll spend time in the kitchen to help oversee, and assist in training Daphne."

"That's sweet of you, Lady Hope."

"Then, before I leave and when the time is right, I'll initiate a new scheme of things."

Cook gawked at her, baffled. "What's that mean?"

"How would you like to be the honorary cook? Whenever you wished, you could be in the kitchen and give advice, but you wouldn't have to do any of the actual work. And you could live in your same old room. You wouldn't have to go anywhere or do anything you didn't want to do."

"That'd be heaven!" Wadding the handkerchief in her big hand, she anxiously leaned forward as the chair creaked ominously. "Will my lord go along with it?"

"I shall see that he does," Hope vowed.

"You're like a miracle come to me, Lady Hope." The tears came again, and she dabbed at her eyes.

"But you must give me time, so we cannot allow the information to reach Lord Amberton's ears. Make certain that all who must know will agree to that," she cautioned. "It will be best if I can choose the perfect moment to approach my lord on the subject. Men can be so disgustingly persnickety when it comes to change, especially when they themselves do not initiate it."

"I'll do anything you say, m'lady!" Cook gazed at her with worship written clearly on her face. "You're an angel!"

Hope flushed. "Surely not that."

"You are." She slowly moved her head from side to side with marvel. "Just think! I didn't like you. I thought you were a mean-tempered little nag. I sure was wrong! You're the sweetest, kindest lady that ever walked the earth."

"Oh, no. Don't flatter me so!" Hope laughed.

"But it's true.

"Thank you, Cook, and after I am gone, I promise I

shall come back to visit now and then to see how things are going," she vowed enthusiastically. "But I must avoid those times when your lord is at home. That wouldn't be safe!"

"He was a good little boy."

"So I understand. But he isn't now." She rose. "Go to the kitchen, Cook. I shall quickly dress and be right along to help with breakfast."

"Bless you, m'lady." She stood up, performed a ludicrous curtsy, and trundled toward the door.

"Oh, Cook?"

The woman turned.

Hope studied her, questioningly. "What made you come to me? At this time?"

The servant sighed. "I know people ain't been eating much. And I saw those dirty dishes. That was you, wasn't it, ma'am?"

"Yes, it was."

"So I decided I couldn't keep going on like this. I had to get help, and you were the best one to ask. I can tell that you know about cooking, and I thought you'd be nervy enough to handle my lord."

"Thank you." She smiled at the last dubious compliment. "I'm glad you came."

"Things'll be better now," Cook said with relief.

"I certainly hope so."

When the door closed behind the servant, Hope frantically washed up in icy water, threw off her nightclothes, and began to dress herself. She certainly prayed things would be better. They had to be, at least while she was here. But would Lord Amberton agree to her plan? On most estates, retired servants were given cottages some distance away from the main house. That wouldn't do for Cook. She wanted to be in the midst of the everyday flow. Well, somehow, some way, she'd convince the marquess to allow it. Also, if Cook's eyesight was badly failing, she might need people to take care of her. Lord Amberton *must* give his consent.

* * *

Unwilling to face the inedibles on the sideboard, Colin sat down at the breakfast table and motioned Mitchell to fill his cup. After his wonderful midnight repast, he wasn't too terribly hungry, but he didn't wish to pass up the meal and be too ravenous at lunchtime. There was always the possibility that something here, probably the ham, would be worth eating. He wondered if Lady Hope would have similar thoughts.

Lady Hope. The very remembrance of her brought about a twinge of desire in his nether regions, and the kiss they had shared had unsettled him more than he cared to admit.

He hadn't meant to initiate that act of intimacy. He certainly did not want to find himself in a tangle with an innocent lady of Quality. Yet his traitorous body had rebelled against his cool logic and the former had won the contest. Damn it all anyway! In the future, he'd have to be extremely cautious. They had already engaged in several encounters that would have been scandalous had they been witnessed. One slip with Lady Hope, made public, would have lasting repercussions in his life.

Colin gritted his teeth and sipped his tea. The potential consequence of misbehavior was not the only thing that had his nerves on edge. His unfulfilled passion provided him a potent reminder of his folly.

He was not accustomed to a kiss being an end in itself. To an Amberton, a kiss was trivial foreplay. He couldn't remember the day when, feeling as he had when he'd kissed Lady Hope last night, he hadn't carried the act to its completion. Oh, Hell! Here he was, desperately wanting to bed a woman who was totally ineligible for the sport. What a muddle!

At that very moment she came through the door, looking slightly flushed and damnably attractive. Wishing him a cheerful good morning, she went straight to the buffet and began to fill her plate.

"Not eating, Lord Amberton?" she called over her delicate shoulder. "The food smells delicious."

"Yes, well, odors can be deceptive," he grumbled.

"I must disagree. Won't you allow me to fix you a plate?"

"No, thank you. I'm not very hungry."

She did it anyway, setting a heaping portion before him.

"Lady Hope . . ."

"Hush, my lord, and eat your breakfast. Otherwise, you will be miserable by luncheon."

Bossy wench. Just because he'd kissed her and joined her in a midnight rendezvous didn't give her leave to order him about. But the food did smell good, and it didn't appear to be over or under cooked. Lady Hope was eating with fine appetite. He took an experimental bite of ham.

It was delicious, but that was not surprising. The meat was already cured. It was probably just an accident that it hadn't been fried to a crisp. He tried the eggs and found them absolutely mouth-watering. The bottom crust of the bread was a bit too brown, but that was insignificant since the overall quality was so much better. What was going on? He eyed Lady Hope suspiciously.

She smiled back, her big brown eyes as innocent as a child's.

"The eggs, my lady, taste much the same as . . ." Just in time he remembered the presence of the servants and halted himself before he revealed their secret of the previous night. "They are similar to some I've had before."

"Indeed?" she asked sweetly. "But that is not surprising. Eggs prepared in this fashion are much the same. I believe it to be a simple recipe."

"Hm. Perhaps. Of course, I know nothing of food preparation, but . . ."

"That is correct, my lord," she interrupted. "You know nothing of cooking, and why should you? Except in the case of the fine male chefs, it is a woman's business. No one would expect you to possess that kind of knowledge. So why bother even thinking of it?"

"Actually, I was thinking of a certain rule I made."

"A rule? Excellent! I am glad that you brought up the subject of rules, for I have another."

He groaned.

"I believe it should be a rule that we all join together in the drawing room after dinner. Last night, I found it most enjoyable."

His temper flared as he recalled how she had flirted so outrageously with his friends. "If that is to become a habit, it seems that we should observe another regulation that you set down."

"What is that?" she queried mildly.

"The one about flirtation, about my friends leaving you in peace."

"Oh, was that an edict? I scarcely thought so for you did not agree to it, and you certainly didn't enforce it."

Hoisted on his own petard! "I was trying," Colin protested, "but how could I expect success when *you* flirt with *them?*"

"Ah . . ." She narrowed her eyes. "So your failure is all my fault."

"I didn't say that! I merely remarked that you weren't making it any easier."

"Once you instructed me that flirting was human nature," Lady Hope countered.

"Just let it be," he growled.

She'd nailed him again. He must not be alert yet this morning. He applied his attention to his breakfast and decided to leave off further conversation with the pesky vixen.

Damn, but she vexed him! One minute, he wished to turn her over his knee. The next, he wanted to make love to her. For all her prattling of propriety, she was a naughty little bundle. And it seemed she was always one step ahead of him. No female had ever accomplished that. She was challenging his masculinity right down to its last ounce of potency. What she needed was a good lesson in male superiority.

They finished their breakfast at much the same time and together departed the dining room.

"I have a busy morning planned," she commented as they passed through the hall. "I plan to do some touring. Could you point me in the direction of the gallery?"

"Certainly." He led her toward the corridor that she would take. "Just stay out of trouble," he admonished.

Lady Hope simpered mischievously. "Trouble?"

"You know what I mean. Stay away from my friends. You're playing with fire."

"Oh, I know how to quench it," she boasted airily, looking up at him with that enticing minxish expression on her face.

Something snapped. Before he could consider his actions, Colin caught her arm and whirled her into the nearest room, which happened to be the library. He kicked shut the door.

"Lord Amberton!" she had time to gasp before he pulled her into his arms and brought his mouth down hard on hers.

She struggled in his arms, but Colin had no doubt that he could gentle her. He was far too experienced in the art of making love to fail at it with this delectable innocent. As he predicted, her lips began to soften. When she clung to him, he eased his grip on her, lightening it to a caress. He deepened the kiss, his tongue teasing her lips and the fragile tissue of her mouth. At first she stiffened at this new experience, but soon he had her purring with delight. Shyly she followed his lead and tentatively kissed him back.

Ha! She knew how to quench a man's ardor? She couldn't even control her own. She was so inexperienced that he could have her right now on the library floor if he wished. What a lesson he was teaching her! And he was enjoying it immensely. Tenderly he skimmed his hand across her exquisite derriere.

It happened so quickly that Colin could never have reacted in time to avoid it. Lady Hope pulled away from him, drew back her hand, and punched him hard in the nose with her fist. He reeled backward, blood gushing from his nostrils.

"Jesus!" he cried, staggering to keep his balance.

"Oh, my lord, I am so sorry!" she wailed, quickly slipping her arm around his waist and guiding him to a chair.

Groaning, Colin fished out his handkerchief, but it plus Lady Hope's small lacy square were not enough to stem the tide. She unwrapped the cravat from around his neck and shoved it against his nose.

"I shall fetch assistance!" she frantically declared, rushing from the room.

His face throbbing, Colin closed his eyes and tried to lean his head against the cushions, but the gesture only sent the blood pouring down his throat. He coughed, moaning. Damn but she packed a punishing right!

Lady Hope returned with what seemed to be every servant in Amberton Hall, along with his friends in varying stages of dress, and Mrs. Sommers. Her caterwauling must have echoed through the entire house. It was terribly embarrassing, especially since his cronies instantly summarized what had probably happened and began to laugh outright.

The lady took command, hovering at his side and barking commands to his staff. She replaced his ruined neckcloth with a towel and examined his nose. "It doesn't appear to be broken, thank heavens," she announced and pinched his nostrils together with an iron grip.

"Ouch!"

"Be still, my lord. This will stop the bleeding."

He obeyed, staring helplessly at the company and wishing he could throttle his chortling friends. In fact, every male in the room was amused by what had happened to him. The footmen were hiding their grins behind compressed lips. Mitchell's shoulders were shaking. The kitchen boy—what the hell was he doing here?—was aping his elders and snickering. Dobbs, his own valet, was standing at Lady Hope's side, his mouth trembling. What a setdown for a proficient ladies' man! He'd never live it down.

The females were kinder. Mrs. Dawes wore her most matter-of-fact expression. The maids were wide-eyed and open-mouthed. Mrs. Sommers was white-faced and horrified.

Lady Hope shifted position, unconsciously bringing her luscious breasts directly into his line of vision, but he wasn't interested in feminine attributes just now. Especially here. Lord, what would have happened to him if he'd tried to touch one of those twin treasures?

The corners of her lips twitched. "Let us see if the bleeding has stopped," she suggested, removing the towel from his nose. "Ah yes, everything is fine now."

It didn't feel fine. His nose was like jelly. His face was covered with hardening blood.

"Now we shall clean you up. Cook? Mrs. Dawes?"

The big woman lumbered forward with a bowl of water, while the housekeeper brought linen cloths and exchanged them for the soiled towel.

"Dobbs?" Lady Hope presented the valet with the bloody cravat. "You must wash this immediately before the blood hardens."

Gingerly holding the article between the tips of his thumb and forefinger, Dobbs stared at it with distaste. "It is ruined, my lady."

"It can be salvaged. Go along now and do as I say."

Dobbs lifted his disdainful chin. "No."

The staff gasped.

Eyes blazing, she rounded on him.

"Leave off, Lady Hope," Colin hurriedly interceded.

"No, I shall not. I will not brook impertinence and disobedience on the part of a puffed-up hired hand."

"Hired hand!" sputtered Dobbs. "I am the finest valet in the kingdom!"

Colin's friends doubled over with laughter and were forced to seek chairs.

"Good! Then you should have no trouble in cleaning

it!" Lady Hope grabbed the stained neckcloth from his hand and wrapped it around his neck. "Proceed. I have no further need of you here."

Dobbs's face contracted with horror. Deflating somewhat, he removed the cravat. "But it . . . it's ruined, my lady."

"Perhaps you are not so fine after all," she sneered. "Very well, *I* shall teach you the proper way in which to do it."

The valet's jaw muscles churned. "I'll do it," he muttered and departed to a faint smattering of applause.

Lady Hope turned back to Colin. "You should fire him," she recommended, beginning to cleanse his face. "You should not put up with such insolence."

Colin closed his eyes. "Dear God, you are the most domineering woman I've ever seen."

"No, I am not. I merely have high expectations, particularly from those I employ."

"Your servants must hate you."

"They couldn't, my lord!" his own cook burst out. "They must love her! They'd always know where they stood, and they wouldn't be afraid to come to her with a problem. She'd fix it up!"

"Now I've heard everything," he murmured. Cook? Taking Lady Hope's side? What a day this has been, and it was only just begun.

"Thank you, Cook," said Lady Hope pleasantly. "Now I believe we are finished. Everyone may return to their duties. Lord Amberton will be fine."

There was a general shuffle as the room cleared.

"Perhaps you would like to lie down," the lady told him when they were alone.

"Maybe I shall."

"I really think you should. Go up to bed. I'll find Dobbs and send him to you."

Colin was seized with panic. "Please leave Dobbs alone, Lady Hope. He's the best valet I've ever had."

"He wants proper conduct."

"Please?"

"Oh, very well!" She laughed lightly, then sobered. "I really am so very sorry that this unfortunate event took place. You were naughty, my lord."

"So were you," he retorted.

"Perhaps." She squeezed his shoulder. "I shall leave you now. See you at luncheon? You should be much improved by then."

"I suppose." He watched her glide toward the door.

Before she left the room, she paused and turned. "Lord Amberton?"

"Yes."

"You need not be concerned for my safety. You see? I am most adept at putting out fires."

"Dammit!" He started up from the chair, but was forced to sit back down because, God help him, he was laughing too hard.

11

As soon as the door had closed behind her, Hope's bravado fled. Oh, what a shocking stunt she'd committed! How scandalous! How mortifying! The fact that Lord Amberton had deserved the severe retribution, and more, didn't make one particle of difference. Hope Blissfield had bloodied the nose of a marquess in a most unladylike manner, and it was the greatest transgression she'd ever enacted. What if Gerald somehow found out? Oh God.

Knees turning to water, she bent her head, leaned against the wall, and drew in several huge, ragged breaths. Why couldn't she have given Lord Amberton a smart, feminine, little slap? Instead, she had dealt him a stunning blow, just like a man fresh from Gentleman Jackson's boxing salon. Thank heavens she hadn't broken any of his bones. Lord Amberton would never have forgiven her if he'd had to go through life with a crooked nose to mar his handsome face.

She couldn't blame him if he never forgave her at all, yet he must have done so. He wouldn't have laughed so hard if he harbored a grudge, would he? Dear, dear, why did it matter so much anyway? He was a deplorable rake who merited his punishment. She shouldn't bother herself with his feelings.

But she did. Her skittish mind had not quite returned to its normal logical state since Lord Amberton's tender kiss the night before. Now, freshly assaulted again, and with a passion that had nearly destroyed her willpower to resist his advances, she was as addled as a half-wit. At a time when she should be wishing the very worst for the marquess, she was throbbing with desire for his regard. In truth, she should not give a snap of the fingers for his opinion of her.

She must, however, consider what others thought of the deed she'd done. Her act was so sensational that tales of it might not be silenced. Servants would whisper. Lord Amberton's friends would tattle. As soon as the snow thawed enough for travel, the entire district would probably be well aware of the event. By spring, all the *ton* would know. She would be censured!

With a miserable sigh, Hope forced up her chin and made herself look around at those still remaining in the front hall. Quickly turning away from her, Mitchell cleared his throat and fastidiously straightened his black coat. Two footmen tightly pursed their lips to stifle their snickers. Agatha, draped weakly over the newel post and talking with Lord Kelwin, unhappily met her gaze. The earl turned and regarded her solemnly.

Hope set her jaw. She had no choice but to brazen this through. She could haughtily pass by the servants and Kelwin. Agatha was a different story. Her friend would definitely pursue her, and Hope had no desire to talk with her until she had regained some measure of aplomb.

A wonderful idea stabbed through her scrambled thoughts. She *could* escape Agatha. The kitchen was even now preparing for lunch. Hadn't she promised to help? With tremendous relief, she whirled in the opposite direction and strode toward the service area.

"Hope?" Agatha called.

She quickened her pace, nearly dashing through the green baize door.

"Hope!"

Once inside the labyrinth of corridors, she took to her heels and burst into the kitchen to the great surprise of all its occupants. "Cook! Please help me hide!"

"Poor lovey! Come in here." The enormous woman speedily shuffled her into the scullery, so startling a maid who was washing dishes that she dropped a frying pan with a splash of water and a piercing clang.

"Laks! I thought something 'ad me, I did!"

"Shut up, Rosie, and clean up your mess," Cook commanded, ushering Hope to an ancient stool. "Now don't you worry, m'lady. I won't let no one find you. No, they won't get past me!"

"Thank you." Gratefully she collapsed onto the wobbly seat.

Cook disappeared, firmly shutting the door.

"Did I splash you, m'lady?" The little servant anxiously knelt and began to wipe Hope's damp slippers with a linen cloth.

"I'm fine. Don't bother," she said kindly.

"Just ain't used to seein' a lady come in here." She rose, picked up the fallen pan, and began to dry it with the same towel she had used on Hope's feet.

"No, Rosie!"

The maid squealed and dropped the pan again.

"I'm sorry," Hope said, glad to be diverted from her own problems to those of Amberton Hall. "I didn't mean to frighten you again, but, Rosie, you cannot use that cloth. It's dirty."

The girl stared at the piece of fabric.

"It's soiled from my shoes. And you must wash the frying pan again. There is dirt from the floor, even if you can't see it. Food must never touch anything dirty."

"Oh."

"Remember, while working with anything to do with food, one can never be too clean."

"Yes, m'lady, I'll remember! Cook says to do everything you say . . . that you know all there is to know 'bout the kitchen."

"Well, that is a high compliment indeed, but . . ." She let her voice trail off and leaned her head against the dingy wall.

"It sure is nice, havin' a lady at Amberton Hall!" the maid piped, returning to her dishwashing.

And, oh, how the residence needed one! But despite the complication of being short-staffed, Hope wondered how many otherwise elegant homes were, in truth, just like this one behind the scenes. Not hers, she thought with pride. Her servants were absolute treasures, and she was an incomparable mistress. Even if she did go around hitting gentlemen in the nose with her fist!

"Get out o' here!" she heard Cook shout.

Hope sprang to the door, pressing her ear against it.

"We were just . . ." Lord Kelwin's voice echoed.

"Out! Out!" screeched Cook.

"Well I never!" the earl exclaimed.

There was a loud, sharp crack.

"That was Cook hitting the table with her rolling pin," said Rosie knowledgeably.

There was no more conversation. In a few short moments, the scullery door opened. "They're gone now, m'lady."

"Oh, thank you, Cook!" Tears prickled Hope's eyelids. "I . . . I know it's silly and cowardly of me, but I simply couldn't face anyone right now."

"Don't you worry none, lovey. We'll keep you safe." The big woman led her out into the kitchen. "Nobody'll get you. Not even m'lord!"

"I . . . I don't think he would try. He didn't really seem angry about w-what happened."

"'Cause he was guilty," stated Daphne.

"Shut up," ordered Cook.

"He tried somethin' with m'lady, and he deserved what he got," the girl muttered. "Just like Denny from the stable tried with me. Don't you think I didn't let 'im have it, too! Grabbed me on the bottom, he did, and I kicked 'im in . . ."

"Get busy with them pies!" Cook directed. "M'lady don't want to hear about your trifling!"

"Women have to stick together," Daphne said stubbornly. "Men're all the same. Don't matter if they're lords or stableboys. They all want one thing."

Flushing slightly, Hope sat down at the table. The servants weren't fooled. They'd calculated that Lord Amberton had attempted to take liberties with her. Knowing that they realized what had happened should have made it all the more mortifying, but it did not. These women, at least, were on her side. She was glad she'd come to the kitchen. Daphne's discourse might be a bit too impertinent for a proper servant-to-lady relationship, but Hope didn't care. It was so nice to have staunch supporters here, even if they did inhabit the region behind the green baize door.

Of course, Agatha was her ally, too. Hope felt rather guilty about having run from her, but she hadn't been in any mood to answer her companion's inevitable questions. Besides, Agatha surely would have scolded her, not for defending herself, but for doing it in the way that she had. She'd made a scene, and ladies didn't make scenes.

Daphne interrupted her reverie. "M'lady, about the filling for the pies . . ."

Determinedly pushing the whole terrible episode from her mind, Hope threw herself into supervising the luncheon preparation. She showed Daphne the proper mixture for the apple pies, minutely instructed her on oven temperature, then set her to shredding potatoes to be combined with diced onion and melted cheese for flavorful fried patties. She directed the other girl, Mertie, in the preparation of a platter of diverse vegetables. While Cook kneaded the dough for Hope's favorite light rolls, Hope herself whipped up a mushroom sauce for the tournedos and wrote down the recipe for the steaks' quick grilling. It would be a simple lunch, but a delicious one. Finally, she hung up her borrowed apron.

"I'd best go to my chamber and freshen up for this delectable repast," she told them. "Everything should be well in hand."

Her new friends nodded confidently. "Bless you, m'lady," said Cook and wiped her eyes, once more overcome with emotion for what Hope had done for her.

Hope took the servants' stairway to avoid meeting Lord Amberton or his guests. Happily, Agatha was not to be seen either. Martha, stowing clean undergarments in the chest of drawers, told her that her companion had been searching for her.

"I knew where you were, my lady, but I didn't tell. 'Tis a fine thing you're doing for that old cook. All the servants are talking about it."

Hope was not surprised that word had spread so quickly through the residence. Nothing was sacrosanct to a household staff. But now that the news was widespread, it wouldn't be long before Lord Amberton found out. She would have to discuss the matter with him as soon as possible. She dreaded it. Though he had taken his severe rebuff this morning with unusually good humor, she couldn't expect to find him in equally fine spirits when he learned of her invasion of the kitchen.

At breakfast, he'd seemed to have an inkling that she might have been involved in the meal, but he hadn't directly accused her of it. What would he say when he found out for sure? After all, she had gone against his express orders, no matter what Cook had requested.

Hope stretched her weary back and began to wash up. Kitchen work was fatiguing, especially when there was such a small staff. She might as well speak to Lord Amberton about that, too, and about modernization of the facility.

With Martha's help, she changed her gown, then sat down at the dressing table. After luncheon, she would request an interview with the marquess. Hopefully, the good food would put him in the best mood possible. She would also sweeten his temper by being kind and amiable. And she would get it over with as speedily as she could. She certainly didn't wish to risk being importuned again!

Agatha was dismayed to find that she was the only female present when the company assembled in the drawing room to await the announcement of luncheon. She had been certain that Hope would be present. Where was the young lady hiding? No matter, Hope would make her appearance before much longer. Her robust appetite would drive her out into the open.

It had hurt when Hope had run away from her. Agatha knew that she had been rather hard on her friend during this difficult situation, but she owed it to her to express her opinion. Hope's impulsiveness and her strong will worried her.

It disturbed Hope's brother, too. Whenever Lord Blissfield met with Agatha, he lectured her on the subject and threatened to hold her responsible for any lapses of conduct. Agatha was afraid of the straitlaced earl. He might not be able to fire her, but he could muddle her chances of finding top-drawer employment when Hope married and no longer needed her. If he heard of this tangle, he would be very angry.

Agatha frowned unhappily.

"I assume that you haven't found her yet." Lord Kelwin seated himself in a chair next to hers.

Agatha shook her head. "No, but I do thank you for helping me try."

"It was the least I could do! I'm sorry we didn't find her, but don't be disturbed," he said kindly, briefly squeezing her hand. "I am certain that no harm could have come to her."

"I am not concerned about her physical condition. I know she is all right in that way." Flooded with warmth from his touch, she forced a small smile. "But she was so overset! That is what distresses me."

"She'll get over it. The lady is rather bristly, isn't she? She must be difficult to work for," he sympathized.

"Oh, no!" Agatha disputed loyally. "You have it all wrong, my lord! Lady Hope is the kindest employer and the sweetest person."

He eyed her with disbelief. "She gives the impression of being obstinate and argumentative."

"She is merely under great strain," Agatha rationalized. "But . . . well, I suppose one could consider her to be a bit . . . ah . . . opinionated."

Lord Kelwin laughed.

"But she truly is an angel!"

"I shall take your word for it, Mrs. Sommers." He continued to grin, though his words were serious. "I do have the feeling that Lady Hope has definitely overset Colin's well-being more than any of us realize. She challenges him. Actually, she challenges all of us with her rules and regulations, even though she may mean well."

"I know." Agatha sighed. "I have tried to warn her, but there is little more I can do. I can only hope that Lord Amberton and the rest of you will put up with it all. In fact, it wouldn't hurt for the gentlemen, excepting yourself, of course, to listen to what she says and take it to heart."

"Excepting me?" he asked curiously. "Why?"

She flushed. "You are different from the others."

"Am I?"

"Yes." Agatha nodded emphatically. "Your manner is much more pleasing. You are more responsible."

"Why, thank you, Mrs. Sommers."

"In fact," she added recklessly, "it is hard to believe that you are a part of Lord Amberton's circle of friends. He and the others have such deplorable reputations. If it were not for his title and wealth, I doubt that the marquess would be received by any decent person. He is . . ."

Agatha stopped short, horrified that her tongue had gotten away from her. By criticizing his friend, she was being impossibly rude to this pleasant man. She had stepped beyond her station in life.

"Yes?" Lord Kelwin prompted.

"Forgive me," she whispered. "I go too far."

"But I would like to hear your opinion. Mrs. Sommers, we are not in a London drawing room. We are snowbound together, a situation which lends itself to informality. Please speak freely."

"Very well." She smiled shyly. "I . . . I was just going to say that Lord Amberton is a rake."

Kelwin chuckled. "I believe you were going to say much more than that, Mrs. Sommers, but, yes, you are right. He is a rake. There is something I'd like to point out though." He sobered. "Colin and I have been friends for a very long time. Believe me, there is a reason for his being the way he is."

"His father?" asked Agatha.

"His father, and his entire male ancestry. But there is one thing he's doing about it."

"He plans to reform?" she probed, excitement welling up within her as she remembered what she had speculated when Hope had held Lord Amberton's coat to her cheek.

"Gad, no. But he refuses to carry on the Amberton curse. He vows never to marry."

"I see."

"You do not find it admirable?"

She lifted a delicate shoulder. "It would be far more commendable for him to improve himself and to assume the duties that his rank has accorded him."

"I doubt that he could, with no more reason than that. It would take a very strong will to overcome the influences in his life. It would require a very strong *woman*, perhaps."

Their gazes met. *Hope*. Agatha suddenly knew that he was thinking the very same thing as she. Only a determined lady like Hope could break the fatal Amberton predilection to vice. And Hope, whether she perceived it or not, was attracted to the handsome devil.

Agatha experienced a sudden chill. Lord Amberton was dangerous. He was a heartbreaker.

"She could do it," Lord Kelwin said quietly.

"No, my lord." Agatha shook her head. "I could never encourage such a thing. Do remember that I have scant influence over her."

Lord Kelwin smiled persuasively. "Unlike his father, Colin isn't satisfied with his lot. He possesses the sort of inner spark of consciousness that it would take to kick over the Amberton traces. He also has a great fortune, Mrs. Sommers. He could do much good."

"No!" cried Agatha. "Hope is my friend. I could never support her in such a pursuit."

"I think they're attracted to each other," he persisted.

"My lord, I understand that you want the best for your friend, but you cannot ask me to sacrifice mine to the cause. Hope needs a gentle, settled husband."

"Lady Hope needs a man who's virile enough to control her," he disputed flatly.

"And then there's her brother," she murmured. "If I aided Hope in something like this, he would ruin all chances of my future employment."

"Perhaps that might not prove to be a factor," Lord Kelwin mused. "At any rate, I'm not suggesting that we embark upon a course of matchmaking, only that you would not discourage such a *tendre* if it did occur."

The door to the drawing room opened. Expecting to see Mitchell enter to announce the meal, Agatha was relieved when Hope, appearing quite calm and collected, glided in. Glad, for once, to escape Lord Kelwin's company, she hurriedly rose and went to greet her friend.

"My lord, I am happy to see that you were able to join us for lunch," Lady Hope said politely, as Colin escorted her toward the dining room.

He gave her a sidelong glance, astonished to see by her expression that she seemed totally truthful in the remark. The amount of blood she had caused to stream from his nose had frightened her earlier. By now, he'd expected her to be over her shock and to have become indignant about his role in the whole affair.

"Thank you, Lady Hope," he responded. "I believe you really mean it."

"Of course I do. I do not wish you any harm."

"But I wish harm for you?" he inquired.

"I didn't say that." She met his sideways glance, her brown eyes unquestionably innocent.

"No, but I suppose I did have ulterior motives. I don't now." He lowered his voice. "I attempted liberties. I should never have done so. I owe you a grave apology."

"You are forgiven," she hastily responded. "I, too, beg pardon for causing you injury."

"I cannot blame you, Lady Hope. I deserved it."

"My lord," she whispered, "is there any chance of preventing word of what happened from leaking out?"

"I'll do what I can," he promised. "We'll discuss it later."

"After lunch?" she appealed. "In the library?"

"Yes, that will be fine. And do not worry. We'll keep the door open. You will be safe from me."

Colin seated her at the table and took his place, steeling himself for the inevitable teasing that he would surely suffer from his friends. Since he'd retired to his chamber immediately after the incident, that confrontation had not yet taken place.

Mechanically beginning his meal, he noticed that his friends were in high humor, but happily they were exercising uncharacteristic restraint in the presence of ladies and holding back their jesting for the present time. In fact, the major topic of conversation concerned the excellence of the repast. Everyone seemed to be enjoying the luncheon immensely.

Lingering over the taste of the food, instead of impulsively swallowing it, Colin found that it was absolutely mouth-watering. The beefsteak was just the way he liked it, well seared on the outside and juicy and rosy within. The rolls were light as a feather. The vegetables were nearly as good as if they were fresh from the garden. Breakfast had been delicious; now luncheon was superb.

And that morning, Cook had shocked him with her defense of Lady Hope. There was something havey-cavey going on. He eyed the lady in question.

Lady Hope smiled guilelessly at him.

"I see that you are savoring your meal," he observed.

"Yes, my lord. It is quite above the ordinary."

"I wonder what we shall have for dinner," Colin reflected.

"Oh, probably a choice round of sirloin with Yorkshire pudding." A look of guilt flashed in her eyes. "Er . . . well, that is my guess. Being snowbound limits the selection to what can be provided by the estate."

"Who cares?" Jamie Bridgewater proclaimed. "When the food is this good, who could miss turbot or oysters?"

"Very true," Sir Roger agreed and added in an undertone, "Some of us have no need of oysters anyway."

Lady Hope blushed at this mention of that aphrodisiacal shellfish.

Colin felt his own cheeks burning. Dammit! He should have known that he wouldn't make it through this encounter without some reference to the morning's events.

Mrs. Sommers smoothly changed the subject. "I'm sure it won't be long before the roads are clear, but I shall never forget this storm. I don't think I've ever witnessed anything like it before."

The general discourse turned to the weather, each diner remarking on his or her experiences with inclemency.

Colin let the talk sweep over his head, his mind engaged in speculation concerning the quality of the cuisine. He had no doubt that Lady Hope had something to do with it, and he intended to get to the bottom of it. She must have defied him and confronted Cook, but whatever she had done, she'd met with success. The little minx was ensconced clear up to her pretty neck in this stew pot.

Yes, he'd find out what was going on in the kitchen of Amberton Hall! But he wasn't so sure that he wished to enforce his regulation. Apparently, Cook was no longer annoyed. His guests were pleased. Furthermore, he was enjoying the simple repasts far more than his meals in London! French cooking might have its place, but this solid English fare made a man feel warm and comfortable inside. It was just the thing for a cold winter day.

Suddenly, he found that he regarded Lady Hope in a newly favorable light. And when she smiled at him, he smiled back, as if they shared a secret.

12

"I'm looking forward to the roasted sirloin, and I've always been partial to Yorkshire pudding," Lord Amberton declared as Hope entered the library.

She quailed. This was certainly unexpected. She knew he suspected that she was involved in the meal preparation. However, she'd anticipated first discussing the morning's disgrace. With this opening statement, he'd caught her off balance as usual. Dreading his displeasure, but determined to defend her actions, she bravely sat down beside his desk.

"You've been to the kitchen, haven't you?" he asked without preamble.

"Yes, my lord. You know I have," she sweetly replied.

"I am not referring to our midnight repast."

"I assumed as much." She nervously straightened her skirt. "My lord, if you will listen to my explanation without rancor, I am sure you will agree that I have done the right thing in going against your wishes."

He did not precisely smile, but his violet eyes were mirthful. "Lady Hope, a man cannot be bad-tempered on a contentedly full stomach. In fact, I suggest that we move to the fireside where we may be even more comfortable."

She nodded, relieved, and rose to accompany him to the hearth. Lord Amberton sat on the sofa, but Hope ignored the unspoken invitation to sit beside him. She chose a chair a safe distance away.

Once again, he began the conversation. "Now, Lady Hope, please inform me about what is going on."

"Did Dobbs tell you I was involved?"

"No." He lifted a questioning eyebrow. "How is my valet associated with this little intrigue?"

She shrugged. "Servants' grapevine. That's how I knew that I should discuss this with you as soon as I could. That, and the drastic improvement of the food."

"No, he didn't tell me," he repeated. "Dobbs has become afraid of you, madam."

"Afraid?"

"Something about 'hired hands,' I believe," he drawled.

Hope couldn't help giggling. "That was naughty of me, wasn't it?"

Lord Amberton grinned. "It was rather lowering for a man of Dobbs's self-esteem. But we digress from the subject, my lady. Do tell me of your meddling with my household."

"Well, that is certainly not a genial way to look upon it," she objected, but she smiled.

"Now, Lady Hope," he answered, chuckling. "You may have properly chastened me for my sins, but you must allow me the opportunity for a small amount of mischief."

Hope laughed. After what had happened that morning, she was surprised that she did not feel intimidated or constrained with him. Without the slightest hesitation, she told him everything, from Cook's early-morning visit to her room to her own assistance in the meal preparation.

"Poor Cook is so yearning to remain here in the hall, and Daphne is excited about moving up in position," she finished.

"Very well," he said.

"You'll consider my proposal?" she cried, bouncing to the edge of her chair.

"Not just consider it, my lady. If everyone is satisfied, I see no reason why it isn't immediately made official."

"Oh, thank you!" If she hadn't retained a degree of wariness, Hope would have hugged him. "I'm sure that you won't be sorry!"

"I'm certain I won't, but there is one drawback."

"What is that, my lord?" she quizzed, ready to meet and solve any dilemmas.

"I cannot be at ease with your spending time in the kitchen. You are my lady guest, and you should not be asked to labor. I feel that I am taking advantage of you."

"But I don't mind!" Hope assured him. "Really I don't! I have so much time on my hands, and, as you may have guessed, I am an energetic person. I will be glad to assist."

"There's more to it, too, isn't there?" he pondered.

"What do you mean, my lord?"

The marquess hesitated thoughtfully. "You truly care about those less fortunate. You were quick to spring to your abigail's defense, and now you have taken up Cook's cause."

"I try to be considerate of working people," she admitted. "Life is not always easy for them. And I find that a contented staff is much more willing and productive than a disgruntled one."

"But fraternization . . ."

"I would not precisely call it that. I will not stand for impertinence or disobedience, as evidenced by my encounter with Dobbs over your neckcloth, my lord," she explained. "My servants understand this. Those who abuse my goodwill do not last long in my employ."

"A big, happy family," he observed somewhat cynically.

Was he making fun of her? Hope realized that her methods of management might be considered a bit unorthodox, but they worked for her. She firmly believed in them.

She lifted her chin. "I care for my servants, and my servants care for me. What is wrong with that?"

"Nothing, I suppose," he mulled, "especially for a lady who has no husband to look after her."

"I assure you, my lord," she said archly, "my ideas

would not be different if I were wed. May I ask where this discussion is leading? It seems an unusual topic for you."

"Perhaps I am trying to learn something of household management."

Hope eyed him suspiciously.

"Don't believe me?" He chuckled. "Frankly, Lady Hope, I was wondering what my servants thought of me. Cook should have come to me with her troubles."

"I would guess that because you are here so seldom, your staff, even the old retainers, are rather in awe of you. Then too, people would expect a woman to comprehend the workings of a kitchen far better than a man would do."

"So, once more we are back to exploring the differences between men and women, which leads us to what happened this morning."

Hope shifted uncomfortably in her chair.

"Again, I apologize for allowing myself to lose control. I can only beg my friends and the servants to keep the matter to themselves, but there's always the possibility that the news will spread." He sighed. "There is nothing else that we can do."

"No, but at least no one knows *exactly* what happened."

"Lady Hope, the fact that I am involved could leave little doubt in anyone's mind. I pray that your reputation is not besmirched. Naturally, I don't care about mine."

"You should," she murmured.

"Oh, for God's sake! We both know that my reputation was made on the day I was born." Restlessly he stood up and began to pace the floor.

"Just because your ancestors . . ." she began.

"Don't start up with me, Lady Hope!" His travels brought him ever closer to the sideboard and the brandy bottle, until he finally seized it and poured himself a glassful.

"Lord Amberton!" she chided, also getting to her feet. "If you wish refreshment, why not ring for tea?"

"Do you want tea, Lady Hope?" he demanded.

"No, not really."

"Neither do I! I want a glass of brandy and, by damn, I'm going to have it!"

"Go ahead then!" she snapped. "Drink yourself into an early grave!"

"At least I'll be alone." He took a great gulp. "I won't have a female there pestering me."

"So now you are blaming women for your vices?" she asked snidely.

"I'm blaming one in particular for this drink," he countered. "Don't you know what you're doing to me?"

"No." Hope stared innocently at him. "What?"

Lord Amberton took a deep breath and set his glass aside. "Suffice it to say that you make me forget to behave like a gentleman."

She smiled crookedly, relieved that his tantrum had ceased. "I do fear that *you* make me forget to behave like a lady," she murmured.

"Does that make us even?" Grinning, he walked back to the hearth.

"Dangerously so."

He rubbed his chin thoughtfully. "Perhaps we can come up with a truce."

Hope returned to her chair. "Very well, let us start with something simple, like your drinking."

He snorted. "Or your meddling."

"My lord! Because of my meddling, you have a—what did you say?—a 'contentedly full stomach.' "

"All right, all right!" Lord Amberton threw up his hands. "My drinking, then. I'll promise to drink only in moderation, if you'll vow not to chide me for it."

"Done!" She extended her hand, but instead of shaking it, he kissed it lingeringly. She drew it back, nerves tingling.

He cleared his throat. "Your hand is much too soft and sweet to be engaged in kitchen work, you know."

She flushed, a strange sense of longing settling deep within her. "I . . . I will only be advising. And writing down directions."

"Please do nothing more. I would dislike seeing your silky skin roughened."

"I will be cautious, Lord Amberton," she said awkwardly, then brightened. "About the kitchen . . ."

"Oh, God," he moaned and collapsed onto the sofa. "I know what's coming next, and it's going to cost me money."

"You can afford it. Now let us discuss the modernization! A man of your rank should be embarrassed to possess such an outdated relic!" Hope scolded merrily and proceeded to spell out her plan.

Following their conversation, Hope hurried to the kitchen to tell Cook the good news that Lord Amberton had agreed to all her suggestions. After happy celebration, she discussed the dinner menu and wrote down explicit instructions for Daphne, promising to look in on things later. Then, with a long period of time on her hands, she decided to follow her earlier intent of exploring the gallery.

Instead of bothering the marquess for directions, she sought Mrs. Dawes, finding her overseeing the sorting of linens in a massive second-floor closet. Graciously, the housekeeper consented to guide her in person. They descended the stairs and proceeded down an unused hall that Hope had never even noticed.

"Amberton Hall is even bigger inside than it seems from its outward appearance," she remarked. "One could easily become lost here."

Mrs. Dawes smiled and nodded. "Yes, my lady."

"I imagine that it takes a very long while for new employees to orient themselves."

"It probably would. However, there have been no new permanent staff members for many, many years." She opened a pair of creaking, strap-hinged doors. "Here we are, my lady."

The long gallery, Hope found, must have been beautiful in its day, but now it looked rather neglected. It was clean enough, though the impressive march of windows could have been made to sparkle by a good wiping with vinegar and water, and there were clusters of spider webs nestled in the high corners. Its major fault was in the uneven flagged floor. It was the original, no doubt, whose paving had heaved alarmingly over the centuries. As an indoor exercise walk, which had been its initial purpose, it would now be treacherous. Gazing at it, Hope wondered why it had not been repaired. Surely, resetting the stones could not be such a monumental undertaking for a man of the marquess's means.

"Mrs. Dawes, this floor . . ." she began.

The housekeeper shrugged impotently. "Lady Hope, I greatly appreciate your observations on the state of the house, but I haven't the staff or the funds to carry out any more than we are already doing. As a matter of personal pride, I manage to squeeze out the money to hire temporary people to clean the place thoroughly once a year. I do know how to keep a house."

Hope flushed slightly. 'It was not my intention to be overly critical."

Mrs. Dawes drew herself up into a square, brave stance. "Beg pardon, my lady, but you are. I heard of your instruction of the maid in the Blue and Gold Drawing Room, and of the footmen in the Rose Salon. Then you turned your attention to the kitchen."

Hope's flush deepened. "But . . ."

"I, and Mitchell, too, would like nothing better than to see this house kept the way it should be," she went on. "After all, it is our home, as well as an exhibit of our abilities."

"I'm sorry," Hope murmured, genuinely apologetic. "I am just so terribly distressed when I see a marvelous home like this, which does not glow with perfection."

"I agree with you." The woman nodded, visibly deflating. "Please forgive my impertinence."

"Of course . . . if you can forgive me. I fear I am a deplorable busybody, Mrs. Dawes." Hope wrinkled her brow.

"But there must be something we can do. Perhaps I could speak with his lordship about expanding the budget."

The housekeeper sighed. "It will do no good."

"Nevertheless, I shall do it anyway," Hope vowed. "Poor Mrs. Dawes! It must be difficult to work under such circumstances. I cannot understand why Lord Amberton is so unfeeling."

"Oh, he is not *uncaring!*" she protested. "He just isn't *here.* And on the few occasions that he is, he doesn't see. Please, my lady, it will just make him cut up stiff."

"Good!" She chuckled. "That's what he needs!"

She turned her attention to the portraits lining the wall opposite the windows. Here were displayed the images of generations of Ambertons, staring sightlessly from their great, gilt frames. None of them looked very happy. The youthful, brutally handsome men all bore premature lines of dissipation about their mouths and eyes. Their lovely ladies wore expressions of long-time suffering.

"Which are Lord Amberton's parents?" Hope asked.

Mrs. Dawes led her to the spot.

Lord Amberton's father looked like the other men, dark and breathtaking, a dangerous heartbreaker. His mother was fair-haired and beautiful, with fine slender hands like his lordship's. But it was her eyes that captivated Hope.

"They're violet!" she cried.

"Yes," the housekeeper concurred. "Unusual, aren't they?"

"So that's where he gets them," Hope mused. "What sort of woman was she?"

"My lady was the kindest and most gentle of ladies," she recalled with a sad smile. "Too tender, I suppose, for an Amberton. It was an arranged marriage, but she deeply cared for him, at first. Who can resist that fatal Amberton charm?"

Who indeed? Hope thought cynically. "What happened then?"

"He made her life miserable with his drinking, and gambling, and womanizing. He didn't act like a married man should!" Mrs. Dawes dabbed a tear from her eye. "And she was such a dear sweet lady!"

Briskly she turned to point out a painting of Lord Amberton as a child. Hope couldn't help but smile back at the pretty little boy. But, somehow, it was heartrending to see him so bright-eyed and fresh-faced, untouched by future excesses.

Next, the housekeeper showed her a portrait of the marquess's younger brother. "The young man was taken away last summer. No one ever knew the reason why. He became ill one night with horrible stomach cramps. By morning, he was dead."

Hope eyed him curiously. "What kind of man was he?"

"Lord Jemmie was much like my lord, Lady Hope. You might say he was a younger image of Lord Amberton."

Hope refrained from asking more about the young man. Lord Jemmie must have been a multiple-bottle man who also delighted in gambling and womanizing.

"Did Lord Amberton have any sisters?" she inquired.

"Yes. Lady Susan is wed to a fine, upstanding gentleman." Mrs. Dawes pointed to a painting of a lovely young woman. "They have three children, two girls and a boy, and are very active in charitable work. I suppose she will have to curtail that now, for we recently heard that she is expecting again."

"Do they ever visit Amberton Hall?" Hope questioned.

"No, ma'am, but my lord keeps in touch with them."

Hope sighed. At least one Amberton offspring had managed to overcome that dreadful heritage. Lady Susan sounded like a very useful member of society.

"The Amberton children were beautiful," she observed. "They must have been a great comfort to poor Lady Amberton."

"Well, the little Lady Susan was. I am ashamed to admit that my lady cared little for her sons. I suppose they reminded her of their father."

Mrs. Dawes quickly went on to show her the rest of the long line of portraits. By the time they had finished, Hope felt as if her head was saturated with tales of the notorious Amberton family. They had a seemingly endless history, most of it disreputable where women were concerned. Goodness, but those men had been such ardent lechers! How thoughtless they were toward their wives! It was no surprise that Lord Amberton had been adversely affected by his ancestry. Unfortunately, it was practically inevitable.

When they had returned to the main hall, she remembered her vow to approach the marquess on the subject of the housekeeping budget. Luckily, instead of being in the billiard room with the rest of the gentlemen, he was at his desk in the library, glancing over his account books and drinking a glass of brandy. He looked up warily as she entered.

"Drinking, I see," she caustically observed, pleased to observe a slight grimace of guilt cross his face.

"Dammit, this is the remainder of that glass I poured when you were here!" he defended, rising. "I have not cheated. Moreover, this is my house and . . ."

"So it is, and that's what I want to talk with you about." Feet aching, she dropped into the chair nearest him.

"No point in offering you a seat, I see," he said sardonically. "Now what sort of a peal are you about to ring over my head? More complaints? Further regulations?"

"Oh, don't be so stiff-rumped," she cheerfully chided.

"Stiff-rumped?" He was forced to laugh. "What an expression for a lady!"

"We shall not discuss my social degree."

"Then what? Another rule?"

"Perhaps." Hope smiled up at him. "Just sit down, my lord, and be still! I cannot speak with you towering above me like some great threatening menace."

Shaking his head in merriment, the marquess obeyed. "Now what? I am at your mercy . . . as is beginning to be a customary thing."

"I doubt if that could ever be!" She leaned forward deliberately. "I'll get right to the matter at hand. My lord, I have been exploring the gallery and have found the floor to be in piteous disrepair."

"Indeed? Tell me, my lady, are you a stone mason?"

"You know I am not."

"Neither am I," he said brightly. "Next topic?"

"Lord Amberton, this is not a subject for amusement," Hope warned. "You are allowing this house to go to wrack and ruin!"

"Very well," he acceded. "I'll have someone find out about resetting the stone."

Hope stared at him, dumbfounded. "That was easy."

"I've given up. You defeat me at every turn."

"Hm, well then . . . Shall I move along to another concern?"

He feigned a gasp. "It had best not be the kitchen!"

"No, that issue is settled, and Cook, by the way, is ecstatic. This latest issue pertains to your staff. It is too small to care properly for the house. You must hire more people."

He moaned.

"Please?" she begged. "Consider it? I shall confer with Mrs. Dawes and present you with a written proposal. I shall be as fair and economical as possible, my lord."

Lord Amberton rolled his eyes. "What will you come up with next?"

"Nothing. I swear it!" she cried. "Do allow me to pursue this. You will not be sorry. And after all, you have nothing to lose in merely looking over my ideas."

"Why are you doing this?" he quizzed.

"Because I think Amberton Hall is wonderful," she said earnestly. "It is so beautiful, and it could be more so! You have a serious responsibility as its caretaker, my lord, so that it will be here in the future."

"What if I don't care?"

"I do not believe that," she scoffed. "No one, even a resolute rake, wishes to see the demise of something so magnificent."

He slowly exhaled. "All right, Lady Hope, if you wish to take the time to set down a plan, I will look at it."

"Oh, thank you!" she trilled.

"Mind you, I'm not saying that I'll adopt it."

She smiled happily. "You will though. I know it!"

"And I want something in return."

Hope eyed him cautiously. "What is that?"

"I'd like you to cease meddling in my household affairs."

"Dear me," she murmured with chagrin. "You know me well enough to realize that your request will be most difficult. What shall I do with my time?"

"If the kitchen doesn't keep you busy, I'm sure you'll come up with something. Just don't let it involve me. I'm having a hard enough time avoiding the brandy without your driving me to it." He lifted the glass and took a small sip. "This is like a mere taste of water to a man dying of thirst."

"That may be, but just think, my lord! You will enjoy your few drinks all the more."

"We'll see," he grumbled.

"I have confidence that you will overcome this deplorable habit." She rose and strolled to the door. "See you later."

"Make it *much* later!" he called after her.

Hope waved mirthfully.

What a day it had been! And it was still far from finished. She was suddenly very, very weary. Her emotions had certainly run the gamut today. She wished she could take a nap, but there was still much to do. She must visit the kitchen, inform Mrs. Dawes of her budget success, and, horror of horrors, she had to face Agatha, whom she could avoid no longer.

13

The Garden Suite was vacant. Not even Martha was at work within. Astonished, Hope went immediately to Agatha's room and found her abigail there, folding Agatha's plain, serviceable undergarments. The widow was nowhere to be seen.

"Martha, have you seen Agatha?"

"Yes, my lady. She has gone to the drawing room."

"Strange," she mused. "Was she looking for me?"

"No, my lady, I don't think so. She took her sewing basket. Maybe she just wanted to sit somewhere else for a change." The little maid eyed her like a cat that had lapped up the cream.

"What is it?" Hope demanded suspiciously. "You know something. Is it about Agatha? Or me?"

Martha emphatically shook her head.

"Then what is it?"

A look of consternation crossed the abigail's pert face. "It's . . . it's about me, my lady."

"What happened?" Hope cried. "Have you been accosted again?"

"No, ma'am! Well . . ." She smiled dreamily. ". . . not in a way I didn't like."

Hope collapsed into the nearest chair. Could there be

any more turmoil on this frantic day? And there was still the evening to be endured.

"Perhaps you'd best inform me, at once, what this is about," she said with a sigh.

Once more, the expression of distress contorted the girl's comely features. "We were going to tell you together, my lady, but . . ."

"You and who else?"

Martha blushed. "John Coachman."

"John Coachman? I might have guessed!" She arched a wary eyebrow. "Do not tell me that you have been so foolish as to allow John Coachman to cause you to be in an interesting condition."

"Oh, no, my lady! He wouldn't dare! He tried, but . . ." She giggled. "I didn't hit him as hard as you hit Lord Amberton, though. Leastways, his nose didn't bleed! But I give him a pretty good whack."

Hope flushed deeply. "I would prefer that you do not mention the name of Lord Amberton in my presence," she said tightly.

Martha's face contorted. "I'm sorry, ma'am!" she wailed. "I didn't mean to make you mad. Really I didn't! I just thought you gave him what he deserved. I was proud of you, my lady. All women should be! You stood up to . . ."

"Please!" She lifted a hand for silence.

"You're a real heroine, Lady Hope!" the maid babbled. "You struck a blow for us all when you busted him in the nose. Why, even John thought you did just what you should, and . . ."

"Martha!" Hope shrilled.

The girl startled and fell silent.

"That's better," Hope said, lowering her voice to its normal range. "Now, let us not talk about my deed. I don't think that is what you and John Coachman wished to discuss with me."

"No, my lady." She glanced tremulously toward the

door as if she wished that the young manservant would miraculously appear. "This is hard."

Hope was fast losing her patience with her abigail's nervous procrastination, but she managed to speak quietly and encouragingly. "Martha, you should know that you can come to me with any problem and speak as freely as you wish, but I am willing to send for John if you would like to have his support."

The young servant determinedly stuck out her lower lip. "I've been 'round you for years, my lady. I oughtta be able to say this on my own."

"That's right. Now, sit down." She paused while the girl obeyed. "And speak frankly, else we shall be here all night."

Martha took a deep breath and lowered her gaze to her lap. "John asked me to marry him," she said slowly. "An' I want to do it!" she finished with a rush.

"I think that's wonderful!" Hope exclaimed, reaching out to grasp her maid's tensely folded hands. "I am not surprised. I thought you two were sharing a *tendre.*"

Tears shimmered in Martha's eyes. "But in the kind of jobs we have, we're not supposed to get married."

"Who says so?"

"It's not done." The girl looked up optimistically. "Is it?"

"That's what you want to ask me about, isn't it? You wish to be wed and still remain in my employ."

"Yes, my lady," Martha whispered, "but I've never, ever heard of any lady's maid who was married."

"Well I, for one, see nothing wrong with it," Hope declared. "I've known both you and John Coachman for a long enough time to be certain that you will not allow your marriage to interfere with the performance of your duties and your loyalty to me."

The abigail stared at her as if she disbelieved what she was hearing.

"As far as I am concerned, you may wed and *keep your*

jobs." She gave Martha's hands a final squeeze and sat back smiling.

"Oh, my lady!" Bursting into tears, the maid threw herself at Hope's feet, wadding snatches of the lady's skirt into her damp fists. "You are so good! You are an angel, Lady Hope!"

"Not quite that! Now, Martha, catch hold of yourself." She took the girl's shoulders and gave her a little shake. "Goodness! You must calm yourself so that you may go and tell John what has transpired. You mustn't worry him with your tears. Men are afraid of weeping women."

With a great snuffle, the maid sat back on her heels, fumbling in her apron pocket for a handkerchief.

Hope presented her with her lacy one. "Yes, I give you my blessing to wed. And furthermore, I intend to have a party to celebrate. For a wedding gift, I will buy you a fine dress to wear, and I'll raise John's wages."

"My lady!" Martha threatened to cry anew. "We are so lucky to have a kind mistress like you!"

Hope swiftly rose, when she saw that her maid was on the brink of throwing herself into her lap. "Dry your eyes and go to John. I will congratulate him at a later time. Right now, I'm going to search for Agatha."

The abigail got tremblingly to her feet. "We will serve you really good, all of our lives, Lady Hope."

Until you are several months pregnant, thought Hope, but she thanked her graciously and left the chamber.

So! Martha and John! She wasn't surprised. They might have their spats, but they'd been smelling of April and May for quite some time. And the arrangement would work. In their positions, they would not have to be apart for any appreciable length of time. Hope was happy for them, and yet she was somewhat sad, as well. The maid had found her heart's desire. Why not the mistress?

Hope shrugged off the poignant emotion. Martha was probably easy to please in the qualities she sought in a man. Hope, most definitely, was not.

Thoughtfully, she descended the stairs. Just what exactly

did she want in that perfect, elusive male who would become her husband? He must be attractive, at least to her, but that was not the most important trait. Kindness, compassion, responsibility? Oh, yes, those were important. Compatibility? Hope laughed to herself. If she held out for a gentleman who was completely congruent to her way of thinking, she would probably have a very long wait. Love. That was the real key. She and her husband must love each other beyond all boundaries. Love was the balm to any insufficiencies.

Still smiling, she opened the drawing room door and stopped short, mouth dropping open as Agatha sprang away from Lord Kelwin's embrace.

"Hope!" The widow tittered like a schoolgirl.

The earl merely grinned, bowed, and took Agatha's hand and folded it fondly in his elbow.

"Hope," her friend repeated skittishly.

Lord Kelwin bent toward Agatha's ear. "Shall I tell her, my dear?"

"No." Agatha giddily shook her head. "Hope, Lord Kelwin has done me the honor . . ." Her final words blurred into incomprehensible murmurings.

His lordship stepped into the breach. "Lady Hope, Agatha has done *me* the honor of accepting my proposal of marriage. I fear you must seek a new companion."

Hope staggered sideways into the doorjamb.

"Oh, my dear friend!" Agatha dashed forward and threw her arms around her. "I won't do it, if it causes you so much grief!"

"Grief?" Hope gasped, recovering and giving her a sound hug. "I am ecstatic! I could not be happier for you!"

"Are you sure?" she quavered.

"Of course! It's the most wonderful news I've ever had!" One arm around her companion's waist, she stretched out her hand to Lord Kelwin. "My lord, you are correct. The honor is *yours!* She will make you the best wife a man could ever dream of!"

"And he has two little girls!" Agatha sputtered. "I shall be a mother as well!"

Instead of taking Hope's hands, Lord Kelwin circled his arms around both of the ladies. "I was afraid that she wouldn't want to take us all on."

"She will be as marvelous a mother as she will be a wife." Hope chuckled. "I should know! She's been trying to 'mother' me for several years. Agatha, I hope your new children will not be as inclined to misbehavior as I am!"

"Oh, Hope." She flushed, embarrassed.

"Well then, I shall leave you two lovebirds." She withdrew from the three-way embrace. "Agatha, I intend to arrange for a beautiful wedding for you, and that includes the prettiest dress imaginable. Just decide on the date. And, my lord, are you prepared to announce your betrothal immediately?"

"I see no reason to delay." Besotted, he gazed at his future wife.

"Then I shall make sure that dinner tonight is something special. Merciful heavens, I cannot believe all that this day has brought forth!" Turning, she entered the hall and closed the door, leaving them blissfully gaping at one another.

Hope started toward the kitchen. In light of all that had happened, Agatha wouldn't call upon her to explain her own activities. The widow would be too wrapped up in thoughts of her lord and future husband. Kelwin and Agatha! Who would ever have guessed that the lofty peer would even notice her widowed companion? Under ordinary circumstances, he probably wouldn't have done so. But this was a strange time, in an unusual season.

Her smile faded. An uncomfortable lump filled her throat. The two women who were the closest to her were both now betrothed, yet there was no one for Lady Hope. What was wrong with her? Tears prickled her eyelids.

"Come on, Roger!" The billiard room door opened.

Drat it! Lord Amberton's friends! She couldn't bear to fence with them now, not while she was in such a state.

Hope darted into the Rose Salon and turned the key in the lock. Leaning against the satiny wood, she let loose a sob.

"Lady Hope!"

She whirled. Through the mist of her tears, she saw Lord Amberton arise from his seat at the pianoforte. He hurried forward.

"Merciful heavens," she groaned, shoulders shaking. Too stricken to hold back the flood, she gave up all attempts at composure and wept.

"Hope, Hope . . ." He enfolded her in his arms. "What is it, my dear?"

She couldn't answer. She couldn't tell him that she was distraught at finding herself single in a sudden world of couples. He wouldn't understand. No one would! Shaking her head, she simply pressed her face against his hard, muscular chest and cried.

Lord Amberton did not goad her for a response. He held her tenderly and stroked her hair. "It will be all right."

"No. No, it will not."

"Can I *make* it all right?"

"No, you cannot."

"But I'll try." He guided her to the sofa.

It seemed like hours before Hope came to her senses and found herself sitting on Lord Amberton's lap, her arms around his neck, her head on his shoulder, and her reflexive defenses stupefied by his seductive cologne.

"Goodness!" She tried to straighten, but he held her firmly, though gently.

"Drink this," he softly ordered and held a glass to her lips.

It was brandy. She felt that she should comment on that fact, but she was too utterly vulnerable at the moment to mount a protest. She sipped the strong liquor, half-choking when it seared her throat.

"It is only my second glass since we effected our agreement," the marquess assured her.

Hope looked up into his twinkling violet eyes. "Very good, my lord," she murmured helplessly.

Once more, he compelled her to drink. "It will help."

Hope obeyed. The potent spirits seemed to suffuse her veins, spreading a pleasant warmth throughout her body. She knew she should leap from his lap, but the effort was just too strenuous, and she was far too comfortable. She'd locked the door. No one would catch them.

Lord Amberton dried her face with his handkerchief. "Do things look better now? Perhaps if you told me what was wrong, I could do something about it."

"You wouldn't understand."

"Try me."

Hope struggled to smile. "You would think me an absolute ninnyhammer. Suffice it to say that my loss of equanimity was a purely female reaction to the happiness of others."

His quizzical expression did make her laugh.

"You see?" she asked him. "I don't expect your comprehension, but I do appreciate your kindness in comforting me."

"Rakes have their uses."

Regaining her rationality and nudged by her conscience, she edged off his lap and onto the cushion beside him. "I believe you are too warmhearted to be a true rake, my lord."

"Colin," he directed.

"What?"

"Please call me by my given name. Earlier in this contretemps I called you by yours. I don't think that I shall cease doing so; therefore, you must follow suit."

"It isn't proper."

He grinned. "A great deal has gone on today that isn't proper."

"How true." She flicked him a shy glance. "Very well, but only in private. I shall not have the others making speculation."

"I suppose I must settle for that."

Lord Amberton—Colin—offered her another sip of his drink, but she declined. Relaxing against the down-filled squabs, she gazed around the room. The Rose Salon seemed to glow in the waning afternoon light. There was no more dust. The furniture gleamed with polish. A lively fire sizzled on the hearth. It all seemed snug, homey, and cared for. The footman who'd fallen victim to her scolding had seen to that. She smiled in remembrance of the occasion. She was a busybody. That was true. But the Rose Salon was so much more pleasant for her interference. Or was it because of her maudlin sentiments? No matter, at least she was good for something.

"Colin?"

"Yes, Hope?" His eyes sparkled.

"Are you comfortable?"

"Why, yes, Hope, I am." His expression transposed from a look of playfulness to one of intrigue.

"Then I am good for something, at least," she repeated her thought out loud, realizing too late that the statement was leaving her open to all sorts of raffish commentary.

He didn't take up on the opportunity, but remained serious. "I do not grasp your meaning."

Hope lifted a shoulder and plumped up her spirits. She certainly was not going to admit to her bout with self-pity. Then he would certainly come up with some caustic witticism.

"Never mind," she said lightly. "It was only a passing notion. Do you know, I would dearly love a cup of tea! Then I have the most amazing news to divulge. It's about my companion, Agatha Sommers, and your friend, Lord Kelwin!"

Colin sat back and let his guests carry the conversation in the drawing room that evening. Dinner had been a celebratory affair, and the high *esprit* had continued right on thereafter. Amberton Hall had probably never been the setting for such a joyous betrothal.

Nor were the festivities limited to the upper echelon. The servants' hall was also the scene of a party. Hope's two employees had announced their intentions, too, and she had made sure that they would be feted.

Sipping the champagne that she had allowed to be served, Colin watched the lady as she chatted with her companion and the earl. She was beautiful tonight in her blue velvet gown. He could almost forget that he had been driven to assault her that morning because of her challenge and not strictly due to her loveliness. It would also be easy to ignore his vow to refrain from attempting to claim her again. Never had a woman so possessed his senses.

If he imbibed in another glass of champagne, he might even envy Drew Kelwin for having the courage to wed. It could be nice to have that kind of commitment with an entrancing lady. But he was an Amberton, so it wasn't for him. Kelwin was different. The fellow was steady.

But even though Drew had professed his enjoyment of the marital state, the news had come as a shock. His friend must have been cocksure of what he wanted in a wife. This betrothal had happened so quickly, and the earl was not an impulsive man.

As he watched, Hope caught his eye, detached herself, and glided toward him. "Why are you sitting here by yourself? Why don't you engage in the fun?"

"What am I supposed to do?" he asked sardonically. "Jump up and mill about the room?"

"You could show some enthusiasm." She sank down onto the edge of the sofa. "After all, you are the host."

"This is your party," he countered, "or perhaps it would best be termed a *wake.*"

"For shame, Lord Amberton!"

"Colin," he corrected. "No one is within hearing distance."

Hope laughed. "Very well! But do not think you can turn the subject and escape my chiding. This isn't a wake; it is an observance of happiness. Happiness forever after!"

He snorted. "Fustian."

"Don't you believe that they will be happy?" she probed, arching a sculptured brow.

"Oh, probably. Drew has become a dead bore. I can easily picture him sitting in front of his hearth, feet propped up, cup of tea in his hand, fawning over his wife and children."

"And what is wrong with that?"

"It's dull and tedious."

"Well, I like that!" she snapped, incensed.

Groaning, Colin looked into the flashing brown eyes. "Now how have I offended you?"

"On two occasions, you and I have sat in conversation before the fire in the Rose Salon. I did not receive the impression of your being bored."

"That's a different matter entirely. You are not my wife, and we don't have children. No children, as yet," he amended mischievously.

She flounced against the back of the sofa, crossed her arms, and lifted her chin. "You are *so bad.*"

Colin chuckled. "And you thought I wasn't a true rake."

"Humph! I still don't think you are," she airily told him. "You are playing make-believe."

"I do not 'play,' Hope. At least, not in your frame of reference."

"Ha! All men are nothing but little boys at heart."

"Did I seem like a little boy this morning?" he couldn't help inquiring.

She blushed deeply.

"Answer me, dear," he urged. "With your vast knowledge of the male of the species, you should have no trouble in replying."

Hope pursed her lips into a delicious pout.

"You can't answer!" Colin gleefully observed. "The sharp-witted lady has been rendered speechless."

"No I haven't," she said at last. "I am merely considering which of my many responses would be the most applicable."

"I have you in a corner."

"You have not!" An uncanny smile cavorted across her face. "I am going to prove that you, like all other men, are a child at heart. An act is more evidence than a statement, is it not?"

Just what was she about? Seeing the pent-up mirth in her eyes, he answered her slowly and warily. "I suppose so."

"Good! Then I shall set out to prove my point for all to witness. Do remember that you must participate wholeheartedly in my scheme. And in order that things will be more interesting, we shall make a wager on the outcome. A guinea, perhaps?"

"One moment, my dear," he said suspiciously. "Before wagering, shouldn't I know a few more details?"

"Is a guinea too rich for your blood?" she laughingly queried.

"Change in the purse. I want to know what role I must perform in this farce."

"Don't you trust me?"

"No," he said flatly, "not when it could affect my liquor allotment."

"It won't. You'll enjoy the plot I'm hatching, and so will your friends," she assured him.

"Yes, no doubt they'll delight in laughing at me. What would you have me do? Play with toy soldiers? Build a tower with wooden blocks?"

"Nothing of the sort." She stuck out a lush, tempting lip. "By your hesitance, my lord, you again reveal that you are not a true rake. True rakes will wager on anything."

"All right!" he grumbled. "I'll take the bet, but if you cause me embarrassment, you'll be sorry."

Hope giggled. "You are going to have such fun. So shall we all! Tell me, do you have a sled?"

"What?" he cried.

"A sled. You know," she teased, "the device that children use to slide down hills in the snow."

"For God's sake," he moaned.

"Do you?" she prodded.

"I don't know. You'll have to ask one of the servants."

"You're no help at all." She hopped to her feet and left the room, innumerable minutes passing before she returned. "We're in luck! There were not one, but two sleds in the attic!"

"Lord preserve us," he mourned.

"Just wait and see. You'll enjoy yourself!" Hope faced the company and loudly cleared her throat to call for attention. "There will be entertainment tomorrow," she announced to the company. "We are going sledding! Lord Amberton and I have a wager concerning his being a little boy at heart."

His friends guffawed and gawked at him as if he'd lost his mind.

"But it's cold outside," Sir Roger complained.

"We'll bundle up well, and we'll build a fire," Hope parried.

"I think it sounds like a marvelous idea," Agatha ventured. "I doubt that I'll slide down the hill, but it will be invigorating to be out in the fresh air."

Lord Kelwin agreed instantly, while the other guests reluctantly consented to be present.

Hope clapped her hands with glee. "Oh, what fun we'll have!"

Colin eyed her with wonderment. She was mightily excited by the proposed outing. Her eyes were dazzling, and her cheeks were becomingly flushed. She really wanted to do this, for more reasons than the wager. If he was a little boy inside, she certainly was a little girl.

Surreptitiously, he replenished his glass of champagne. He stood up and walked to the window. As he drew back the draperies to peer out, he heard Hope launch forth on a recital of her youthful adventures in the snow.

Childhood! That was a time in his life he'd prefer to forget. The little boy he had been was a child who was constantly fighting back tears and unceasingly striving for the approval that never came until he was old enough to drink and carouse. Hope would lose her bet. The young lad she imagined he'd been had never existed.

Ha! She would see! On the morrow, Miss Know-It-All would get her comeuppance.

He turned back to his guests. At least, the lady had regained her usual spunk. She'd overcome the turmoils of her day and would sleep well, happily dreaming of tomorrow's adventure, while he. . . . He would lie awake far into the night, aroused by the memory of her in his arms.

14

The sun, making an appearance for the first time in days, blazed down on the afternoon gathering, turning the particles of snow into shining, crystalline prisms. Though the air was still bitter cold, a thaw had begun to take place. The surface of the hillside was rendered lightning fast and ideal for sliding.

Despite the frigid temperature, nearly all of the residents of Amberton Hall had turned out for the sledding, for Hope had declared the day a holiday for the servants as well. Catching her spirit of fun, the staff, both outside and inside employees, had joined together and pitched in to make the event as pleasant as possible. The sleds had been cleaned and renovated. A path had been shoveled from the hall to the nearest hill. Snow had been packed down to make several sledding runs. A huge bonfire had been built on the summit. Everything possible had been done to achieve a successful adventure. Even the kitchen staff, under Hope's supervision of course, had gone all out to prepare a sumptuous buffet meal for the returning revelers.

Standing by the fire, Hope surveyed the scene with pride. Never had she dreamed of such a curious occasion. The *ton* (and her brother, Gerald) would be shocked at such seeming fraternization between the classes. Everyone was so bundled up that it was difficult to distinguish servant from master. The sleds were divided equally, one for Lord Amberton and his guests, the other for his staff. There, however, the fellowship ceased. The servants kept to one side of the fire and the slope, while the ladies and gentlemen stayed on the other. Both groups surreptitiously eyed the other, each waiting for one who was nervy enough to be the first to tackle the hill.

"Well," said Hope, "now we are ready to see Lord Amberton behaving himself like a little boy and enjoying it immensely. I shall win my wager."

"No, you won't," Jamie Bridgewater dryly observed. "Colin was never a little boy."

She narrowed her eyes. "Would you care to wager that you, too, will be acting like a child before this day is out, Lord Bridgewater?"

"Ha! It wouldn't be gentlemanly to cheat you so, Lady Hope."

"Dear me, and I could have used the money," she bantered, wondering if they'd guessed how wealthy she was.

"In a pig's eye," Bridgewater retorted, removing her doubt.

Sir Roger pressed close to the blazing logs, chafing his gloved hands. Plainly, he was not a cold-weather enthusiast. He looked daggers at Hope, blaming her rightly, she gleefully supposed, for his discomfort.

"I'm freezing," he grumbled. "This outing is absurd. It is the product of a silly, muddled, female mind."

Hope, warm in her fur-lined, red velvet cloak, lifted her chin high-spiritedly. "Sir Roger, I believe beyond a doubt, that you are the most obnoxious man that I have ever met."

"From you, love, that is a compliment indeed. If you found me agreeable, I don't think I could sleep nights from worrying that something had gone wrong with my august self."

"Oh, but there *is* something wrong with it!" Hope countered, laughing. "You have obviously languished so long in gin mills that you've lost your gentlemanly demeanor, if you ever had any to begin with, of course!"

"Gin mills! I'll have you know . . ." He stopped, realizing that everyone, especially the lady, was snickering at him. "I'll bet she doesn't even know what a gin mill is," he muttered.

"I certainly do!" Hope piped. "It is an establishment of such ill repute that no person of Quality would set foot within."

The bachelors glanced at each other and chuckled, causing her to believe that each one of them had indeed sampled the dubious pleasures of the dregs of London. She shook her head. How could gentlemen of such impeccable birth lower themselves to rub shoulders with such debris, human or otherwise? A ghastly picture of the kind of women who must frequent such establishments rose in her mind. Had Colin ever held one of those dreadful creatures in his arms, or kissed her red-painted lips? Hope felt like striking him again, just on general principles.

"Your eyes are suddenly flashing with fire," he abruptly said into her ear. "What are you thinking?"

"I am deciding how I will spend your guinea," she pertly rejoined.

"Ahh . . ." He arched an expressive brow. "But here we are, and I have yet to see any little boys."

"You shall, my luckless lord. You shall!"

"You are terribly confident, Lady Hope."

She cocked her head flirtatiously. "Of course I have confidence, *for I am always right!*"

The gentlemen groaned, and Agatha rolled her eyes heavenward.

"Let's be about this farce," Sir Roger begged. "Let's get it over with. It's cold, dammit!"

"Gad, but you're becoming repetitious," Lord Bridgewater remarked.

The baronet glared down his nose at his friend.

"I can see that you're telling the truth though, Rog," the

viscount went on. "Your ears are as red as Lady Hope's cape."

In a frenzy, Sir Roger jerked off his hat and threw it on the ground, tying his woolen scarf over his head like an old beggar woman. He glowered at Hope. "In honor of the occasion, I suggest that the instigator of this absurdity should be the first of us to go down the hill. Unless she is afraid!"

Hope hesitated, eyeing the sled and the steep downward trek. It had been a long time since she had slid down a hill. How did one steer? More importantly, how did one stop? There was an excellent possibility that she would make a fool of herself, but she could not give Sir Roger the pleasure of seeing her renege.

"I'll go with you," Colin volunteered.

His friends laughed raucously.

"I am not afraid," she archly informed them, "but very well, my lord, I shall accept your accompaniment. Since you are a part of the wager, you should be one of the first, too."

Her companion quickly moved toward them. "Hope, I wouldn't do that."

"Nonsense, Agatha, I shall be fine! I did this every winter when I was a little girl." Head high, she marched to the sled and sat down. "Come along, Amberton, unless you are having second thoughts!"

His grin couldn't have been broader. "No, I wouldn't miss this for the world."

As soon as Colin took his position behind her, Hope immediately perceived the reason for her friend's warning and the gentlemen's merriment. Why hadn't she remembered how intimate tandem sledders must be? The marquess's nicely muscled legs were scandalously propped on either side of her. His arms encircled her waist in a most familiar manner. She stiffened her back and stared straight ahead.

"Can't retreat now," he whispered, his breath tickling her ear.

Her cheeks burned. Good heavens! Even with all the layers of clothing, she could feel the solid planes of his chest against her. It was vastly unsettling.

"Push us off!" he cried.

Hope's excitement overcame her mortification as the sled raced down the hill. Wind and flakes of snow blew in her face. Her hood flew back and her skirts flapped wildly. What a ride! She cried out in exhilaration.

It was ended all too soon. The sled plunged into a snowbank at the bottom of the hill and turned over, flipping them off. They rolled a short distance and came to a stop, his body covering hers.

Momentarily stunned, Hope gazed up into his eyes, watching mesmerized as the dancing violet irises deepened to a penetrating shade of purple. His mouth seemed to soften. Reaching up, he touched her cheek.

"Colin," she murmured.

"Hope."

She sighed and closed her eyes, lips parting.

The next thing she knew he had leapt up and was hauling her to her feet. She was disoriented by the sudden motion. Had he not been going to kiss her? Had she not wanted him to? Dear God, how she'd wanted him to!

Belatedly, she remembered the audience at the top of the hill. What she and Colin had already done had been scandalous enough. If they'd gone a step further, they'd have really been in the suds. Why, he might have been forced to ask her to marry him! She should be grateful he'd come to his senses. Was she?

"That was a fine sleigh ride!" Colin's good cheer was forced. The moment had stirred him too.

"Yes! Yes, it was!" she exclaimed in a voice that seemed too high-pitched to be her own. "It's too bad we can't do it again."

"Why not?"

"We just can't," she said slowly, shaking the snow from her skirt and trying unsuccessfully to avoid gazing into his marvelous eyes. "But I shall always remember how much fun it was."

He thoughtfully studied her. "So will I," he uttered under his breath, then picked up the sled's rope, took her hand, and started back up the hill.

Agatha had left Lord Kelwin's side and was waiting for her when they reached the crest. "Hope, how could you do such a thing?" she hissed, ushering her away from the company and toward the fire.

"I just didn't think."

"You must *start* thinking! My goodness, he was embracing you all over!"

"I know." She sighed, tingling with the memory.

"And that little episode at the bottom of the hill . . . I could scarcely believe my eyes!" Agatha scolded. "What on earth was *that* about?"

"We fell off the sled," Hope replied innocently.

"There was far more to it than that."

"My breath was knocked out by the fall," she snapped.

"And was he trying to breathe it back into you? Hope, you were almost kissing!" Agatha shuddered. "It was scandalous."

Hope stretched out her hands to the warm flames. "Please, Agatha, do not ruin my good time by being critical."

Her friend ignored her plea and pounded on. "I cannot keep from it! Since we have been at Amberton Hall, you have become so outrageous that you will be lucky to emerge from here with any reputation left at all. *Good time?* How could you enjoy such shocking freedom?"

"I don't know, but I did. Maybe if you were not so stuffy, you'd enjoy yourself more," Hope irritably told her.

"I am not stuffy!"

"Oh yes, indeed you are."

Agatha tensed defensively. "If behaving like a proper lady is stuffy, then I guess that is what I am."

"And as a result, you're going to miss out on all the fun. Why don't you go down the hill with Lord Kelwin?"

Hope blithely challenged. "He'd probably like it, and so would you."

She gasped. "Andrew is a gentleman. He would never dream of asking me to participate in such an appalling activity."

Hope laughed cynically. "More's the pity. Why don't you ask him? He might surprise you. After all, he's just as big a rake as any of these rascals present."

"No, he isn't!" the widow asserted.

"Just watch this. We'll see his true colors! Lord Kelwin?" Hope beckoned. "Agatha would like to ride down the hill."

"Hope!" her companion shrilled.

The earl's face lit up. He started toward them. "Of course, my dear! I'll be glad to escort you."

"I am going to murder you, Hope." Turning, Agatha dashed off toward Amberton Hall with her laughing fiance in hot pursuit.

Hope giggled and directed her attention to the sleigh riders. Sir Roger had abandoned his aggravation and was embarking down the slope, shouting with gusto. Colin, who had pushed him off, waved at her.

"Sure you don't want to go again?" he called.

"Not on your life!" she answered, wishing with all her heart that she could. But Agatha was truly right. It was too improper, unless one went alone, and that wouldn't be any fun at all.

She strolled up to the gentlemen on the edge of the hill and smiled down at Sir Roger, picking himself up from the snow. The servants had also begun to slide. She laughed merrily as she witnessed the dignified Dobbs speeding downward. Everyone was having fun. She felt enormously proud of herself for arranging the outing.

Sir Roger tramped up, grinning. "All right, little vixen, I must give you credit. That was most entertaining."

Hope chortled. "More fun than billiards?"

"I'll admit that the billiard table was becoming a bit

stale." He winked at her. "But unfortunately for you, you've lost your guinea."

"No!" she cried.

"He's right," Lord Bridgewater seconded, glancing pensively from her to the marquess. "From what I saw, Colin looked anything but a little boy!"

Hope blushed deeply.

"Oh?" Colin protested. "In all fairness, you're too quick to judge. Just watch this, Jamie!" He flopped onto the sled and raced down the hill on his stomach.

"You see?" Hope boasted. "I win after all!"

But she knew that she hadn't. He was only playacting for her benefit. From the glimpses she'd had of his past, she realized that he hadn't had a very happy childhood.

When he returned to them, however, there was a boyish look on his face and a sparkle of mischief in his eyes. Maybe she was wrong. Her sledding party just might have reminded him of a piece of youthful gaiety, or perhaps it had given him one that he'd missed. She would wait for his comment on the matter of the guinea. Only Colin Amberton knew the truth of how he felt.

Colin leaned on the mantel by the warm, crackling fire and, catching Hope's eye, silently lifted his cup of mulled wine in salute. Her spontaneous party had been an outstanding success. Who would have ever guessed that jaded fellows like himself and his friends would have found such honest enjoyment in the pursuit of a childish activity? Hope was a diamond of the first water for coming up with the idea. Even Sir Roger had ended up having a good time, and when Drew Kelwin succeeded in coaxing his reluctant betrothed to accompany him down the hill, the event had become absolutely hilarious. Hope had won her guinea, but he wouldn't give it to her tonight. He would think of some special way to make the presentation.

The fun had been good for the servants, too. Though the older ones hadn't coasted, most everyone had attended and enjoyed watching the antics. Seeing their rise of spirits,

Colin realized that being confined to the house was hard for them, also.

The only drawback would come to him later. He would spend another restless night lamenting his celibacy. The memory of Hope's lush body entwined with his would be much too scintillating for comfort. For his own peace of mind, he should stay as far away from her as possible, but she was such a lovesome temptress that he was unable to resist her allure. He strolled across the room to where she sat, alone for once, on the sofa, while Kelwin and his betrothed took a turn about the room, and Jamie and Roger began a game of chess.

"Were you toasting me, sir?" she asked sweetly. "Or challenging me with the fact that you are partaking in alcohol?"

He grinned. "Toasting you, madam. Besides, the mulled wine was your idea."

"Indeed it was. As I have said, I have nothing against drinking in moderation." She eyed him curiously. "Why were you toasting me?"

"In gratitude," he replied honestly, dropping down beside her. "The sledding was fine entertainment. I hadn't recognized how much we needed a breath of fresh air."

"It truly was fun, wasn't it?"

He nodded. "I'm also grateful to have good meals to look forward to. And although I didn't mention it, I appreciated the Rose Salon being put in order. That was your doing, wasn't it?"

She looked rather abashed. "Well, I did make complaint to a footman."

"Your 'complaints' have a way of inspiring action. I suppose I must admit that a bachelor does have his shortcomings in managing a household."

"Goodness, Colin," Hope fluttered, "you are giving me far too much credit."

He shook his head. "I don't think so. Furthermore, I'm certainly hoping that your improvements will remain long after you've left."

She laughed. "You have a willing staff. All you have to do is to make your wishes known to them. And I will write down that plan for the hall's betterment. I just haven't had a chance to do so yet."

"Don't run yourself ragged," Colin implored. "There's plenty of time."

"Well, actually, there is not." She smiled wistfully. "Did you not notice, when we were outside, that the snow has begun to melt? Martha informs me that John Coachman thinks that we shall soon be able to travel."

"Don't be too hasty! I will not allow you to take chances."

"We won't court danger."

Colin suddenly wished that another blizzard would come and cause her to prolong her stay at Amberton Hall. It was not just because she had taken charge and made many facets of his life more pleasant. He would miss her for herself. He would miss matching wits with her. He would miss being tempted by her. Lord, he'd even miss her criticisms! He wondered if she would miss him, too.

Of course, he could visit her on occasion, though the very thought of it shocked him. He'd never been interested in social calls on well-bred ladies. Could such a tame sport become a desirable pursuit for an infamous Amberton? Being snowbound with Lady Hope Blissfield must have addled his brain.

That, and the baffling Kelwin. Drew was totally smitten with his chosen fiancee. The dimwit was actually looking forward to his wedding! Even though the earl had expressed his enjoyment of marital bliss, Colin still couldn't get over it. How could the man be so pleased at becoming leg-shackled?

At least, Roger and Jamie had long held true to their single status, though even they had proclaimed that they would marry someday. When that happened, Colin would be left alone. Ah, so be it! That was the price of being an Amberton who, astoundingly, had a small grain of conscience where ladies and offspring were concerned.

Covertly, he watched Hope gracefully sipping her mulled wine. If he were not the man he was, he suddenly knew he would wish to make her his wife. The idea struck him like a thunderbolt. He had never met a woman who had made him feel like that. Of course, he'd never spent so much time in the company of a young lady of Quality, but he doubted that it made a particle of difference. Among her sex, Hope was special. She might be stubborn, opinionated, and bossy, but underneath it all, she was a darling. And Colin Amberton, England's most dedicated libertine, was falling in love for the very first time in his life. He didn't like it. He didn't like it at all.

"What is the matter?" Hope's voice pierced his stupor.

Colin struggled to grope his way out of his muddled state. "The matter?" he repeated inanely.

"You looked rather startled."

He stared at her, fighting the desire to take her in his arms. "Did I?"

"Yes, you did." She eyed him keenly. "You looked like you'd been stung by a bee."

"I don't know. I—just—don't—know."

Her smile faded. Her eyes widened with alarm. "Colin, are you ill?"

"No! I mean . . . I just felt peculiar for a moment," he managed.

Hope nodded sagely. "The lack of spirits, no doubt. I have heard it said that one who is accustomed to great quantities of alcohol often feels odd upon cutting down that intake. Have you honestly made an effort to follow my direction?"

"Yes, dammit!" he growled, recovering.

"My, but you've had a swift change of temperament," she observed pointedly. "We were chatting quite pleasantly, and now you've become cross."

"Stop trying to henpeck me," he quarreled.

She began to laugh. "What an absurdity, my lord! It couldn't be done. You are far too shrewd to allow yourself to be harnessed up in leading strings."

Maybe so, but wasn't that just what she'd done? Looking back over her visit, he could see how frequently he had bent his own will to hers. His drinking was a good example. It would have been easy to cheat, but he hadn't.

"My dear," he said, "you underestimate yourself."

"Not where you are concerned! I may appear to get my way with you, but it is only because you permit it. There is no woman on this earth who could dictate successfully to you, Colin Amberton, and you are well aware of it."

"Am I, indeed?"

"The proof lies in the fact that you remain a bachelor," she teasingly went on. "Over the years, I imagine that countless ladies have cast themselves in your path and devised all manner of traps in the fruitless attempt to become your marchioness. You have escaped with ease."

"Perhaps," he replied enigmatically.

If she only knew how wrong she was! Petite Lady Hope had done the impossible. She had caught him.

Colin's heart lurched as, once more, he confronted himself with the truth. What was he going to do? He couldn't marry her, and she was too good to become his mistress. Ah well, he would surely recover when she was gone. The parting, however, was going to be painful.

He looked across the room at Drew and Mrs. Sommers who were now engaged in a comfy coze by the fireside. Their life together was just beginning, while his with Lady Hope was coming to a screeching halt. Dammit, he envied his friend!

Hope followed his gaze. "Are they not an ideal couple?"

He shrugged. "Whatever that is."

"First you are pleasant, then touchy, and now you appear to be in the doldrums," she chided. "I just don't know what to do with you tonight."

Colin retreated to his comfortable guise of seductive flirtation. "Oh, I could tell you, my ravishing lady! Better still, I could *show* you."

"Behave yourself, my lord!" Her eyelashes fluttered co-quettishly.

"Hope, that is difficult to do . . . when I am in the presence of such a delectable morsel as yourself."

She pretended dismay. "Comparing me to your dinner, sir?"

"Merely feasting on your charms."

To Colin's relief, they passed the rest of the evening in the comparative safety of razor-sharp banter. And this was the manner in which he'd get through the remainder of her visit. Participating in deeper discourse was like walking on quicksand.

15

Ensconced at Colin's desk, Hope spread out her papers and began to put the final touches to her scheme for the improvement of Amberton Hall. Over the past few days as the thaw continued, she and Mrs. Dawes had explored every room in the house and assessed what must be done to return each one to superior condition. Their critical examination had disclosed far more neglect than appeared to the casual observer. Nothing, except for the floor of the gallery, the kitchen, and most of the working rooms, was actually shabby, but wall coverings were dingy, fabrics were somewhat faded, and carpets were rather worn. The complete renovations of the beautiful home would require great expense. Hope sadly doubted that the marquess would sink as much money into the project as she wished he would.

Then would come the added expense of the extra servants needed to keep everything in prime shape. Her calculations on that were much more attractive, since Colin was seldom in residence. If, however, he allowed his home to become the showplace Hope knew it could be, there was every possibility that he would take a greater interest in it. He might even choose to hold sizable house parties. That would require a much larger staff.

Idly flicking her chin with the pen's feather, she studied

her figures and wondered if she could cut corners. After all, she had promised to be economical. Unable to bear striking out any phase, she decided to leave it as it was. This was the way it should be done. If Colin wanted to pare it down, he could do so himself.

Of course, he might just ignore the whole thing. Although he'd vowed to consider her ideas, he'd been acting strangely lately. He refused to indulge her with any serious conversation, engaging only in outrageous flirtation.

Hope sighed. She had spent a great deal of time on this endeavor, but there was nothing she could do if he merely tossed it on the fire. She had kept her word in preparing it and should forget it now, but there was something more at stake. If the plan went forth, she could assist in all facets of it. Not only would it be fun to return the old mansion to its former grandeur, but it would give her the excuse to stay in contact with Colin.

She looked up as the door opened and he entered the room. "Well, this is timely!" she said with a rush. "I was just about to send for you."

He wryly regarded her. "I see you have made yourself at home at my desk."

Hope refused to let him get the better of her. "Yes," she declared. "All the materials I needed were right at hand."

Colin arched an eyebrow. "Went through my drawers, did you? And did you read all the letters from my stable of mistresses?"

"Certainly not!" she flushed slightly, then added curiously, "Are there some of them here?"

"No, I fed the drivel to the flames. Are you sorry?"

"I wouldn't have read them anyway!" Hope professed with horror, but she silently admitted how tempting it would have been. What sort of missive would a mistress write? Something suggestive and seductive? A spark of jealousy flared. She couldn't help sticking her lower lip out just a bit.

He laughed. "You'd have read every word, love. Admit it!"

"Do not call me 'love,' " she admonished. "You use the word too triflingly."

"Do I?" Momentarily, his violet eyes darkened.

"Yes you do. Anyway, you should not mention those women in my presence."

He stared at her in mock surprise. "This, from one who prefers frank speech?"

"I do prefer it," she countered, "but all too often you forget that I am a lady."

"I wish you weren't," he bemoaned.

"Well I am, and there's an end to it!" Hope rose. "Now do sit down and look over these papers. I have finished my study of Amberton Hall."

"Keep your seat. You look elegant presiding there." He pulled up a chair beside her. "You are in greater control than any Amberton who's ever sat at that desk."

"I wish you would not belittle your ability to manage this estate."

Colin chuckled. "Some of us know our limitations."

"There is nothing you could not learn." She gathered up her report and handed it to him. "Here are my recommendations. If anything isn't clear, I'll be happy to explain. Do remember that the figures are only estimates, since Mrs. Dawes and I were unable to determine the actual prices."

His smile faded very swiftly after he had begun to read. Hope anxiously watched him, her spirits plummeting as a frown crossed his face. He wasn't going to agree to the entire scheme. He might, however, endorse a portion. She found herself holding her breath.

After what seemed like hours, the marquess returned the papers to the desk. "There is a tremendous amount of redecorating here."

"Upon close inspection, Amberton Hall is a bit threadbare, Colin," she quietly informed him, picking at her skirt. "It could be a diamond of the first water."

"I would seldom be here to enjoy the fruits of all this expenditure."

"Perhaps you would wish to spend more time in residence if your home were as beautiful as I visualize."

"There is more to a house than beauty." He shook his head. "Amberton Hall holds nothing for me."

"But it is your seat!" Hope protested unhappily.

"Don't think I do not appreciate your efforts, Hope. I really do." He eyed the stack of documents and grinned self-consciously. "Even if I did wish to turn this old museum into a true jewel, I wouldn't have the first idea how to go about it. I don't know a thing about household fixtures and furnishings. I'd be as like to buy linen for draperies and satin for sheets."

Her heart tripled its beat. There might be a chance for her plan after all! She excitedly leaned forward.

"I am willing to oversee it all, Colin. In fact, I would be happy to do it. And I am experienced. I refurbished my own home, you know."

"No, Hope, I couldn't ask you to do that. Furthermore, for propriety's sake, your brother would never allow it."

"But I would *enjoy* it!" She bounced exuberantly on the edge of her chair. "Gerald has no say in this matter or in any other. I do as I please. He probably wouldn't find out anyway."

He rolled his eyes heavenward. "Hope, you underestimate the ability of gossip to travel. I know that we've begged discretion from everyone here, but no one is so perfect that they can avoid letting something slip, now and then. Even a hint is all it takes. There has been so much scandal already. We can't afford more. Heed me, madam, I know what I'm talking about. I'm the world's best authority on notoriety."

"Fustian! Everyone would consider my aiding a nearby neighbor in the redecoration of his house to be perfectly innocent."

He laughed sarcastically. "Not when that house is Amberton Hall."

"Fiddlesticks!" she said airily. "There is nothing that anyone could make of it."

"Don't be such a schoolgirl." His voice was almost rough. "You know the accusations people would let fly."

She propped her elbows on her knees and cradled her chin on her hands, staring at the carpet that had so suddenly looked worn. "There must be some way to succeed."

"Hope, I haven't decided to do this yet."

She glanced up at him and saw his dark gaze firmly fixed on her gaping décolletage. Quickly, she straightened.

"A magnificent view," the marquess remarked.

"Keep your mind on our business," she upbraided weakly, her body suffused with a warm flush.

He smiled lazily. "It's difficult."

"Make the attempt! Colin, please, we must settle this matter. I am leaving tomorrow."

"Tomorrow!" He jolted from his stupor.

"Yes." Hope's stomach gave a sickening lurch as she thought of their parting. "John Coachman informed me, just a while ago, that we could travel."

"Are you certain it will be safe?" It was his turn to slide to the edge of his chair. "I will not permit you to take chances."

"John Coaehman is cautious. We shall be secure."

Colin got to his feet and urgently strode to the window, peering out. "There is still a lot of snow. Perhaps you should wait."

Hope toyed with the pen, making illegible scribbles on a blank sheet of stationery. Did he truly care? Or was he merely being polite? Her heart seemed to ache. No, she didn't want to leave, but in all conscientiousness, she couldn't put it off.

"Thank you for your kindness, Colin, but we must go."

"So I can't persuade you." He turned, grinning crookedly. "With your permission, I believe I could use a drink of brandy."

She nodded, smiling.

"Will you have a glass of sherry?"

"Thank you." Hope moved to a seat by the fireside. "About the plan . . ."

"I promise to give it my complete consideration," he pledged, and pressed the glass into her hand.

Hope's nerves tingled as their fingers touched. Oh, how she would miss him! After the stormy beginning of their acquaintanceship, who would have ever believed it would come to this? How could she have lost her heart to this impossible man? Would she ever see him again?

She put her thoughts into words. "You will come visit me, won't you?"

"Me? Go calling on a *proper* lady? Now that would be scandalous in itself." Colin took a quick sip of brandy.

"But we are friends."

"Yes, I suppose we are. Strange, isn't it? Given the nature of our first meeting."

She smiled wistfully. "That's just what I was thinking. So much has happened since then." She felt her savoir faire crumbling under the pressure of the imminent farewell. "Colin, what are we going to do?"

He frowned. "About what?"

"About us," she murmured boldly, holding her breath.

"What do you mean?"

"Nothing. Nothing at all!" Blushing, Hope forced herself to laugh. "I imagine that we can manage to overcome any hints of scandal, and . . . and anything else."

Tears prickling her eyelids, she hurriedly returned the subject to the improvement of his household.

"Do you know," Sir Roger drawled, taking a sip of his after-dinner port. "I'm actually going to miss Lady Hope's pert company."

"So will I," Jamie Bridgewater agreed, "though I didn't get very far with my flirtations. She only has eyes for you, Colin."

"That's right, Colin. Too bad that you vowed never to wed," Kelwin stated. "A female like Lady Hope would never be dull. She would make you an excellent wife."

The marquess forced a laugh, which sounded fake even to his own ears. "My friends, we all know that no one would be an excellent wife for an Amberton. Why should I wish to spend my life, even the small portion necessary to provide heirs, with a woman who'd undoubtedly grow to detest me?"

He shifted uncomfortably under his friends' speculative gazes. Surely they couldn't have guessed that his feelings for Hope had gone beyond the normal sentiment of a rake for a beautiful female.

"Even if I did change my mind, I wouldn't wed Lady Hope," he felt compelled to explain. "I like her, and I wouldn't want to make her miserable, which is exactly what would happen if she married me, for I wouldn't change my style of life one iota."

"Maybe you wouldn't, but she would change it for you." Sir Roger chuckled. "She already has. See how she curtailed your drinking!"

Bridgewater laughed. "Face it, Colin, you already do everything she says, even when she isn't around to check up on you!"

"No I don't!" Colin hotly protested.

The gentlemen grinned knowingly.

"I am only attempting to make her stay as pleasant as possible," he said defensively. "When she is gone, I intend to return to my normal, disreputable self."

"Will you?" Drew asked softly.

Colin frowned at the earl. "Just because you are going to leap into the abyss again, Drew, doesn't mean that the rest of us must follow. That's what you're about, isn't it? And as for the rest of you, everyone will see that the lady has had no effect on me. Tomorrow, when she has left, I intend to get totally foxed."

But inwardly he knew he wouldn't. Hope's dictum had showed him the benefits of sobriety. Since he'd begun rationing his drinks, he'd never felt so good. He didn't intend to go back to his previous amount of consumption. But he certainly wouldn't admit it to anyone!

Nor would he acknowledge, even to Hope, that he planned to follow her suggestions on refurbishing

Amberton Hall. After his discussion with her, he'd taken her papers and surreptitiously inspected his house. Her ideas had piqued his interest. It might be fun to improve the place, but he would not ask for Hope's help. It was all too unsettling to be in her company.

"So now that it's become possible to travel, what shall we do?" Sir Roger mused, thankfully changing the subject.

"We've been invited to the Renville house party," Bridgewater reminded. "Hadn't we planned to attend?"

"I won't be going," Kelwin said immediately. "When I'm certain it will be safe for my mother to travel, I'll be fetching her to meet Agatha. Colin, you wouldn't mind if I brought her to Amberton, would you? I'm not asking you to stay here. Your servants will care for us admirably."

Colin felt a rush of panic. Lady Kelwin was rather a stickler. She would cxpect to be treated with very high standards. Perhaps he should remain home, but how would he cope? He'd best ask Hope for advice on meals and the like.

"You're welcome, of course," he assured his friend, wishing that other arrangements could have been made.

"But you're coming with us, Colin," Jamie declared. "Remember? Helene Wyndham will be there."

Helene! He hadn't thought of the baronet's widow in days. Before they'd left London, he sent her those unmistakable signals that he wished to make her his new mistress, and she had indicated her willingness. Helene was ripe for a lover. If he didn't attend her, she'd choose someone else. Suddenly, however, he wasn't so interested in her anymore.

"I'll think on it," he said vaguely. "I'm not so sure she appeals to me."

Once again, his bachelor friends stared at him, the wonderment plain on their faces.

Colin awkwardly rose. "Let us join the ladies. They've planned entertainment for our last evening together."

They adjourned to the Rose Salon, where Hope and

Agatha, awaiting them with a tea tray, greeted them cheerfully.

"I've often wondered what gentlemen talk about over their port," Hope hinted.

"What a pity you will never learn." Colin sat down beside her and accepted a cup of the hot brew. "Perhaps we discuss the same things you ladies have been chatting about."

She laughed. "Somehow, I doubt it."

He watched her small, nimble hands pouring the drinks. He would miss seeing that. She had certainly added a touch of class to the gathering.

"What is our special entertainment?" Jamie asked her.

"Lord Amberton will perform on the pianoforte," she announced.

"What?" Colin nearly dropped his cup, while his friends roared with laughter.

"*That* should prove amusing!" Sir Roger chortled.

"They don't know, do they?" Hope realized, regarding Colin with persuasive brown eyes. "You will show them? Please?"

He couldn't deny her. "All right, but just a tune or two. And in exchange, I insist that everyone else shall make a contribution to the evening."

The guests groaned. Hope made a moue of distress. "Very well," she said, "we have a bargain."

"No!" cried Sir Roger. "You can't answer for all of us, Lady Hope!"

"Care to wager on that?" Drew Kelwin asked.

"She's a bloody dictator." The baronet pouted, but acceded. "All right," he grumbled.

Hope smiled. "Ready to commence, my lord? I have set out your music."

"Set out . . . I thought it would be just two simple tunes." Colin eyed her expectant face. "Oh, so be it."

Setting aside his cup, he went to the pianoforte. She hadn't made it easy for him. The first piece was a minuet of small difficulty, but the second was a concerto. He sat down, limbered his fingers with a few scales, and commenced. Luckily, he survived the light melody with few mistakes and finished it to a round of applause.

"I didn't know you could play!" Bridgewater exclaimed.

"Neither did I," echoed Kelwin, "and I've known you longer than anyone here!"

"I quit playing long ago," Colin told them, flushing with elation. "You'll see that when I attempt this next piece."

"You will play beautifully," Hope said confidently, crossing the room to stand at his side. "I shall turn the pages, so you will have no distractions."

No distractions? The sweet scent of her cologne and the sideways view of her shapely breast were nearly disabling, but when he began the concerto, he found himself becoming engrossed in the music. When he struck the final note, there was absolute silence.

Colin laughed. "Terrible, wasn't it? I told you I hadn't played in years."

"Why, it was magnificent!" Sir Roger exploded. "Why did you ever quit playing?"

He shrugged self-consciously. "Rather an effeminate sport for a man."

"Not when you play like that!" Jamie scoffed. "When next I visit your house in London, I'll expect to see a pianoforte in the salon."

"Balderdash." Colin started to rise.

"Wait!" Drew stopped him. "Do you know a waltz?"

"Yes, I suppose I can think of something."

"Then Agatha and I will perform our entertainment together. We shall dance," the earl announced.

"I can't waltz," wailed his betrothed. "Remember? I am a vicar's daughter."

"I'll show you, my dear."

"No, Andrew, I'll make a fool of myself!"

He fondly took her hand and drew her to her feet. "Love, when you are in my arms, you are never a fool. Play, Colin!"

"They are a wonderful couple," Hope murmured, as Kelwin swept his future countess around the room. "She is following him to perfection. Oh, how I love to waltz!"

"Then do that for your offering," he suggested.

"Maybe I shall. Sir Roger or Lord Bridgewater would probably be agreeable to accomplish their turn with dancing."

Colin visualized her in the arms of one of his friends. She would be so winsome and graceful. She'd look up at Jamie or Roger with those soft, innocent eyes . . .

"Waltz with me," he said impulsively and struck a glaring, wrong note. "Damn."

Hope giggled.

"Will you?" he urged.

She hesitated. "If you like."

"Oh, I definitely *like!* I assume that Mrs. Sommers can play well enough to accompany us?"

"Yes."

"Then let's have our turn." He preemptively ended the music, leaving Drew and Agatha off balance in mid-twirl.

"Colin!" his friend complained, stepping squarely on his fiancee's toe.

"Ouch!" cried the widow.

"My darling! I am so sorry!" Kelwin sputtered, horrified. "Are you all right?" He would have picked her up and carried her to a chair, but she laughingly batted his hands away.

"It isn't so bad as that, Andrew. I shall recover momentarily."

"That was naughty," Hope chided Colin.

"It came back on me too, didn't it?" He grinned remorsefully. "Now we'll have to wait until she recuperates."

"My turn," Bridgewater announced. "I shall do a recitation."

The company groaned.

"Make it short," Sir Roger implored.

Jamie strolled to the center of the room. "When Adam was born, there weren't any women . . ."

"Adam wasn't born!" shouted the baronet. "He was created. And if he *had* been born, there would have been one woman at least."

"Shut up!" Bridgewater retorted. "Allow me to finish."

"Please do. End our misery!" Sir Roger begged.

Jamie sniffed. "When Adam was born, there weren't any women. In his birthday suit, he went swimmin' . . ."

"Did he swim in a lake or in a stream?" Colin asked.

"That's it," grumbled the viscount. "I quit!"

"That might be for the best," Hope decreed, laughing. "It doesn't sound like a rhyme suitable for mixed company. Sir Roger, will you entertain us?"

"All right. For my performance, you must guess who I am." He marched across the room, shaking his finger at Colin and speaking in a high, shrill voice. "You shall curtail that drinking! Behave yourself! Cease that flirting! There will be no dallying with the servant girls!"

Abruptly, he dropped to his knees and folded his hands beseechingly, gazing up at Hope. "Oh, please, my lady! Forgive my grievous sins! I promise I shall change my wicked ways! No! No! Don't hit me! Aagh!" He fell prostrate.

The group laughed until the ladies were in tears.

"Have I really been that odious?" Hope asked, wiping her eyes.

"No, much more so!" Roger stood up to take his bow, then kissed Hope's hand. "Actually, my lady, you have livened up this party more than I can ever say. We may have started out on the wrong foot, you and I, but I am glad that fate placed you on the doorstep. Whenever we meet in London, I pray that you will grant me a dance."

"Consider it done." She smiled.

"You'll have to stand in line, Rog, for I'll be there before you. In fact, I cannot wait that long." Colin rose and took Hope's hand. "Lady Hope will now exhibit her talent at waltzing. Mrs. Sommers, will you accompany us?"

"Of course, my lord."

As soon as the music began, Colin realized what a mistake he'd made. In his arms, Hope was not only everything he thought she'd be. She was more. His stomach twisted with pain and desire. God, but he wanted her!

She looked up at him, her eyes filled with an equal longing. She, too, must be experiencing the shattering passion. Would she lie awake tonight, as he would surely do?

He drew her closer. Her gaze locked with his, and she did not protest the improper nearness. She was his for the moment, but there it would end. There was no future for them. No, he wouldn't ask her to dance in London or anywhere else. His heart couldn't bear the torture.

"I cannot continue playing," he heard Agatha whisper unhappily to Kelwin. "Their feelings for each other are far too obvious, and nothing can come of it."

As the melody came to a swift ending, Colin took both of Hope's hands in his and brought them to his lips. "You are a marvelous dancer."

"So are you," she said trembling.

"I shall always remember this, my lady."

"I, too, my . . . love." Whirling away, she dashed from the Rose Salon.

"I must go to her." Agatha squeezed Lord Kelwin's hand, favored Colin with a hard frown, and hastily followed.

"I believe that we could use a glass of brandy." Colin strode woodenly to the bell rope and gave it a yank, then paused to attempt to regain his poise.

"That's it, Colin, stand in the corner like a dunce," Sir Roger said roughly. "For if you allow her to leave here without declaring yourself, that is exactly what you are."

Colin turned. "Perhaps I am, but I'm doing the right thing, and I will not discuss it further!"

Jaw clenched, he went to the door, tossed an obscenity over his shoulder, and left the room.

16

"My lord, the ladies are leaving," Mitchell said, quietly interrupting Colin's solitary reverie by the library fireside.

"Thank you. I'll be along." Tenting his hands and resting his chin on them, the marquess briefly continued his study of the dancing flames as the door clicked shut behind his butler.

So the time had come for Hope and Agatha to depart. Colin could scarcely recall that there'd ever been a moment that he'd desperately wished for the ladies to leave. Despite his bachelor guests, Amberton Hall was going to be very quiet . . . and very dull without them.

He should be glad, especially in light of the previous evening's events. With Hope in his arms, he had lost his poise. He had revealed far too much of his inner feelings, and everyone had seen it. Gad, he'd acted like a lovesick puppy, instead of a dashing man-about-town! At least no one had laughed, though their critical comments had been just as bad.

When had he fallen in love with her? Colin shook his head. It didn't really matter. He couldn't have her. He was an Amberton.

Mitchell returned. "My lord, I am sorry to disturb you, but the carriage is waiting. You asked to be informed . . ."

"Yes, yes," Colin said brusquely. "I'm coming."

"The company has assembled in the hall."

"I'm coming! Cease nagging me!" Irritably, he leapt to his feet.

"My lord!" The servant quailed. "Such was not my intention, sir!"

Embarrassed by his lashing out, Colin took a deep breath. "I apologize, Mitchell. I . . . I have a lot on my mind."

"Of course, my lord." A mildly shrewd expression crossed the butler's face. He bowed, stepped back, and held the door as the marquess strode out.

Colin was surprised to see the household staff gathered together to bid the ladies godspeed. It was as if they were tendering farewell to the mistress of the house, instead of a mere guest. Hope, with her directives and proposed reforms, had obviously touched them.

He paused, waiting while she moved along the line of servants with a smiling word for each one. Dammit! Why couldn't she just get it over with? She finished with a final, short discourse with Mrs. Dawes and turned to chat with Jamie and Roger. Colin started forward.

"My lady, it goes without saying that you will be missed," he told her, forcing a grin. "I do believe that you've won the hearts of everyone here."

"But some people won't do nothin' about it," Cook intoned in a low, raspy voice.

Colin cleared his throat in warning.

Shoving her hands in her apron pockets, Cook innocently eyed the ceiling.

"You have a wonderful staff, my lord," Hope replied.

"Thank you, I value them highly."

"Somebody's makin' a big mistake if he lets her go," came the opinion of ancient wisdom.

Roger and Jamie chuckled.

Flushing, Colin took Hope's elbow and directed her toward the door, while the two bachelors, Drew Kelwin, and Agatha fell in behind.

"Don't be angry with Cook," Hope said softly. "She has gone through a trying time."

"I won't say a word to her. She might hit me with her rolling pin." Grimly, he took her through the door and descended the front steps. "After what you have done for her, she probably feels dependent upon you."

"It will pass. With Daphne's help, all will be well with her." She slipped her arm through his, clinging slightly as her small booted foot slipped on a patch of ice. "It's still a bit slick, isn't it?"

"Yes." He frowned. "Perhaps you'd best postpone your trip for another day or so."

"Oh, no. We are all packed and ready, and I do have complete confidence in John Coachman. We shall be fine."

"No doubt, but still . . ."

"Colin, it's best that I leave now. Don't we both know that?"

Her unspoken thought seemed to hang crackling on the air. Colin felt rather ill. If he were any other man, it wouldn't be happening like this. He would have gone down on his knee to her. He would have asked . . . But he wasn't any other man. He had impediments and a vow to remember.

"Yes," he finally said. "Yes, Hope, we both know that."

He escorted her to the open coach door and glanced inside, where her abigail was already waiting. The servants had looked ahead to the ladies' comfort. There were hot bricks for their feet and plenty of carriage robes for their laps. There was even a hamper of delicious smelling tidbits on the seat. For such a short journey, the travelers would be snug and ridiculously pampered. Colin was pleased. He wanted her to be cozy.

He handed her into the vehicle. "Take care, Hope. I'll see you in London, during the Season."

She nodded, blinking rapidly. "Good-bye, Colin."

From the corner of his eye, he saw Drew conducting his fiancee to the opposite side of the carriage. He wavered, thinking to speak with Hope for a few more minutes while his friend took his leave, but decided against it. It was better to cut it off now.

"Good-bye, my dear." He closed the door and went to join Roger and Jamie on the steps of Amberton Hall.

The horses, with flared nostrils blowing puffs of steam in the chilly air, stamped restlessly in the slushy snow. John Coachman touched his hat, made a bow, and climbed up onto the box. He took up the reins to depart, but Kelwin was prolonging his adieu, chatting with Agatha through the open window. Dammit, thought Colin. Why couldn't the earl get on with it?

He set his jaw. If not for his past, that could have been him with Hope. Ah well, soon he'd conquer such sentiments in the arms of another. Helene? Perhaps. He supposed that lush siren would be as good as any. If not, he'd present her a bauble and move right along to another candidate. That was the Amberton way, after all.

Beside him, Roger shivered. "I'm freezing. I'm going inside. Drew can pitch his sweet talk without my audience."

"Me, too," Jamie seconded. "Colin?"

"I'll wait."

"Why can't you just let yourself go, and accept what's happened to you?" Bridgewater muttered.

"Accept what?" he asked with a hint of challenge.

The viscount uttered an obscenity and followed Roger into the house.

Colin stiffened, shuffling his feet, while Kelwin continued his lengthy colloquy. Eventually, Hope turned and peered out the window, her stare melding with Colin's. He wanted to shrug, and gesture, and laugh at their two lovebird friends, but he couldn't. That might have been them. And it just wasn't funny.

Nor could he look away from her eyes. Even from the short distance, he could see her expression of naked hurt. It pierced his heart. He could endure his own loss. He couldn't bear hers. He should have talked with her. He should have explained.

"Hope!" He hurried forward.

"Colin?" Frantically, she lowered the glass.

Agatha diverted her attention from Drew and looked quickly from one to the other, then made a great pretense of searching for something on the seat. "Oh, dear! I seem to have left my sewing basket. Martha, come back to the house and help me search for it. You, too, Andrew!" She bounded out the opposite door of the carriage.

Colin scarcely noted the scramble. "Hope, I . . ." He covered her little gloved hand with his. "I . . ."

Her brown eyes glowed with anticipation. "Yes, Colin?" she breathed.

He swallowed hard. If he could have been granted one wish in his life, he would have asked that Hope be his wife. But he couldn't have that. She was too good for him. *He was an Amberton.*

He squeezed her hand. "I pray your stay here was not too disagreeable."

"Oh." Disappointment flooded her features. She made a faint choking sound.

"Is something wrong?" he asked urgently.

"No." She slowly shook her head. "I . . . I just thought you were going to say something else."

He couldn't ignore the implication of her words. After last night, they both were fully aware of the emotion that lay between them. Unable to meet her gaze, he bent his head, caressing her fingers.

"I'm sorry, Hope," he murmured, his heartbeat pounding loud in his ears. "I can't be the man you deserve."

"Colin, you don't know . . ."

"Yes, I do. Listen to me! Something happened here that should never have occurred! I don't know if it was the storm, or the isolation . . ." He chanced a glance up at her, but she was staring straight ahead.

"Hope, I would be the poorest of husbands. I like to drink. I like to gamble. I *like women.* Lots of them! Do you understand me? These things constitute my way of life! I like them!"

"Fustian," she said coldly. "I do not think that you truly like those things. I don't even think that you like yourself. But there is one certain thing I believe about you. And it is that you are afraid to be who you really are inside."

"You are wrong. I've tried to tell you! I am a rake and a libertine. A cad. The worst of lechers!"

She snorted. "Please spare me the superlatives. If you must struggle so desperately to convince yourself of your own worthlessness, do wait until I have departed. I have no enthusiasm for nonsense like this."

Colin groaned. "I'm not making sense. I just want you to know that, despite my character, I've grown to care for you in my own way. It isn't your fault that nothing more can come of it."

"Of course." Hope abruptly withdrew her hand from his grasp. "You need stand no longer in the cold, my lord. I perfectly understand. I wish to thank you for your hospitality and for the passing flirtation. I have never known such a true rake, so the experience was vastly amusing."

"Hope, it wasn't just . . ."

"Ah, here comes Agatha! We shall be on our way."

"Dammit, Hope!"

"It is *Lady,* Lord Amberton. Not *dammit.*" Biting her lip, she flounced back against the squabs.

Colin stepped back from the carriage, pain washing over him. He'd meant to explain his position, but everything came out wrong. He'd ended up hurting her worse, and making a fool of himself.

Drew Kelwin handed his fiancee into the carriage and joined him as John Coachman, at long last, gave his team the office.

"Well, Colin," his friend said crossly, "from the looks on both of your faces, I don't think you asked Lady Hope for her hand."

"What the hell gave you the idea that I would?" he snapped.

The earl laughed sarcastically. "Because you love her? Because she loves you?"

"If you'd stop to consider the entire situation, you'd realize that I'm doing the right thing," he grumbled.

Kelwin grimaced. "Don't give me that balderdash!" "Reconsider it, Colin. You're making the greatest mistake of your life!"

Colin cast a final glance at the departing coach. "She deserves better than an Amberton," he said, and turned on his heel toward the house.

"I thought he was going to ask me," Hope whispered, her constricted throat making it almost impossible to utter a word. "But it seemed that all he was trying to do was to tell me why he *wouldn't* marry me. Oh, why did I have to fall in love with a man like that?"

Try as she might to keep from it, a tear slipped down her cheek. Chewing her inner lip, Hope turned her face to the window and battled to keep back the sobs, but her shoulders began to shake.

"My poor dear." Agatha gathered Hope into her arms. "Just let it out. I know how it hurts."

"I don't want to cry in front of you and Martha!" Hope wailed. "The two of you are so happy. I don't want to make you sad for me."

"He's a mean man," pronounced her abigail.

"No, he's a darling!" she contended, tears momentarily abating. "He just doesn't want to admit to it!"

"Maybe he'll come round in his thinking," Agatha soothed. "It's plain to see that he loves you."

"Do you really think that he might?" Hope gasped.

"I wish I knew. But if he doesn't, it might just be for the best. Ambertons have certainly not been model husbands."

"Colin would be," she stated with confidence. "I am convinced that he is different. A man who can play music like he does has great depth of feeling."

Agatha merely sighed and patted her friend's arm.

Hope fingered her cloak. "What can I do? There must be something I can do!"

"There is nothing, short of compromise, and you don't want to force him into marrying you."

"No," she quietly declared. "I wouldn't want him that way. He will have to make up his own mind then, won't he?"

"I fear so," she said bleakly.

"Agatha, I just don't know if he can." Twisting her face into her friend's shoulder, Hope let loose her sobs.

Miserably swirling the brandy in the glass in his hand, Colin stared up at the portrait of his father. The man had been handsome, but that was the only good thing that could be said of the previous marquess. He certainly hadn't been comely inside.

Colin's gaze shifted to the next Amberton, to the next, and on down the family tree until the jaded, dissolute noblemen faded away into the murky shadows of the late afternoon. They were all handsome men. They were all perfectly worthless.

"You bunch of bastards," he growled, drinking deeply. "Because of you, I can't have . . ."

He couldn't say it aloud, but he could speak it to himself. He couldn't have Hope. The generations before and, yes, he himself had prevented it. Lady Hope was beyond his touch. He bore the title of a marquess. He was blessed with the handsome countenance of his forebears. Thanks to his man-of-business, he was wealthy. But she was far above him. Lady Hope Blissfield was too good for an Amberton.

Admitting it made him feel sick all over. He'd never wanted a woman in the way that he wanted her. Oh, he desired her in the loin-aching way that a man needs a woman, but he wanted her in other ways, too. He wanted her at his side every minute of every day. He wanted to laugh with her, even to fence with her, and to care for her as one would a precious piece of porcelain. He wanted her to have his children, and for them all to be a family.

He stared at his ancestors. They gazed back, their cynically curved lips mocking him and his soft heart. Inside he might be different, but they wouldn't allow that.

Refilling his glass from the bottle he'd set on a table, Colin crossed the gallery's uneven floor and sat down on the cold, stone window sill. These men were dead and gone, but their influence lived on in him. He was an Amberton. He was just like them. Why did it have to be this way?

It didn't. He could almost hear Hope whisper in his ear. That was what she would say if she were here and knew his thoughts. She was right. He didn't like the way he was. *And he didn't have to be that way.*

He could change! He could be that loving husband, doting father, conscientious landlord. It might not be easy, but with Hope at his side, he could be all of those things. He didn't have to end the Amberton dynasty. He could *change* it! With her encouragement. With her love. He grinned. With her bossiness!

Colin leapt to his feet. "What do you think of that, Father?" He strode toward the painting of his sire. "I'm in love, and I'm damned happy about it!"

The former marquess's mouth remained set in its arrogant leer.

"I'll play the pianoforte, and, by Jove, I'll even play with my children! I hope you spin in your grave at the sight of such domesticity!

"Sir, you don't look so pleased. Have a drink!" Colin laughed, drew back his arm, and hurled his glass of brandy into the painted face.

The liquor washed across his father's smirk. The glass crashed to the floor, shattering into millions of crystal shards. There was a sharp intake of breath in the direction of the door.

Colin whirled. "Mitchell!"

"My lord." The butler's eyes were bulging. "It . . . er . . . was growing dark, so I brought candles."

"Thank you, Mitchell, but I won't be staying. I've had my fill of this room."

"Yes, sir." The servant warily edged past him and deposited the candelabrum on the table.

Colin smiled at him. "How long have you been at Amberton Hall?"

"Since I was a boy, my lord."

"A good many years then, eh?"

The butler observed him uneasily. "An appreciable time."

"Then you're in for a change. Amberton Hall is going to be completely different," he announced. "I intend to repair and redecorate. We'll add all the staff you could wish for. And I'm going to get us a mistress."

Mitchell's mouth dropped open. He narrowed his eyes.

Colin chuckled. "Oh, not the kind of mistress you might expect of me. I'm speaking of a real lady. A marchioness! If she'll have me," he added ruefully.

The old retainer's face burst into a broad smile. "She will, my lord!"

"Well, I'll have to plan my campaign carefully. I'm not in her best graces just now. But, Mitchell, I feel lucky!"

"Yes, sir!"

Colin strolled toward the door. He'd immediately inform his friends of his decision and get them off his back. Also, he'd probe them for suggestions on how to proceed with his suit.

But before leaving the room, he paused. "One thing more."

"My lord?"

"I want these portraits removed and put in storage as soon as possible. I intend to replace them with something more pleasant. Perhaps we'll hang them again someday. But not for a while."

Humming a waltz, he sauntered down the hall.

17

As each day dragged on into the next, Hope unhappily grew more and more convinced that her relationship with Colin had ended. Though she still believed that she had touched his heart, it must not have been enough to change his raffish mind. She consoled herself with the thought that she, at least, must be the only female on the earth who had come close to winning his love.

Luckily, she was so busy that she had no time on her hands to wallow in her tragedy. There were Agatha's and Martha's weddings to arrange, spring planting to think about, and her trip to London for the Season to be planned. She must also devote some attention toward obtaining a new companion, but she tried to ignore that. It would not be easy to replace a friend like Agatha.

Although she was constantly occupied with these endeavors, Hope sometimes felt a strange, almost overwhelming sense of loneliness. This was underscored by Martha's chattering happiness and by Lord Kelwin's visits to Agatha. The two betrothed women were an everyday reminder of her single state. Kelwin, though he seldom mentioned the marquess, made her think of Colin. She was secretly glad when the earl departed to fetch his mother, and she gained some respite from seeing him.

Without threat of interruption from Kelwin, Hope and

Agatha plunged so deeply into their plans for the wedding and for the entertainment of the dowager countess, that Hope felt as if she were being plucked from another existence when, one day, they heard the sound of a coach on the drive. Surely the Kelwins couldn't have arrived so quickly! As one, the two ladies sprang to the window.

"It's Gerald!" Hope cried with a sense of dismay, as she watched her brother emerge from the carriage and hand down his wife and children. "For goodness sake, that's all we need! Now he'll be plaguing me to find a new companion, and I don't have time to think about it just yet."

"Perhaps he'll do it for you," Agatha suggested, quickly gathering up the papers on which they'd been listing menus and guests.

"Oh, no, I won't allow it! I can just imagine the type of person he'd choose." Hope hurried into the hall to greet her family.

She knew at once that something was amiss. Dorothy was as sweet as ever. The children were exuberant to see their beloved auntie. But her brother was stiff and unsmiling.

"We must converse without delay," he frankly declared.

"Now, dear," gently put in his wife. "We have only just arrived."

"All the better," he proclaimed. "You will wish to rest and freshen up from the long trip, my dear, and the children need a nap."

Hope eyed him with trepidation. Ah well, perhaps it was best to have this confrontation now. She sent Thompson, her butler, to arrange for refreshments, and Mrs. Watkins, her housekeeper, to escort her brother's family upstairs. Steeling herself for battle, she led Gerald into the drawing room.

The earl greeted Agatha, proffered his best wishes for her forthcoming nuptials, and indicated her dismissal from the room.

"Now," he said without preamble, as soon as the widow

had closed the door, "we'll address the disturbing point at hand. Why were you staying at Amberton Hall?"

Hope stared aghast at him. "How did you know?"

"Scandalous news has wings, dear sister. It doesn't matter how I found out."

"It certainly does to me!" She stalled for time to get her thoughts in order. "I refuse to discuss the matter unless you divulge the name of your informer." She flounced down into a chair, crossed her arms, and stubbornly lifted her chin.

"If you must know," he revealed, "it was Thompson."

"My butler?" she shrilled. "I thought he was loyal to me!"

"He is, my dear. He was shocked and concerned by what had transpired. For fear of negative repercussions, he decided it best to contact me."

"The traitor! The tattlemonger! I shall fire him!"

"No, you will not. He did what he thought was best, and he was right. He has your best interests at heart."

"Balderdash! He has caused you to set out on a fool's errand, Gerald," Hope explained. "The reason we stopped at Amberton Hall is simple. A storm drove us to seek safety, and that is all."

"I'm afraid not, dear sister. Would you care to account for the bachelor party in progress?"

Hope irritably pressed her lips together, forming a fine line of resentment. Oh, what she would do to Thompson! But first, she must pacify Gerald. She was actually grateful to her butler when he suddenly appeared with a tray of tea, sweets, and sandwiches. His appearance afforded her a brief, calming moment.

"Gerald," she began, when the servant left, "we had no choice. The blizzard was so savage that it was too dangerous to proceed further. As it was, we were fortunate to reach a safe haven."

"Pardon me if I doubt you," he stated. "I am too well aware of your inquisitiveness."

"You are naming me a liar?" she burst out. "If I were a man, I'd call you out!"

Gerald laughed.

Hope rose abruptly. Ignoring the tea, she went to the sideboard and poured herself a glass of sherry. Cynically, she thought of all the things Colin would say if he saw her taking wine to bolster her spirits.

"If you wish for something stronger to drink, dear brother," she muttered maliciously, "you may serve yourself. If I did it, I fear I would be far too tempted to throw the stuff in your face."

He accepted her invitation and joined her, helping himself to port. "I pray that Lord Amberton did not initiate you into the habit of frequent imbibing."

"Don't be ridiculous! The marquess was a gentleman at all times!" She flushed, remembering the moments when he was not.

Lord Blissfield keenly observed her. "Are you certain of that?"

"Yes!" she snapped, crossing her fingers for luck. "If you don't believe me, just ask him!"

"He'd only lie to me."

"Lord Amberton is a man of honor!" she gasped.

"He is a disreputable scoundrel."

"No, he is not!"

He frowned. "You are awfully defensive of him. You haven't fallen under his spell, have you?"

"No!" Hope shrieked. "Nothing happened, Gerald. I will not allow you to make more of this than what it was, and I refuse to discuss it any further!"

"Very well," he recanted, taking her arm and leading her to the sofa. "We shall leave it for the moment and speak of another pressing matter."

"What is that?" she asked sourly, sipping her sherry.

Her brother helped himself to the sandwiches. "You are going to need a new companion."

"I am aware of that. I thought to obtain one in London."

He shook his head. "I scarcely see how you can appear

in society without a proper chaperon, especially after the Amberton disaster."

"Then I shall write to employment agencies and conduct interviews here."

"You wouldn't consider coming to live with us?"

"No, and please don't waste time haggling over it." Hope smoothed her skirt. "We've covered that ground before."

"All right." Noting her familiar, anxious gesture, he smiled in a patronizing manner. "Actually, I have a candidate in mind."

Hope groaned.

"Now hear me out!" He paused to finish his tidbit and reach for another. "Let us consider Auntie Evaline. She needs a home."

"You make her sound like a stray dog or cat."

"Certainly not!" he protested. "I myself support her, but the day is quickly approaching when she cannot live on her own. Her living with you would solve more than one problem."

"You're trying to push her off on me." Hope couldn't keep from laughing. "You're afraid she'll have to live with you."

Two spots of red arose on her brother's cheeks. "That is absurd!"

"You are oh so guilty, Gerald!" she chortled. "My answer is no. Aunt Evaline is the most obnoxious woman I've ever encountered. Furthermore, she's too old."

"I have always been of the opinion that Mrs. Sommers was too young. I have little doubt that she took advantage of the situation at Amberton Hall to nab Kelwin. In fact, I am not so sure that she didn't encourage you to go there in hopes of finding just such a victim."

"Lord Kelwin loves her madly!" Hope exclaimed. "And Agatha was far more distressed with our situation than I was! Don't you dare criticize her! *Don't you dare!*"

He shrugged. "Just a man's opinion."

"Well, keep it to yourself!" She leapt to her feet. "I love

you, dear brother, but often I find that I cannot bear your presence."

"Sit down, Hope," he said wearily. "We haven't finished."

"Oh, yes, we have! For the moment, at least! I am going upstairs to chat with Dorothy. You may indulge in wolfing down that tray of food. I do note that you are developing a paunch, Gerald."

With that parting shot, she sailed from the room, her thoughts as turbulent as the snowstorm had been.

Two weeks had passed before Colin got up his nerve to mount his horse and ride to Shadyside Park to beg Hope for her hand. In the meantime, he'd vacillated between traveling to Blissfield Hall to ask her brother for the permission to pay his addresses, or to confronting the lady first. Actually, an interview with Lord Blissfield was the proper way to conduct such a matter, but in his case, he thought it might be best to allow Hope, if she accepted his suit, to clear the way. Although he disliked hiding behind her skirts, he questioned whether her seemingly straightlaced brother would welcome him.

Aside from this anxiety, there was one other matter that delayed his mission. He'd had a perfect gold guinea made into a necklace, in hopes that the reminder of their sleigh-riding wager and the symbol of her victory in it, would convince her of his sincerity to mend his ways. Also, from his vast experience with the fairer sex, he knew that a gift always sweetened a lady's regard.

Trotting along on his horse, Colin wasn't surprised to see that Hope's estate was as well-groomed and orderly as the lady herself. The drive passed through twin brick pillars and into a small woodland park from which all undergrowth had been cleared, leaving only large old oaks and elms. It crossed a wooden bridge over a shallow, rocky brook and proceeded along the perimeter of a gently sloping lawn, edged with clipped boxwood, to the house itself, a three-story, symmetrically windowed brick of eighteenth-century vintage. As he drew up before the black-lacquered front door, an immaculate, liveried footman appeared instantaneously to take his reins. The marquess lightly hopped down and started up the trio of stairs.

His carefree step belied his inner turmoil. Colin was nervous. This was an errand of the sort he'd never thought to make. More than a few times on the way over, he'd considered putting off the venture and thinking it over at even greater length. Once, he'd actually had his horse turned halfway around in the opposite direction before he'd summoned his courage and continued on. Now that he was even closer to seeing Hope, he again considered flight.

He didn't have the chance to change his mind. No sooner had he set his foot down on the stoop, than the door opened. A stiff, staid butler peered out, suspiciously ogling him up and down before he deigned to bow.

"Good afternoon, sir," Hope's retainer intoned words that dripped with distrust.

The man seemed so formidable that Colin himself almost bowed in return. "Good afternoon. I am the marquess of Amberton, come to call on Lady Hope."

The servant's nostrils fluttered. "I shall see if she is available." He took Colin's whip, hat, and gloves and escorted him to a cheerful yellow salon.

Colin paced. It seemed like an interminable time was passing. What if she wouldn't see him? No, Hope was inquisitive, so that wasn't likely. Perhaps she was merely freshening up. What if she'd guessed the nature of his mission and couldn't come up with a good excuse to turn him down, one that wouldn't hurt him? Sometimes the best of men were refused, let alone someone like him. Oh, God, he'd feel like a fool if she declined his suit.

He stopped at a window and gazed out at the road he had traveled. He almost wished he could raise the sash, leap to the ground, and take to his heels. This business of proposing marriage was absolutely torturous. Behind him, the door opened briskly. Taking a very deep breath, he slowly pivoted.

"Lord Amberton, I understand," said a solemn male voice.

He recognized instantly who this must be. The man had the same bright blond hair and gold-flecked eyes that she did. Hope's brother, too, was rather petite, at least for a man, but his bearing was decidedly masculine. Colin guessed that he might prove a surprise to an opponent in a bout of fisticuffs. In fact, the man's expression just now indicated that he'd like nothing better than to plant a hard right to Colin's face.

"I am Blissfield, Lady Hope's brother." The earl bowed stiltedly.

Colin echoed the gesture, but he did it with grace. "Lord Blissfield."

How much did the man know of his and Hope's acquaintanceship? Had she managed to keep secret her stay at Amberton Hall? On more than one occasion, she had worried about her brother's reaction to the event. Colin definitely determined to remain silent about it and allow the earl to take the lead. He hadn't long to wait.

"I wasn't pleased to hear of my sister's visit to your house," Blissfield began as if Hope had had a choice in the matter. "No, it was more than that. Truthfully, I was appalled."

"I wasn't happy about it either," Colin carefully replied. "Unfortunately, it couldn't have been prevented."

"Really." There was sarcasm and total doubt in the man's response.

"*Really,*" Colin responded.

"Believe me," Blissfield went on, "I am sadly aware of my sister's sometimes outrageous curiosity. She was fascinated by Amberton Hall. In my opinion, she used the snow as an excuse to stop there. You should have sent her on her way."

Colin pinched his lower lip with his teeth. No matter what the reputation, the Amberton title, having been conferred on a favorite by the flirtatious Queen Elizabeth, was much older than that of the Blissfields. He disliked having his word questioned by this upstart earl. He'd met men in duels for doing as much. But this was Hope's brother, and he managed to hold his temper.

"You are in error, Blissfield," he mildly countered. "If I'd turned her away, you might be here for Lady Hope's funeral instead of a visit. The storm was as violent as any I've seen."

"Well . . . perhaps." The earl turned to the sideboard. "Allow me to offer refreshment, Amberton, before you go on your way. Port?"

"Honestly, tea would be more welcome."

"Tea?" Blissfield arched an eyebrow.

"Yes, thank you." Colin could easily see disbelief written all over the man's features. Blissfield could scarcely fathom the idea that the infamous marquess of Amberton preferred tea to wine. Ha! That should set him back.

Lord Blissfield rang for the butler and placed the order, then nodded to Colin. "Now, my lord, perhaps you will sit down and explain why you are here. You asked for my sister, I understand. I cannot permit you to call on her, of course. That should come as no surprise to such as you. As it is, we shall be fortunate if her reputation is not already in shreds, without adding to the situation."

Tensely, Colin seated himself in a chair by the hearth, while Hope's brother took a chair opposite him. His heart raced, and his abdomen suddenly felt as though someone had tied knots in his insides. If he had only known that Lord Blissfield was present, he could have postponed his visit.

He had no choice now but to forge ahead. This was going to be difficult. He knew that this gentlemen would not look favorably on his suit. He'd probably forbid the match. Then what?

Hope was of age. She could marry him in spite of the earl's protestations. But did she care enough for him to do so?

Perhaps it would be best to get right to the point. He would have to attempt to win over this frank and boldly prejudiced lord. Maybe he would be surprised. Blissfield was obviously worried about his sister's reputation. The man might welcome an honorable way out.

"Is Lady Hope aware of my presence?" Colin asked casually, feeling his way along.

"Certainly not!" Blissfield exploded. "I'm only grateful that Thompson had the good sense to inform me before he sought her out! I don't want her within miles of you. Good God, man, you know what you are! Why can't you understand my point of view?"

Colin mastered his flash of anger. "I wish you would understand mine. My intentions are honorable."

The earl's eyes widened with horror as his perception dawned. "You . . . you mean that you wish to . . ."

"I wish to marry the lady," Colin finished.

"Lord above!" Blissfield started up from his chair, then collapsed back into it, uttering a long, low whistle.

At the moment, the butler chose to arrive with the tea tray. As the man served, Hope's brother overcame his shock, and his face turned an angry red. By the time the servant left, he was seething.

"No, no, and *no!*" he erupted.

"My lord, allow me to explain," Colin said urgently.

"No!" Blissfield roared. "I love my sister! I want her to be happy! I'll never sanction her betrothal to a damned, disreputable Amberton!"

Colin struggled with his rising temper, trying to speak calmly in hopes that soft tones would soothe the earl's agitation. "I want her to be happy, too, and I'll do whatever it takes to make her so."

His adversary wrenched up from his chair, violently shaking his head. "Dammit, I have a responsibility! What do you think my father would say? He must be spinning in his grave at the very thought of this. Wed Hope to a rogue such as you? Hell and damnation! Aren't you aware of your reputation?"

"Yes," Colin acknowledged. "I intend to make amends."

"Aren't you aware of your *family's* reputation?"

"It can be overcome."

"Impossible! You are not welcome in certain drawing rooms. Decent people avoid you! Mothers with young daughters cross the streets when they see you coming." He exhaled with a loud whoosh. "And you come to me, asking for my sister's hand? What lunacy, my lord!"

"You are wrong, Blissfield. My title . . ."

"Devil take your title! If it ever held any honor, that was long ago besmirched. It would require generations of good deeds and unobtrusive living to remove the tarnish." He finally lowered his voice. "You may have the best of intentions in the world, sir, but it won't work. And I won't allow Hope to be dragged through the dirt of the Ambertons, past and present."

"I don't believe that would happen," Colin protested tightly.

"I know it would. You'll never change. Once a rake, always a rake!" Blissfield ran a quivering hand through his hair and dropped back into his chair. "Tell me, Amberton, do you have sisters? If you did, you might possess a small understanding of how I am feeling."

"I have a sister."

"Is she wed?"

Colin nodded shortly.

"To what manner of man?" Blissfield demanded.

"He is gentry. He owns a very productive estate in the Midlands and is a member of Parliament."

"A country politician. Quite a comedown for the daughter of a marquess, is it not?" Hope's brother said disparagingly.

Colin snapped. "He's a good and decent man!"

"Excellent! But he's far beneath her socially. The lady couldn't do any better. Because she's an Amberton!"

"Be careful, Blissfield," he warned in deadly tones. "I've had just about enough of your insults to my family."

The earl snorted. "What are you going to do? Call me out? That would be a fine recommendation for your suit!"

"I'd be damn well within my right of honor, rake or no," he growled.

"You have asked for my sister's hand, and I am trying to have you understand why I'm turning you down. If you can't take the fire, Amberton, stay away from the flames."

"You pompous ass." Colin acutely wished he could regale the earl with tales of Hope's little transgressions, but he held his tongue. It would only hurt her.

"Pompous, am I? An ass? I'll have you know that I'd rather be the biggest dullard in England, than to be its most notorious libertine!"

Colin stood. He was getting nowhere with this dogmatic lord. He never would. Stubbornness must run in the Blissfield family. He would come back another time and talk with Hope herself, when Gerald Blissfield was not present.

"May I remind you that Lady Hope is of age?" he fired back. "The ultimate decision is hers."

Hope's brother sharply drew in his breath. "You would go against my wishes?"

"I love the lady," Colin answered simply.

The man seemed to deflate a little, slumping down. "If you love her, you wouldn't do that to her. I would be forced to disown her from the family. Furthermore, I will ruin you far more thoroughly than you or your ancestors have ever done to yourselves. *And* I'll destroy her too."

"You wouldn't," he spat.

"Oh, yes, I most certainly would. I am not without social influence. I will see to it that neither one of you is accepted by genteel society. It will even carry over to your children. That, my lord, should show you how serious I am about this situation."

For that moment, Colin was thankful he was a skilled card player. If he hadn't been, his face would have revealed his shock. Lord Blissfield was not only overbearing. He was revengeful. And Colin didn't doubt that he would attempt to do exactly what he threatened.

Poor Hope. If she accepted him, she would lose all contact with her family. She might also be snubbed by the *ton.* Would the day come when she was sorry she'd ever seen his face? He didn't think he could bear having her look at him with loathing.

And what of his own vow? He had pledged to end the Amberton taint. Instead, was he going to add to it? Suddenly his situation seemed insurmountable.

"I see that my words have given you pause," Blissfield relished.

"I bid you good day," Colin replied habitually and started toward the door.

It opened before he reached it.

"Colin!" Hope cried, her eyes lighting with happy surprise, "Why wasn't I told you were here?"

"My lady." He bowed, forcing a smile.

"You needn't be so formal. Oh!" She caught sight of her brother and flushed. "You and Gerald have met."

"Yes." Blissfield rose. "Unfortunately, Lord Amberton is just leaving, my dear. You've only time to bid him *adieu.*"

"No!" She lay her hand on Colin's forearm and looked up beseechingly. "You must stay a short while longer, my lord. We haven't even had time to chat, and I want you to meet the rest of my family."

"Lady Blissfield and the children are resting," her brother told her.

"No, they aren't. They're . . ." She clutched the fabric of Colin's coat. "My lord, what is happening here?"

It was gratifying that she addressed the question to him and not to her sibling. With that small gesture, she revealed where her devotion lay. It also made him feel as if his heart was being ripped from his chest. He couldn't hurt her any more than he already had. No, this would be the end.

"Nothing is happening, my lady," he said and glanced at Lord Blissfield. "Nothing now."

The earl took a deep breath and exhaled it audibly, briefly closing his eyes with relief. "Thank you, Amberton."

"Good-bye, my dear." Wondering if the pain showed in his eyes, Colin bowed again, kissed her hand, and strode into the hall.

Hope chased after him, catching his arm as he grasped his accouterments from the butler. "You will tell me what is going on, Colin Amberton, or I will hang on you all the way to Amberton Hall."

He couldn't help grinning. The darling vixen would probably try to do just that. He halted.

She tilted her head. "There was a reason for Gerald to be so overset, other than his usual sanctimony, which I'm sure was outraged by being in presence of such a knave as yourself."

Colin thought of the little jewel box in his pocket. "If I tell you, will you allow me to make a hasty escape? I am in grave danger of engaging your brother in a bout of fisticuffs."

She smiled. "That is easy to understand. So am I. Very well, my lord. But will you promise to come and see me when Gerald has gone?"

He swallowed. "Not for quite a while, Hope. I am to be a belated guest at a certain house party."

"Oh." Her eyes swam with moisture. "I thought maybe . . . but I am always wrong where you are concerned."

"Here. This explains everything." He gave her the box. "It's rather personal, so your brother did not approve such a gift. That's all that happened."

Flicking her affectionately under the chin with his forefinger, he left the house, mounted his horse, and spurred it into a gallop, before she had time for anything else.

18

Flooded with disappointment by his speedy departure, Hope opened the lid of the small, flat box. She gasped as she stared at its contents. A gold guinea, set beautifully into a necklace! She had won their sleigh-riding wager, but was there greater meaning? What had he said? That gift explained everything? But how? Her mind rotating with possibilities, she trailed back into the house.

The guinea could merely be the honorable payment of a gambling debt. Horribly, it could also denote the finish of any contact between them. Or . . . or . . . Could it symbolize the fact that she had changed him? Gerald could hold the key to it all. Clutching the precious necklace, she dashed to the drawing room where, to her surprise, she found her brother indulging in another glass of wine and leaning weakly against the sideboard.

He straightened abruptly as soon as she entered and scowled at the bauble laced through her fingers. "What is that?" he demanded severely.

He didn't know! Colin had perverted the truth. The "personal gift" was not the guinea. There was something else, something he had obviously discussed with her brother. Hope's heart pounded. The blood raced through her veins. She took a deep breath.

"Gerald, did Lord Amberton ask to marry me?"

His face grew deathly pale. His jaw muscles twitched. It was all the answer she needed.

"What did you tell him?" she quietly asked.

"In short, I told him no." He hurried to her and tried to put his arms around her, but his sister drew bluntly away. "My dear, how could I give my blessing to your wedding a man like that?"

Hope walked stiffly to the sofa and collapsed. "I assume you were nasty. I suppose you insulted him."

"I spoke frankly."

"It's a wonder he didn't call you out," she bitterly mused. "I do believe that for once in your life, you behaved improperly, Gerald."

"I used the only language a man like that can understand!" he loudly defended, sitting down opposite her.

"Cease calling him *'a man like that'!* You are speaking of the man I love!"

"Fustian! You can't love him. He'd only break your heart. Before thc ink was dried on the marriage register, he'd be running off to another woman."

"That's not true, Gerald. He loves me!"

"Then that's his misfortune!" Lord Blissfield shouted. "I won't take a chance on it! I won't give my blessing!"

Hope glanced backwards as she heard a small gasp at the doorway. Dorothy was poised there, her mouth half-open in wonderment. She recovered and entered.

"Do I understand that Hope has received a proposal?"

"Yes, and I won't allow it," her husband grumbled.

"But what is wrong?" His countess carefully closed the door behind her. "My, but I could hear you quarreling all the way upstairs!"

"You want to know what is wrong? I'll tell you what is wrong!" he railed. "Hope's suitor is none other than the marquess of Amberton!"

"Lord Amberton?" she cried. "No, Hope, you mustn't marry him. He has a dreadful reputation."

"You see?" Gerald asked triumphantly. "Everyone knows how contemptuous he is. Doro, you must help me talk some sense into my misguided sister. She thinks she loves the cad."

Hope's sister-in-law glided across the room and sat down beside her, taking her hand. "You really cannot marry him, Hope. Gerald is right. The marquess would make you miserable. I'm sure you have only a case of puppy love. Puppy love is . . ."

"I know what it is, Dorothy," Hope interrupted. "I've experienced it before, and believe me, that isn't what I feel for Colin. In fact, it would shock you if you knew exactly how I felt about him!"

Dorothy's blue eyes widened enormously. "Ladies aren't supposed to have feelings like that about gentlemen!"

"Well, I do," she insisted.

"He has corrupted her!" wailed Lady Blissfield.

"No, he hasn't. Not that he didn't have the chance," Hope admitted recklessly.

"Enough!" Gerald commanded. "You will not marry him, and that is final. He isn't suitable. Have your little cry, dear sister, and let us be on with more important matters."

"Yes, Hope," his wife seconded. "It really wouldn't work."

"I am not going to cry!"

"Whew! That's a relief!" Lord Blissfield rose and returned to the sideboard. "Let us all have a drink and begin anew."

"Another drink, Gerald?" Hope caustically inquired. "After all your criticism of Colin? I'm beginning to think it's a case of the pot calling the kettle black."

"Oh, no, my dear," Dorothy hastily assured her. "Your brother only imbibes when he is vastly overset."

"That's true," he echoed, "though now that this matter is settled, I feel much better."

"It isn't settled," his sister disputed. "I have yet to hear what was said in your talk with the marquess."

"And you aren't going to hear it either."

"Dammit, Gerald! I am weary of men refusing to tell me what happened in a matter of which I am very much involved!"

"Such language," he complained, bringing glasses of sherry to the ladies and returning for his own. "The thing's over and done with. It's time to cease riding this dead horse. Do you know what has occurred to me, Hope? I believe you can get along without a companion for a while. Dorothy and I will take in the Season with you this year."

"That will be wonderful!" The countess's eyes sparkled with monumental excitement. "It has been so long since we've participated!"

"I'll treat you both to brand new wardrobes," he promised. "We'll leave immediately following Mrs. Sommers's wedding. Won't we have fun?"

"Yes," breathed Dorothy. "Won't it be marvelous, Hope?"

"I daresay it will. You've neglected Doro's social entertainment, Gerald. You should be ashamed for going up to town alone, when you've attended your sessions in the Lords."

"The children have needed me," the countess explained, "but now they are older. Ah, but I shall miss them, though."

"We'll bring them too," her husband proclaimed magnanimously. "Why not? And I vow that I shall escort my two ladies to all the events, even the opera!"

The ladies gaped, knowing how much he hated that entertainment.

"I can scarcely wait! My dear, you are the most thoughtful husband in the entire world." Dorothy turned up her cheek to be kissed as he returned to his chair.

Hope smiled cynically. "I do thank you, brother, but if I attend the Season, my *husband* shall escort me."

His good cheer fled. "No!"

"I pray that you will not, however, break your promise to Dorothy."

Gerald ground his teeth. His chest heaved. "Hope, you

are of age, so I can do little to prevent it. But if you persist in this foolishness, I will disown you from the family. Your marriage to Amberton would be just that abhorrent to me."

"You would not do that!" his wife admonished.

"Just watch me," he threatened. "And that, dear sister, is just what was said in our little conference."

"So that is what happened," she whispered. "He didn't wish me to face that hurt."

"Oh, he said all the expected drivel—that he'd change his ways, make you happy, that he loved you."

Hope stood, her face pale with anger. "Well, it hurts far worse to lose him than to lose this family."

"Where are you going?" Gerald cried.

"To the man I love."

"No, you won't!" Her brother and sister-in-law pursued her into the hall.

She paused. "Thompson, please send for my carriage," she ordered her butler.

The servant blanched. "Now, my lady, you do not . . ."

"Do you refuse to follow my direction?" she snapped.

The haughty retainer looked from sister to brother. "Yes, ma'am, I do."

"My God! Am I to be a prisoner in my own home?" she gasped.

Brittle silence was her answer.

"Thompson, you are summarily dismissed from my employ." Hope shook her head in disbelief. "But I am sure that will not overly distress you, since you appear to be in Lord Blissfield's hire, anyway."

He had the grace to hang his head, but he did not attempt to make a defense.

She turned coldly to her brother. "You may have won this engagement, Gerald, but you have not won the war. I shall have my heart's desire."

"Hope!" her sister-in-law wailed. "Gerald! Do not be like this! We are *family!*"

"No, we aren't," Hope contradicted. "I've been tossed out of it."

"Not yet." Her brother smiled smugly. "You haven't stepped beyond the bounds. By tomorrow, you'll come round to my way of thinking. You'll see that he isn't worth it."

"You're wrong. And as far as this family goes, after the events of today, I have no desire to remain a part of it. We used to be loving and understanding. We had our tiffs, but we respected each other's feelings. Since that obviously is no longer the case, I shall seek a new family, one in which I will be loved and cherished."

She turned and started up the steps, then paused, looking over her shoulder. "We no longer know each other, Gerald. Perhaps we never did." As she continued on her way, she heard Dorothy begin to weep.

When she reached her chamber, Hope summoned Martha and Agatha and informed them of what had transpired. "Martha, can you secretly have John hitch up my carriage and wait for me in the stable? You wait there, too, for I want you to accompany me. I won't be returning, so I'll need you at Amberton Hall."

Her maid nodded confidently and darted on her errand.

"Agatha?" Hope smiled sadly. "I know you must highly condemn my lack of propriety, although I have no other choice. I must rely on your discretion in keeping silent my plan of escape. You have been my friend for too long for me to slip away without telling you."

The widow squared her shoulders. "I will accompany you, too."

"No." Hope hugged her. "I don't wish you to fall under Gerald's wrath."

"I am no longer afraid of Lord Blissfield," she proudly announced. "Andrew is his equal, and in a sense, so will I be."

"You cannot imagine how good your stance makes me feel. For you, not just for me. But there is bound to be scandal, and I don't wish you to be involved in it. Go to bed. Pretend you have the headache."

Agatha reluctantly agreed. The two friends embraced each other once more. As her former companion returned to her bedroom, Hope quickly packed her necessities into a small portmanteau. With a bittersweet smile, she folded her prettiest negligee and laid it within. She would wear it for him that very evening. Heart pounding with nervous anticipation, she donned her cloak and sneaked down the servants' staircase.

Martha and John were ready and waiting in the barn. The coachman smilingly assisted the women into the coach and climbed onto the box. He drove carefully along the drive, but the team's scrunching hooves were too noisy to prevent detection. Gerald and Thompson appeared in the doorway of the house and ran forward. With a shout, John whipped up the horses and bolted toward Amberton Hall.

"Goodness!" Hope screeched, jouncing on the seat.

"Don't worry, my lady. My man will get us there safely!"

"If Gerald doesn't apprehend us first. Fiddlesticks! I thought we might be lucky enough to avoid his notice. He'll call for a horse and be right on our trail."

"If he can catch one! They've all been turned out in the paddocks, and the grooms have gone on holiday to the village!" Martha told her gleefully. "And even then he'll have to find a bridle!"

Hope laughed rather hysterically. "At least some of my employees are loyal to me."

"Oh, yes, my lady, for you are loyal to us!" As they swung wildly around a turn, the abigail bounced gigglingly to the floor.

The carriage careened madly down the drive and drew to a sliding halt before Amberton Hall. John Coachman leapt proudly down from his box, lowered the steps, and threw open the door. "Now, how was that, my lady?"

"Lud, John, you should drive a mail coach!" Hope scrambled inelegantly from the vehicle, Martha following with her portmanteau. "Now hide yourself in the stable. If my brother follows, I don't want you to fall victim to his anger."

She sped up the steps as an overwhelmed Mitchell opened the door.

"My lady!" he wailed. "What is this? You cannot . . ."

"I can, and I will." Hope walked past him peeling off her gloves.

"My lady, it isn't *proper,*" he moaned.

"Cease protesting, Mitchell," she laughingly told him. "We've been over this ground before. Need I remind you who emerged victorious?"

"But . . . but . . ." he sputtered. "The roads are clear. You are obviously not stranded. It . . . it just isn't proper!"

"Neither am I. I am here to become an Amberton. Where is my lord?"

He stared speechlessly.

"Shall I search for him?" She flung off her cloak and gave it to Martha.

"No, my lady! Please wait in the Rose Salon. Lord Amberton is in his chamber. I'll fetch him immediately."

"No need. I know the way."

"*My lady!*" he shrilled, reeling against the newel post.

Hope darted up the stairs. Mitchell, recovering, dashed after her. He was too reticent to attempt to stop her physically, but he kept up a patter of protest all the way to the master's door. Ignoring him, Hope threw it open. She caught her breath.

Stripped to the waist, his lordship was pouring himself a cup of tea. He turned, startled, toward her, giving her a full view of his blatantly perfect male chest. He stared.

Dobbs was the first to make active response to the invasion. He leapt into the air, squealing. As soon as his feet again touched the carpet, he sped toward the door, bounced off Mitchell, and stumbled down the hall.

"Colin?" Hope closed the door in the butler's face and slid the bolt.

"My God, woman, what are you doing here?" he managed.

"Coming to you," she whispered.

"No, Hope, this isn't right!" He set his cup aside. "You're going to be hurt."

"Will you hurt me?"

"Not if I can help it, but. . . . Darling, you have to leave before anyone knows of this."

She crossed the room to him. "I love you, Colin, and I do hope that everyone learns of that."

"The scandal! Your brother!"

"You are so beautiful. I never dreamed that a man could be quite so remarkable." Hope shyly reached out to touch the warm, firm skin of his pectoral muscle.

Colin shuddered.

Her eyes widened. "I'm sorry. Do I repel you?"

"God, no. No, Hope. Believe me, that isn't it at all." He stepped backwards. "I have to get a shirt."

"That isn't necessary. I find your physique quite interesting. It doesn't bother me," she assured him.

"It bothers *me*. Please sit down. I'll be back in a moment." He hurried to his dressing room.

Hope chose the sofa by the hearth. "Somehow, I didn't expect you to be so modest," she called over her shoulder.

"Darling, you don't understand! You're too innocent!"

"Well, that will end soon enough, I suppose."

There was a clatter as if he'd knocked over a chair.

"Colin, are you all right?"

"Yes! No! Leave off, Hope, I'll be there very shortly."

She smiled, leaning her head back against the cushions and closing her eyes. Twice he had called her darling in just a few minutes. Oh, happy, happy day!

He appeared, fully dressed, before the hearth. "Come, dear, you have to leave," he began.

"Do sit down, Colin, and let us discuss this." She reached out a hand to him. "Please?"

He reluctantly relented. "Just for a moment, and then you will go. I don't fancy dueling with your brother."

"You will not do that. I won't allow it," she said simply and took his hand. "I heard what transpired in your conversation with Gerald. He told me everything."

He shifted uncomfortably. "It wasn't pleasant."

"I thought it was," she said softly. "You asked for my hand. I found that to be very, very pleasant. My answer is yes, Colin. I want to marry you."

The marquess set his jaw and gazed into the fire. "It's too great a sacrifice for you."

"Let me be the judge of that," she cautioned. "I love you. I will wed no other man. Whatever happens, we can face it together. I don't need society. I need nothing but your love. If I never set foot beyond the boundaries of Amberton, I would be content."

"Now, maybe, but in the future . . ."

"Don't ever doubt me." Hope slipped across the short distance between them. "Together, we are enough."

He opened his arms to her as she prayed he would. Lowering his head, he kissed her sweetly, then expertly deepened the caress, bringing to her attention all of his years of experience. But she didn't care about his past history of mistresses, now. Colin was hers. In her heart, she knew he would never stray.

He trailed the kiss along her jawbone to her ear. "I love you," he breathed. "I promise I shall do my best to be a good husband."

"You will succeed." Tendrils of fire licked at her body. "And now, my lord, what is the next step?"

"Now I will take you home."

Hope jolted upright. "What?"

"Did you really think I would take you to my bed? No, darling, much as I'd like to do just that, we shall go about this in a proper way. In a church, with a ceremony. Only then shall I teach you the rest of it." He grinned. "But I think I'll obtain a special license, instead of waiting for the banns to be read. I'm trying to become respectable, but I honestly don't think I can wait that long."

Hope smiled worriedly. "But if you take me home, Gerald will . . ."

"We'll speak with your brother. If he still refuses to be reasonable, we'll go our own way, but first we must try to make peace with your family. It is the proper thing to do."

She nodded, dreading the confrontation. If only she could have stayed with him from this moment forth! But he was right. It must be attempted.

Colin stood and drew her to her feet. She wished she could prolong their departure, but it was best to meet this unpleasant affair as soon as possible. It would be easier than many of her bouts with Gerald, for she would have him at her side. Hand in hand, they walked to the door.

Hope saw at once that Gerald was totally taken aback. She thought it was pure shock that made him shake Colin's hand, until she saw Dorothy's taciturn smile. Could the countess have pulled off a miracle?

But Lord Blissfield was not entirely forbearing. "You've brought her back?" he asked in tones of pleading.

"Only until our marriage." Colin squeezed her hand, which lay on his arm.

Hope fondly looked up at him. "We shall have a special license, so it won't be long."

Her brother sighed. "I am defeated. I suppose I'll have to walk you down the aisle, dear sister. So be it! I've been made to see that it would do greater harm to take offense than to accept the inevitable."

Hope and Colin exchanged a quick glance. "That was easy," she said.

"Mind you, I'm not enthused," Gerald protested.

"I shall do my utmost to make her happy," Colin vowed.

"Well, she always seems to get what she wants. Apparently you're it, Amberton, but you should have a care. She is, beyond a doubt, the most stubborn, opinionated female I've ever seen!"

"I could use the same words to describe a certain brother!" Hope retorted.

Dorothy quickly rose. "Come, Gerald, I believe it's time we left these two alone for a bit."

"Doro! Ordering me? Surely you've not been taking lessons from her!" He followed his countess from the room. "I'll have you know that I am the man in my house! I'll not become as Amberton is to be!"

"I won't be overbearing, Colin," Hope advised him, as the door closed behind her relatives. "Really, I won't. I shall be loving and gentle and . . ."

He laid his finger across her mouth. "And just as persnickety as a hedgehog? Ah, darling, let us face it. Your wishes have a way of becoming mine, and I do believe I like it. At least, for the time being!"

Bending his head, he replaced his finger with his lips. Always her way? It seemed that in certain sweet aspects of life, he very adeptly took the lead, and his methods had a tendency to drive all logical thoughts from her mind. No, their marriage would be one of give and take. And Hope was exceedingly thrilled to accept that marvelous notion.